The Case Files of Sam Flanagan:

# Sins of the Father

By

## Judith White

World Castle Publishing

Judith White

# WCP

**World Castle Publishing**
Pensacola, Florida

Copyright © Judith White 2013
ISBN: 9781939865076
First Edition World Castle Publishing March 10, 2013
http://www.worldcastlepublishing.com

## Licensing Notes

Cover: Karen Fuller
Photos: Shutterstock
Editor: Maxine Bringenberg

Judith White

# Dedication

For my sisters; Karen Penix, Pamela Lemke and Shelly Drake. Karen, had you been here with us, you would've loved Gran and Helen. I'll tell you all about them when I get to Heaven. Pam, you've always been a rock in a crisis, and for that, I thank you. Shelly, your easy going attitude toward life makes you fun to be around. I love you all!

"Sisters are probably the most competitive relationship within the family, but once sisters are grown, it becomes the strongest relationship." ~~Margaret Mead

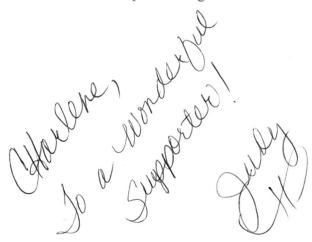

Judith White

# Chapter One

Have you ever wanted to sit down, face to face with God, and get to the bottom of things? Have you ever wanted to question Him as to *what* He is doing and *why*? When this case was solved, I wanted to do just that. I wanted to sit and have a one on one with Him and throw caution to the wind, allowing Him to know exactly what I was feeling and why I was feeling it. Yes, I realize that we shouldn't come to our Almighty Maker and hurl insults at Him, or demand answers to things He says we can't understand at this point in time. But, damn it, doesn't He owe us something in the way of an explanation? Sometimes, life isn't fair. Okay, let's face it; a lot of times life isn't fair. The people who can't speak for themselves anymore—the victims—would always attest to that if they only could. There was something they did, or didn't do, that sealed their fate. And if you asked each and every one of them, they would say they wouldn't make the same mistake if they could only go back in time; if they were only given the opportunity, they would choose a different path. But I need to start at the beginning.

My name is Sam Flanagan. I rent office space on Woodward Avenue in the city of Detroit. I'm a private investigator, but I once worked for the city as a police officer. That lasted for four years, from 1933 to 1937. It was decided by my superiors that maybe it would be best if we parted ways. I don't see it as being relevant to state under which circumstances that was decided. Just know that we *did* part ways, and it was an amicable split.

About eight months prior to my induction into the department, my wife of four years decided her dream to appear on the silver screen was more important than I was. She didn't actually tell me that in so many words, but she left, didn't she? It seemed obvious to me. It was a difficult time for just about everyone in the nation back then. We were reeling from an economic collapse, and were about to put our faith in another leader who could hopefully restore us to the good times. I just wish she had loved me enough to want to stay and wait it out with me. I hold no animosity toward her now, and I'm sorry to say I haven't seen Dee Dee's image on the big screen yet.

Listening to myself tell you these things is like hearing a sob story. It sounds like I feel sorry for myself, but I don't. I actually view it in this way: I'm a private investigator and I love what I do. I was fortunate to have gained experience with a four-year stint on the Detroit police force. For a brief time, I had the opportunity to live with, and love, a beautiful young gal who made me happy. Yep, life can be great!

****

It was April 20, 1943 and I hadn't gone into the office. The reason I didn't go in was that I didn't want to. About three months earlier, I'd accepted a case out of Chicago. I stayed with some great friends while working on it, and my client advanced me one thousand dollars to follow her husband and find out if he was seeing someone on the side. The investigation didn't go as I wanted it to. I couldn't prevent a death, and I felt bad about that. But in the end I solved the how, why, and who...the perpetrator was caught. I never reimbursed my client the portion of the dough I didn't earn, because I figured I *did* earn it by the time I fingered the culprit. I also got a reward for saving the insurance company a large amount of moolah. They were very appreciative. So I decided to stay home, and it wasn't that I didn't need the money; it's just that I didn't need it that day. It was a Tuesday.

In five days' time it would be Easter. My grandmother, Ruby Flanagan, whom I lived with, was dusting furniture and running the sweeper over the rugs that covered some of the hardwood flooring in the living room. She was my father's mother, and at eighty-two years old, talked too loud into the telephone and couldn't see well enough to read. Other than that, she was basically healthy. For the holiday, she had invited her older sister Pearl and Pearl's husband, my great Uncle Derwood, over for dinner, along with their grandson and his family. She'd also invited her best friend, Helen Foster. After Gran straightened up around the house, I was going to take her to the market for the items she needed to prepare the Sunday meal. She had dictated to me a whole list of things she felt she needed, and if we could find half of the things on the list, we'd have a great feast. The trouble was, because of rationing due to the war, food items were not always available.

The market on Gratiot Avenue was crowded. Gran pushed the cart, and as she meandered up and down the aisles, she would name certain items, one at a time, for me to find and bring to her. While standing at a display looking at blocks of cheese, as I reached for the cheddar, I heard my name. I turned around to see who had called it out, and spied my former partner from the police department. Leaving the cheese behind, I walked toward him.

"Why you old coot, you; how the hell you doing, Mac?" I asked as I extended my hand to shake his.

Bill McPherson was tall and slender...everyone called him "Mac." He'd been on the force since 1923 and his face was youthful for his forty-four years. Because of his easy-going disposition and lightheartedness, he was the most popular guy in the department. My four years with him as a partner were good...we'd hit it off instantly. He'd been bumped up to detective in the homicide division five years ago, so he was now a suit instead of a uniform.

"I'm doing alright, can't complain. How about you? You staying out of trouble?" he asked.

"Oh, yeah," I responded. "And I don't mind telling you, it's getting a bit boring."

We talked for a few moments, me asking about the guys back at the station and him asking about what cases I'd been working on. Gran came around the corner with her cart and stopped near us. She stared at Mac, appearing not to recognize him.

"You remember Mac, don't you Gran?" I asked her.

"Mac?" she asked.

"Gran, it's Bill McPherson, my old partner."

It suddenly dawned on her who he was. She put her hand to her chest and smiled.

"Oh my, yes! How are you doing? It's just that it's been so long."

"Well, you're looking beautiful as ever, Ruby Flanagan," he said to her. "It's good to see you." He turned to me. "You hear about Hep Cat?"

"No," I said. "What's happened? Is he alright?"

Apprehension crept up my spine. Hep Cat Martin was in his mid-forties and owned his own filling station and auto repair shop in Detroit. He was one hell of a mechanic and an all-around nice guy. He'd been married forever to Irma and they had nine children, eight pets, and a love for each other that would last into the next life. As far back as I could remember, he'd used his garage at home to practice with a band he put together from the neighborhood, thus gaining the nickname of Hep Cat, or just Hep. I couldn't even recall what his actual given name was at that point. He played a mean saxophone.

"Nothing like that," Mac said. "He's fine. I don't know how he connected with Bill Harris, but he did. He's playing sax with him on a couple of numbers tonight at Baker's Keyboard Lounge. Betty and I are going there to listen to him. Why don't you take a ride on out and join us?"

Bill Harris was a really good jazz trombonist who played the club circuit when he was in town. I'd only seen him once and I liked his music a lot. He'd been making a name for himself throughout the country.

"What time should we be there?" Gran asked.

Mac and I both looked at her. What the hell? I guess she thought the invitation extended to the both of us. Mac started to laugh and he looked at me and shrugged.

"Sure, bring Ruby here along and be there about 8:00," he said. "It's a date then?"

I nodded and told him I'd see them at the lounge that night. I still wasn't sure my grandmother would be joining me, but I kept quiet about that for the moment. He then told us he had to find his wife before she spent him into the poor house and he walked away, waving to us. When he was gone, I turned to Gran.

"You don't really want to go tonight, do you?"

She shrugged. "Sure, why not? I don't have anything else planned. A nice cold one and some music sounds good. Did you get the cheese, dear?"

I sighed heavily, turned back to the dairy display, and picked up the block of cheddar. I returned to where she was standing and put it in her shopping cart.

"If you're not done, let's hurry it up. I want to get out of here," I said and walked away from her, suddenly not in a very good mood.

Judith White

# Chapter Two

At sixteen minutes after seven o'clock, I'd showered and put on my dark blue suit with a white shirt and lighter blue tie. Looking in the bathroom mirror, I combed my damp black hair straight back, away from my face. About a month earlier I'd decided to try and sprout a mustache, but one night I had gotten the urge to shave it even before it had a chance to take off. I leaned closer into the mirror, trying to spy any fine lines that may be forming. I was safe so far. In just a little over two months, I would be seeing my fortieth birthday come upon me, and it was bothering me a bit.

I straightened and gave myself one more look, gazing at myself straight in the eye. Dee Dee had always referred to me as having "Hollywood eyes." She said she loved that they were a deep blue. I felt that I'd pretty much taken care of myself physically so far, standing six feet two inches tall and weighing just over two hundred pounds. I wasn't a knock out, but I was far from being ugly; at least I hoped that was the case. How was a guy to ever know? I had no one to coo over me and tell me I was *the* one. Nine months ago, I had been in the company of a beautiful red head at a dinner club. She was tall and willowy and very attractive…too bad she giggled at everything said and turned out to be dumber than a box of rocks. I never called her again, and hadn't been on a date since then. Tonight at Baker's Keyboard Lounge might have been my chance at meeting someone new, but that was very unlikely to happen now. Instead, I would have another woman on my arm, and it would be my grandmother.

I moved from the bathroom and headed toward the living room, knocking on Gran's door as I passed.

"We should get going. It's almost 7:30," I said, and then continued on my way to get my overcoat, which was lying across the sofa.

Gran stepped out of her bedroom wearing her best church dress, which was dark green with white cuffs on the short sleeves and a white collar. Around her neck was the string of pearls my grandfather had given her the last Christmas they had spent together. Wearing her brown pumps, she also carried a matching brown leather purse.

"I'm ready," she said.

I took one look at her face. She had bright red lipstick on, and her cheeks were just as bright with two circles of red. She looked like a clown.

"What is that stuff?"

I gestured to her cheeks, and made no attempt to hide my disgust. Her hand came up to her face.

"You mean my rouge, dear?" she asked.

"I'm not taking you anywhere looking like that! Go wash your face. You look silly," I said.

Her expression after hearing my words tugged at my heart. I'd hurt her feelings, very badly. I suddenly felt ashamed. All afternoon I'd had a bad attitude about taking her with me to Baker's Keyboard Lounge, and I'd let it show every opportunity I could. I'd been a real jerk.

She set her purse on the coffee table in the living room and walked back into the bathroom. I could hear the water running in the sink. When she came out she was wearing her nightgown and robe, and there was no longer any make up on her face. I felt like a huge heel. She said nothing to me, but walked from the bathroom straight to her bedroom, entered, and closed the door. Oh my God, what had I done?

Sitting on the couch, I waited a few moments, berating myself silently. I couldn't believe I had treated my own grandmother so horribly. What in the hell was wrong with me? Finally I got up and headed for her room, knocking softly when I arrived. She didn't answer and I knocked again—nothing. I opened her door and stuck my head in.

"Gran, can I come in for a minute?"

She was sitting on the edge of her bed with her feet dangling just above the floor, staring at the wall across from her. I entered, sat on the bed beside her, and put my arm around her.

"I'm sorry, Gran; really I am," I whispered.

"You better head out or you'll be late," she said.

"I'm not going without you. Come on, please be my date? I know I've been crabby all day and I'm apologizing. I don't know why I've been such a bear. I'm sorry. You looked great in your dress. That stuff on your cheeks was just a bit too dark. Can't you rub it in a little more?"

She laid her head on my shoulder and I hugged her tighter. "You're right, dear. You've been a rotten bastard all day today," she said quietly. She then got off the bed and left the room, heading for the bathroom again.

I was stunned. My grandmother never swore...she didn't approve of it. But I had to admit, she was correct in her evaluation.

She emerged once again in her green dress, pearls, and brown shoes, but she wasn't wearing any color on her face. I was still sitting on the edge of her bed.

"Do you need another minute for your make up?" I asked her.

"I won't wear any," she said.

But I could hear something in her voice. She'd been excited all day long to get dressed up and fix her face for tonight. She'd wanted to look pretty, but I had ruined that for her.

I rose from the bed and went to the basket of cosmetics she kept on her dressing table but rarely used. I looked through her lipsticks and found a lighter shade, a soft coral, and held it up.

"Why don't you use this one? I bet this color would really look good on you," I said.

She moved closer and grabbed it from me. Looking in the mirror, she applied it to her lips. *It looks so much better than the bright red*, I thought.

"Now put some on your cheeks," I said.

"My *lipstick*?" she asked.

"Yeah, but just rub it in good. The color of your rouge is too bright for you, Gran. This coral is nice with your skin."

She took the tube, marked her cheeks, and then rubbed to blend it. When she was done, it honestly looked rather nice. It gave a glow to her skin...she certainly no longer looked like a clown. I bent and kissed her on the forehead and told her she looked beautiful—and I meant it.

****

We arrived at Baker's Keyboard Lounge fifteen minutes late, but found Mac and Betty seated at a table for four and waiting for us. I hadn't seen Betty in at least a couple of years, but she looked the same. She stood about five feet three inches tall, had thick black hair, dark brown eyes, and a pretty face. Mac had always described her as being on the nervous side, but I'd never seen that in her. Then again, I had rarely been in her company. They had four daughters, ranging in age from twenty-three to seven.

Gran and Betty had never met, so I introduced them to each other as we took our seats. The place was already crowded with drinkers and people just out for a nice evening of entertainment. The place drew large crowds each night of the week, excluding Sundays, when it was closed altogether. People in Detroit flocked to the lounge because of the big name entertainment...Gene Krupa and Dizzy Gillespie to name a couple.

A waitress approached us and asked if we'd like a drink.

"Gran, you want a beer, right?" Then I looked at the gal and asked, "What brands of beer do you carry?"

"Stroh's, Pabst, Pfeiffer, and Champagne Velvet," she answered.

My grandmother's face was filled with excitement. It was like witnessing a young child trying to decide what flavor of ice cream she wanted.

16

"Did you want to stick with the Pfeiffer?" I prompted her.

"Oh, I don't know," she said. "That Champagne Velvet sure is a pretty name. It sounds high class."

I looked up at the barmaid and told her to bring a bottle of Champagne Velvet and a scotch on the rocks. Mac and Betty already had their beverages in front of them. Mac was drinking a beer and it looked like Betty was drinking a Coca Cola.

Ruby Flanagan had lived all of her eighty-two years never having one drop of alcohol pass her lips; up until about three months ago, that is. Her friend Helen had come over one afternoon back in late January with a six-pack of beer, saying they should find out what the fascination with drinking was all about. That day my grandmother got drunk on three beers and passed out, and Helen got sick and high tailed it home. They next experimented with vodka. Helen preferred the harder liquor and Gran stuck with the beer. Now, every once in a while, she voiced the desire for a nice cold one.

"You don't drink, dear?" Gran asked Betty.

Betty shook her head.

"Not really. I've had a glass of wine a couple times, but I don't really indulge in the habit."

"Maybe you should switch to beer. It makes you feel wonderful."

Betty laughed at Gran's statement and turned to me.

"She's delightful, Sam. I like her."

We chatted about this and that, until promptly at 9:00 the music started. Bill Harris was on stage at the microphone, holding his trombone. Behind him were a drummer, a pianist, a saxophonist, and a trumpeter. I didn't see Hep anywhere. He introduced each member of his group and told us he hoped we would enjoy the evening's entertainment. They played what they played best...jazz.

Right before the fourth number, Harris returned to the mike to speak. He took a handkerchief out of his back pants pocket and wiped his brow.

"Now, before we get into our next song, I'd like to tell you a little story. We have a man here who's one of Detroit's own, and he's going to come out on stage and take Earl's place on a couple of numbers." He gestured to his saxophonist. "I happened to meet this guy a few weeks back while passing through the city when I stopped at his station. I wanted to have him look under the hood of my auto, 'cause I'd heard he was the best damn mechanic this town has. Little did I know this guy would be all over me, talking about music. He told me he played the sax, and said he'd formed his own group and suggested he and I play together sometime. I tried to hold him at bay by telling him I'd have to hear what he could do first, maybe next time I was in town. Well, he goes in the back of his shop and pulls out his sax! How would *I* know that in between getting his hands dirty, he practices his blows?"

The crowd broke out into laughter along with the band on stage. He continued when the noise subsided.

"'Now, how the heck am I gonna break this guy's heart,' I thought to myself. He started to play and he blew me away. Ladies and gentlemen, I give you Hep Cat Martin!"

Bill Harris looked off to his left and extended his arm, pointing in the direction from which Hep mounted the stage. The crowd applauded, and I was surprised to hear my grandmother let out a loud whistle.

Hep crossed the stage and stood behind Harris, taking Earl's place. Earl moved off to the side. It was strange to see Hep dressed in a suit, a black one with pin stripes. I didn't doubt that he had gone out and bought it just for this occasion. It also looked as though he'd gotten a haircut. He wore it very short now, which was a bit unusual for him, and the top of it was slicked back. Hep looked a bit nervous.

"We're going to play an original Hep Cat tune he taught the group and myself this afternoon. It's called 'Pinwheel,'" the trombone player announced.

They began to play and they sounded good; really good. Once Hep raised his saxophone to his lips, something magical seemed to take over, and I could see him start to relax. He was included on the next tune, too. After the song was concluded, the crowd roared with applause and I stood. Others followed. Hep bowed and took his leave from the stage. *What an experience for him; what a dream come true*, I thought.

Gran was almost done with her beer and Betty had finished her soda, so Mac and I moved to the bar to get them another. We had looked around for the waitress, but couldn't find her in the crowd. We pushed our way in and one of the bartenders turned to face us. As soon as I laid eyes on him, I knew who he was.

"Johnny? Well, I'll be a son of a gun!" I said.

"Sam? Well, what the hell? How you doing, buddy?"

We shook hands. Johnny Delbeck had grown up next door to my grandmother way back when. In fact, he and his sisters had stayed with us throughout the summer of 1916. I'd run into him a few times since they'd moved, but it had been way too long.

"What on earth are you doing here, Johnny? Don't tell me you don't have the job at Ford Motor Company anymore?"

"Nah," he said. "I'm just standing in for my cousin, Frank, for the night. He works here, but he came down with something and couldn't make it in. He called on me to take his place. Grace and I need the money, so I figured, why not? Besides, it's only for one night."

I introduced Johnny to Mac and they shook hands.

"Nice to meet you," Johnny said, nodding at Mac. He turned back to me and said, "Hey, Sam, I was thinking of maybe contacting you anyway. Your office still on Woodward?"

I nodded that it was.

"Well, Grace and I took in her sister's daughter a few months ago. She was nothing but trouble at home and Grace's sister was pulling her hair out over it. I was hesitant at bringing her down here, but Grace went ahead and offered, so what was I going to say? Anyway, she didn't come home last night. We're a bit worried."

"How old is she?" I asked.

"She's going to be eighteen this coming September. She's pulled this crap before at home, but since she's in our care now…well, we're worried."

"Have you called the police? Told them about it?"

"Nah, we didn't want to do that. She's already known to them up north, where her ma and stepdad live. She got caught a few years ago shoplifting at the five and dime up there. But listen, I have to get back to work here. I work the day shift tomorrow, so I'll stop by late tomorrow afternoon if she doesn't show up by then. Hopefully though, she'll be there when I get home tonight."

I hadn't introduced Mac as my former partner, who was still with the department. Johnny had no idea he was telling me all of this in front of a cop. He moved down the length of the bar to another customer, taking his order.

Mac headed back to the table, but before I could follow him, I felt a hand on my right arm. I turned to see a dame in her thirties standing next to me. My eyebrows rose. Coming up to just below my shoulder, she was wearing a tight fitting royal blue dress. She had a decorative matching blue feather sticking out of her blond hair at the back of her head. Bright red lipstick covered her lips, and her eyes appeared to be too close together. She gestured toward the table.

"Who's the old broad?" she asked. "Why don't you see if you can get rid of her and you and I can make a night of it? Whaddya say, handsome?"

Maybe it was because of the way I'd treated my grandmother earlier, but I was feeling very protective of her. I didn't like this woman's attitude or her audacity.

"What old broad?" I asked, craning my neck to look back at the group I'd been sitting with.

Her face took on a look of surprise. She pointed toward my grandmother.

"The old gal you're sitting with; the one in the green dress."

I turned to her and said, "Hey, that's my wife you're talking about! I take exception to that!"

Her jaw dropped and I headed for the table with the beer, wearing a smirk. When I arrived, I placed the bottle in front of Gran and leaned down, kissing her on the cheek. I glanced back. The blond was watching.

We talked while the band was on break, discussing what plans we had for the upcoming Easter Sunday. Gran told of having invited family over for the day, which led to the story of meeting Padraig and Derwood Flanagan when she was sixteen.

My grandmother's father had come over from Ireland when he was in his early twenties, first staying in Boston for a year. He then migrated to Detroit. One of my great grandfather's friends from Tralee, in the old country, had written him, saying two of his sons were making their voyage to America, specifically Detroit. The brothers were in their early twenties. Could he maybe watch out for them, make sure they arrived safely in the city? My great grandfather O'Malley agreed and helped the two young men to settle in and find jobs. He brought them to church, and that's where his daughters met them. One Saturday night there was to be a church social, and the night of that social, Pearl was on Padraig's arm and Ruby was escorted by Derwood. But by the night's end, they had switched partners.

"Derwood was nice enough," Gran said. "But Paddy was just so darn cute with his red hair and dark brown eyes. And that's how the O'Malley girls married the Flanagan boys."

Betty and Mac laughed. They'd found her story quite interesting, and I never got tired of listening to it. As the four of us rose to take leave of the lounge, Mac nodded to the bar and Johnny.

"He live in the city?" he asked me.

"No, he and Grace bought a place in Dearborn a few years after they married."

"Well, if that girl doesn't show up in another day or two, you should talk him into calling the Dearborn Police Department. You don't want to sit on this too long. And if you need any help, just let me know," he offered.

# Chapter Three

We were home by half past midnight, and Gran went straight to bed after kissing me goodnight and telling me she had enjoyed herself. I still felt badly about my earlier behavior, but I was glad things had turned out right. I removed my clothes and got ready for bed. Wearing my sleeveless undershirt and a pair of pajama bottoms, I brewed myself a cup of hot tea and carried it, along with the new Ellery Queen novel *The Quick and the Dead*, to the living room. I sat on the sofa, put my feet up on the coffee table, and before I knew it, I was on page nine of the book and hadn't remembered anything that I had read. My mind kept wandering to Johnny Delbeck.

Right after Christmas of 1915, my folks, my sister, and I, had moved in for a time with my grandmother and grandfather. They took us in five months after my father had lost his job. He'd been a machinist in a small shop in Detroit, but the business had closed, throwing my father into a depression. By the time he pulled himself out of it, we'd lost our house and he and my mother were broke. I was twelve and a half at the time and my older sister, Eva, was fifteen. The Delbeck's lived next door, where a couple of kids named Albie and Bobby lived now with their parents. I remembered overhearing my grandparents' conversation one night in March of 1916....

\*\*\*\*

"Paddy, that woman is hurtin' in the worst way. We've got to do something for them."

23

"Ruby, that's just a part of nature. I'm sorry she lost the baby, but there ain't nothin' we can do, girl"

"That's what you think, old man! She needs someone to help her with the cooking and cleaning. He's no good to her right now. And she's got those young ones."

"You're a good woman, Ruby Flanagan, that's for sure. Just remember, ya got your own to be concerned about. Don't go overdoin' it."

For weeks my grandmother fixed casseroles, meatloaves, and pies and walked them next door. She would then carry dirty laundry back to the house and wash it. When it was cleaned, ironed, and folded, she would send it back to the Delbeck home. My mother picked up the slack in our own living quarters. At twelve, it took me awhile to put it all together, but I'd soon figured out that the baby that Johnny Delbeck's mother had had lived only ten short days. My grandmother was seeing to it that her neighbor's family was kept fed and clothed while the woman recovered from the shock and depression. A couple of months after that conversation, my grandmother returned from the Delbeck's and sat down in the kitchen with my grandfather. She laid her head down on her arm, which rested on the top of the table.

"I'm tired, Pa. I'm downright tired, and she ain't gettin' any better. She sits in that chair all day long, starin' into space. I don't know what to do anymore."

"I told ya not to take on more than you could do. How can I help ya, girl? Just tell me."

"I got to talk to him, Paddy. She needs more help than any of us can give her. He's got to get her some help, and he's a good for nothin' in this situation."

On a cool, rainy day in late May, my grandfather walked in the back door and into the kitchen with his lunch pail in hand, home from work. I was getting a drink of water from the sink. His ears picked up the sound of someone crying softly.

"What's that?" he asked in his Irish brogue.

"It's Gran. She's been shut in her room crying for about an hour now and won't say what's wrong. No one else is home," I said.

My grandfather went to her and sat on the edge of the bed, not bothering to close the door behind him.

"Tell me I did right, Paddy. Tell me I didn't do the wrong thing. He's sending her off to Eloise. You remember what they did to my sister, Opal, in that place? Oh my dear Lord, Pa, tell me she's gonna be alright!"

I stood in the doorway and saw my grandfather pull his wife into his arms. He seemed shaken, a flicker of fear crossing his face.

"Come on, girl," he said, while patting her head. "You did the best you could. She's gonna be alright."

The mention of Eloise made me gasp at the time. I remembered the kids at school teasing a young girl whose father had been admitted to that hospital. They shouted that her father was crazy, and that he'd be in the insane asylum for the rest of his life. Was Johnny's mother crazy?

Mr. Delbeck knocked on our door three nights later. He told my grandparents that he was taking his wife to the mental facility the next morning, and that he didn't have anywhere to take his children. He was going to farm them out to the county's foster care system until everything was back to normal. They wouldn't all be going to the same home, but what could he do? He still had to work and keep his job.

"You'll do nothin' of the sort!" my grandmother said. "You tell those children to pack a few things and send them over here in the morning. They can stay here."

"Ma," my father, who was sitting on the living room sofa, objected. "How can we take in five more people when we've already got six living in a three bedroom house? They can't stay here!"

My grandmother shot my father a dirty look, and my grandfather stared at him over his newspaper.

"If I were you, Connor, I'd keep my mouth shut. We took you and your lot in, didn't we? If your ma says she wants 'em here, that's how it's gonna be."

And that's how I had gotten to know Johnny Delbeck and become friends with him. He hadn't paid much attention to me before he came to stay at Gran's house. I would be thirteen in about a month and he was fifteen…a huge difference at that stage of life. His four younger sisters shared a room with Eva, while Johnny and I slept each night on the living room floor. When you share space like that with someone, you naturally form a bond. And even though we rarely saw one another since we'd grown older, in my mind, that bond would exist forever.

# Chapter Four

I was going to stay home from the office on Wednesday morning to wash the outside of the windows on the house. Gran wanted them done before Sunday, but it was raining out. A steady downpour was in progress when I woke, accompanied by thunder and lightning. So instead, I stayed home and sprayed a mixture of vinegar and water on the inside of the windows, using old newspapers to wipe them clean. Gran spent the morning on the phone to my Aunt Pearl, and then to Helen.

"Well," she said as she entered the living room. "Pearl is baking a pecan pie and an apple pie and bringing them on Sunday. Helen said she wanted to bring cole slaw."

"That's good," I said. "It'll lighten the load for us."

"Why don't you rest for a bit after you finish that window, dear? You've been busy with that for over two hours."

I turned to her and smiled.

"I guess I will. But I want to get as many done as I can before I go into the office. I'm going to meet Johnny Delbeck there, probably around 3:30 or 4:00," I said.

"Johnny Delbeck?"

"Yeah, I saw him at the club last night, remember?"

"You didn't tell me that," she said.

"I thought I did. Are you sure I didn't mention it?"

"Yep; you didn't say a word. I wish you would have. It would've been nice to see him, dear. He was always such a nice boy. I could've asked him about his mother. I wonder how she's doing?"

****

By the time I entered the building on Woodward Avenue, the rain had been reduced to a light sprinkle. I climbed the flight of stairs instead of taking the elevator and unlocked the door to my second floor office. When I turned on the radio which sat on top of my filing cabinet, I was in time to hear Edward R. Murrow report on the progress of the war that was raging in Europe and the Pacific.

*"...as Adolf Hitler warned today that he would cause so many changes in Europe that it would be impossible to alter all of them. As the Nazi system becomes more firmly implemented in the European economic life, Allied political leaders realize...."*

I turned the radio off; sometimes the war news was just too depressing. While I waited for Johnny to show, I pulled out my bottle of Jack Daniels and a glass that I kept in the bottom drawer of my filing cabinet, poured some, and took a sip. I watched the drizzle float to the ground below and enjoyed the quiet, and wondered if Grace's niece had shown up last night. I was hoping she had, for her sake and the sake of Johnny and his wife. Surely if she had, though, Johnny would've called me...but if he'd called me at the office that morning, I hadn't been there to receive it. I wasn't even sure he still had my home phone number so he could call me there. I glanced at my watch. It was a quarter to five.

I picked up the receiver to my telephone and asked for the operator's assistance in looking up Johnny's home number. I knew the street he lived on, but not the address. He lived in the west part of Dearborn just north of Michigan Avenue on Garrison. From what I remembered, he lived in a pretty nice area of the city. She gave me the number and I wrote it on a scratch piece of paper sitting on my desk, then hung up and dialed his house. After six rings, I disconnected. I was pouring myself more whiskey when my door opened. It was Johnny, and I smiled.

"Hey, I didn't know if you were going to make it. I hope you have good news for me."

He brushed the droplets of rain from his jacket and shook his head. He looked worried as he took a seat across from me and sighed heavily.

"Gee whiz! I had to park two blocks away. People are out everywhere."

"I guess shopping for the holiday," I suggested.

He nodded. "Yeah, probably."

He leaned forward, reaching into his back right pocket, and brought out his wallet.

"I stopped at home after work. I thought maybe you could use this."

Johnny handed me a picture of a young girl, shot from the shoulders up. I looked at it closely. The girl in the picture appeared to be about fifteen years old. She had long, medium brown hair and dark eyes. Her lips were very full and I could tell, since she was smiling, that her right top front tooth was chipped. She was very plain looking, not what I would call pretty or cute.

"This is her?" I asked.

"Yeah. That was taken about a year ago, I guess. Grace is worried sick, and I don't mind telling you, I'm pretty shaken myself. I was almost sure she'd be at home after I got back from Baker's, but she wasn't. You gotta find her, Sam. Oh God, she's been gone since Monday!"

I pulled my eyes away from the picture and leaned down, extracting another glass from my filing cabinet drawer, and poured Johnny some of the Jack Daniels.

"Here, drink this," I said. "It'll calm your nerves a bit."

He took the glass and raised it to his lips, downing the contents in one gulp, and I poured him some more as he wiped his mouth using the sleeve on his jacket. He was shaking from either nervousness or his damp clothing...maybe from both.

"Okay," I said. "Tell me everything about this girl, and start from the beginning."

"We'd gone up to Harrison, where Grace's sister, Vivian, lives with her second husband. He's not Myrna Lou's father. That's her name," he said, gesturing toward the picture. "Myrna Lou Stevic. Anyway, we spent Christmas up there. The whole four days we were there, it was nothing but chaos. This girl isn't a happy person, and you could tell that she didn't want anyone around her to be happy, either. All she did was complain and start arguments with her mother and her two half-brothers. Grace's sister had two boys by this guy she's married to now, who, in my opinion, is nothing but a louse. But hell," he shrugged. "I don't have to live with him. Anyway, on the ride back down here, Grace gets it into her head that she's going to help Vivian out by bringing Myrna Lou down here to stay with us for a while. She figures she'll enroll her in the school here and get her involved with the youth group at church. She's going to save her from herself; set her on the right track. I told her I didn't like the idea, that we didn't need that kind of problem. I kept telling her it wasn't going to work, but did she listen?" He shook his head and took another drink of the whiskey. "The next thing I know, she's already made arrangements for the girl to come down. I was ticked, but what could I do? I went and picked her up at the bus station the first week of January, and she's been here ever since. On occasion, she's been a real pain, but we actually thought she was coming around to the church thing. She seemed eager to go the last month and a half or so. We figured she was enjoying the group, and maybe she was learning what she *should* be learning about the Lord. Gee, this has me all worked up. Like I said, she's pulled this at home, but there was never any indication that she wanted to get away from *us*."

"Tell me about that," I said. "When she left home up in Harrison, how long did she stay gone and where'd they find her?"

"Well, the first time she pulled this stunt, she'd gone to a girlfriend's house and lied, saying her mother said she could spend the weekend there. Vivian called around and found her. Then early last fall she took off again, but came waltzing into the house the next morning. She'd slept out in the garage all night. I even checked our garage a few times, and believe me, she wasn't there.

Well, Monday I took Grace to the pharmacy for some things she wanted to pick up. Jake was at baseball practice at the school and Susan was in her bedroom working on some report she had to hand in before Easter vacation. When we pulled out of the drive, Myrna Lou was sitting on the front steps of the porch with Bonnie, our youngest. We weren't gone more than forty-five minutes. When we got back, which was about 5:00 or so, Bonnie was in the living room playing by herself. Susan hadn't even been aware that Myrna Lou was gone. Grace has called some of the girls from the church, but they said they haven't seen her. She doesn't know what kids she talks to at school. She only knows of a girl named Marion, but doesn't know her last name and has never seen her. What are we going to do, Sam?"

"Let me get a list of the girls that Grace called. Maybe I can get more information out of them."

I grabbed a small pad of paper and picked up my pencil, then looked up at him. He was running his fingers through his hair.

"Aw, damn it! I don't have any names to give you. Grace would know that. I rarely go to church with her, but she goes all the time, her and the kids. She plays the organ at Christ the Divine Lutheran Church. It's about six blocks away from the house. That's where Grace is tonight. She got the kids ready and Pastor Mayhew was going to pick them up. They've got some Easter program they're doing tonight. Maybe you can take a run out to the house tomorrow at some point and talk to Grace. She'd have a lot more information."

"I can do that," I said. "But I think I'll head out to the city and cruise the streets for awhile. Any parks or areas she might hang out at near the house?"

"I'm not sure. There's a park at the end of the street, two blocks down. I see kids there sometimes. There are burger joints and that kind of stuff up on Michigan Avenue. She's probably been in those places."

"Have you called Vivian about this yet?"

Johnny looked down in his lap and shook his head.

"Nope, I wanted to make sure you were going to help us first. At least we can tell her that much. Grace and I can call her tonight."

"Make sure you do. How do you know she didn't catch a bus back home? Of course, I'm sure your sister-in-law would've called, but you never know. Maybe the girl lied to her and told her the two of you put her on that bus."

Johnny's head raised and there was a look of hope in his eyes.

"I still think I'll take a look around Dearborn tonight, though," I said.

Before he left my office, he brought up the subject of my fee. I shook his hand and told him not to worry about that for the moment. This dilemma might all be solved in a matter of hours with one phone call up to Harrison, Michigan. I scribbled my office phone number and the number at the house down on a piece of paper and handed it to him, and told him to call me at any hour about anything. He placed it in his wallet, thanked me, and left.

About fifteen minutes later, I was in my '38 burgundy Chevy Coupe on my way to Dearborn, a small city that neighbored Detroit on its western boundary. The rain was still falling lightly, hitting the rooftop of the car and landing on the windshield. I'd always loved the sound of rain, but tonight I barely noticed it. My mind was preoccupied with finding this girl. I truly hoped the little nitwit had hopped on that bus back to her mother. If she had, I was hoping the woman would whoop her behind good when she found out what she'd put Johnny and Grace through. If she hadn't gone home, I was going to suggest to Johnny and Grace that they do the same thing when I found her. I didn't even know Myrna Lou or the situation, yet I found myself growing angry.

I turned north onto Oakwood Boulevard, then cruised slowly down the street, looking to my left and my right. The street had a hospital, a school, and a Catholic church, but it was mainly lined with residential houses. I didn't see one person out. When I came to Michigan Avenue I turned left. The Delbeck's lived close by. I found their street, Garrison, and drove slowly down it, glancing at

Johnny's house as I passed. Lights were on inside and his car was in the drive…he'd made it home.

I kept on going until I got to the end of the street, where there was a small park with a set of swings and three benches, but the rest of it was just an expanse of lawn. I was surprised to see three young men passing a football to each other. Their hair and clothes were wet, but it didn't seem to bother them.

I stopped the Chevy and turned off the engine. Taking Myrna Lou's picture out of my wallet, I slipped it into the right pocket of my overcoat. As I approached the boys, they noticed me and stopped what they were doing, and began heading my way as I walked toward them.

"Hello," I called out. "I wonder if I could ask you something."

"What?" the young man holding the ball asked.

"Have you ever seen this girl before?"

I showed them Myrna Lou's picture while trying to protect it from the rain. The other two boys started to snicker.

"Yeah, we've seen her," one of them said. "And just about every other guy has seen her, too," he laughed with his buddy.

"What are you two, morons?" the one with the ball said.

He frowned at his two companions and their laughter subsided while they looked at him apologetically. I could tell who the leader of this little group was. He grabbed the picture from me, looked at it closer, and then handed it back.

"Yeah, we know her," he said. "We go to Dearborn High with her. She's in one of my classes. You her father?"

I shook my head, placing the photo in my pocket once again.

"She comes from up north, but she's staying with her aunt and uncle down the street here," I pointed. "They haven't seen her since Monday. I'm wondering if any of you have seen her or know where she might be?"

"Now that you mention it, she hasn't been in class the last couple of days. She was there Monday, though, because we had a paper due in English and she didn't have it to hand in, and Mrs. Dade made a big stink about it in front of all of us. I remember that."

I looked toward the other two and they shrugged. I turned back.

"What's your name, son?"

"Richard Neller, but I go by Rick. I live right there," he said, pointing at the house on the corner, adjacent to the park.

I turned to look and saw a woman standing on the porch watching us. She had her arms folded around her, trying to ward off the cool dampness while under the protection of the awning. She seemed leery of who her son was talking to.

"You a cop?" he asked.

"No, just someone trying to help the Delbeck's find Myrna Lou."

"I know what house she's staying at, and I'll tell them if I see her," he said. "I hope she's not in any trouble."

"I hope so, too," I said. "I'd sure appreciate it if you'd let her aunt and uncle know if you find out where she's at. That would be great. They're pretty worried."

"No problem, man."

I started for my car and the boys returned to tossing the ball. Rick's mother stayed on her porch until she disappeared from my view as I drove down the street. Once on Michigan Avenue again, I drove looking to my left and right. No one was out on the thoroughfare. I might have had a better chance at spotting some activity if it hadn't been for the weather. Stores had closed for the day, and that meant any shoppers had returned home.

Turning around, I retraced my route, driving the length of the main road again, and spotted a White Castle hamburger joint. The front of it was a huge plate glass window and the lights were ablaze, but there were few customers. Pulling into the parking lot, I killed the engine and went in. The aroma that hit me made my mouth water. I was hungry and I was cold. I sat at the counter on a stool that was close to the entrance. A man in his fifties sat several stools away from me. He had a very young boy with him…probably his grandson.

"What can I get ya, mister?" the man behind the counter asked. He was a big man, weighing probably three hundred pounds, was tall, and his hair was oily and stuck to the sides of his head. He wore a white paper cap and a long white apron, which was badly stained with grease. I figured he was somewhere between forty and forty-five years of age.

"I want three of those burgers, and give me some coffee."

"Whaddya want on the burgers?" he asked.

"Anything, everything, just make it quick. I'm starving," I said.

He chuckled as he turned and threw three balls of ground meat on the grill, smashing them with his spatula.

"How 'bout some fries with that?" he called to me over his shoulder.

"Sounds good, and I changed my mind. I want four of those burgers."

I watched as he got the meat going and then threw a handful of french fries into the deep fryer. They crackled and spit when they hit the hot grease. He then poured me a mug of coffee from a freshly made pot. He set cream and sugar on the counter, which I didn't use, and then meandered down to talk to the man and the young boy. I pulled out a cigarette and lit it, smoking it while I sipped on the java.

"Hey, Teddy, what's the Easter Bunny gonna bring ya?" he asked the child.

Teddy shrugged and his grandfather rustled his hair while smiling down at him.

"Something good," the older man said, then added as he looked at the cook behind the counter, "He's been a good boy."

"Well, I have something for you right now."

The man who worked at White Castle reached under the counter and came up with a sucker, handing it to the boy. The child grabbed it, smiling. Teddy's grandfather stood and reached into his back pocket. He took out the money to pay his bill and laid it on the counter.

"Well, got to get the boy home. You take care now, Joe, and have a good holiday."

He helped the boy on with his coat and hat and left, holding the young one's hand. Joe returned to the grill in front of me and flipped the four meat patties, then grabbed the pot of coffee from the burner and topped off my mug.

"Them's good people," he said, nodding toward the door.

"His grandson is a cutie," I said.

Joe let out a boisterous laugh.

"That ain't his grandson, although I can see where you'd come up with that idea. Teddy's his son. He married late in life and the boy was a gift he never thought he'd get."

"Oh, I just figured...."

"I know what ya figured. Most people probably think that if they don't know them." He pointed out the front window behind me. "Paul owns that shop there across the street."

I turned, looking through the drizzle to a darkened business. The sign read "Paul's Barber Shop" in red lettering.

"Paul's been cuttin' my hair for more than twenty years now. You ever need a barber, go to him," he told me.

"I don't live here. I have a place in Detroit," I said.

He smiled and pointed his beefy index finger at me.

"I knew it! I didn't think I'd ever seen ya around here. I got a thing for faces."

He turned and lifted the basket of fries out of the hot oil and used his spatula to lay the meat on buns. He arranged it all on a dark green plastic plate and set it in front of me, along with ketchup and mustard. He then poured himself a mug of coffee and turned back to me, resting his elbows on the counter.

"Okay, so what brings ya into Dearborn?" Joe asked.

I lifted one of the sandwiches to my lips and took a bite before answering him. Dang, it was good. Joe sure knew how to put together a good burger. I grabbed a paper napkin from the dispenser that was sitting in front of me and wiped the mustard and ketchup from the corner of my mouth.

"Well," I said. "I'm actually trying to help out a friend. His wife's niece has been staying with them and she seems to be missing. You get a lot of school kids in here, Joe?"

"Sure do; sometimes too many. There've been times when they come in here after school and take up the whole counter and all they do is buy a soda. Can't make no money like that. I have to give them a time limit so I can make room for some payin' folk in here."

I reached into my overcoat pocket, where I still had the picture Johnny had given me, and I handed it to Joe.

"Ever see her before? That's the one I'm looking for. Her name is Myrna Lou Stevic."

He eyed the picture and then looked up at me.

"What'd you say her name was?"

"Myrna Lou Stevic."

His gaze returned to the photo and he started to nod his head.

"Yeah, she's been in here quite a bit, but she hasn't been in this week so far. She doesn't look like this when she comes in."

"What do you mean?" I asked.

"Well, when I see her, she's got a bunch of war paint on her face. I don't know what she's trying to prove with all that makeup, 'cause she looks silly, I think. And she's not what I would call a little lady, either."

My eyebrows went up and I waited for him to explain himself as I filled my mouth with a couple of fries. Before he got the chance to go on, the swinging double doors that led to the back of the restaurant opened and a young man passed through them and entered the eating area. He was heavy set and had a fleshy baby face. He was badly pigeon toed. Joe watched him while he removed the dirty dishes that sat on the counter where the barber and son had sat when I first came into the eatery. He put them into a bus tub that was hidden under the counter and wiped the area with a damp towel.

"Hey, Ernie," Joe called out. "Come here a minute."

The young man left his towel behind and walked our way.

"Ernie, I want you to meet our new customer," Joe said. "This is...uh...."

"Sam," I said, after swallowing a bite of food.

Ernie looked at me and smiled, showing a mouth full of rotten teeth. He extended his right hand toward me. I grabbed it and shook.

"Nice to meet you, Mr. Sam," he said with a lisp. "I hope you come back and see us again."

"That's all I wanted," Joe said, as he patted Ernie on the back. "You can take that bus tub back now. When you finish with those dishes, I'll make you something to eat for your break."

Ernie turned around and did what he was told. Joe nodded toward the back of the restaurant and spoke to me in a lowered voice.

"He's twenty-six years old and doesn't have the brains God gave a twelve year old, but he's the most polite young man I know and the hardest worker I've ever employed." He looked down at Myrna Lou's picture again and pointed to it. "Now this one," he said, "comes in here with that bright lipstick and that crap on her eyes, and she's telling Ernie how good lookin' he is; telling him she'd love to go steady with him. As she tells him these things, the other two girls she's with are laughing hysterically. Real funny, huh? And Ernie's buying it all. He's blushing and smiling, and I could just imagine his little heart going pitter patter. Well, I can tell you, I was seeing red. I told her she ought to be ashamed of herself, and she tells me to mind my own business. I told her this *was* my business and if she didn't knock it off, she wouldn't be welcomed here anymore. That seemed to shut her up."

"You know the girls she was with?" I asked.

"Nah...I mean, they come in here, but I don't *know* them. I don't even know their names. But I can tell ya this. She came in here about a week and a half, maybe two weeks ago with some young fella and about four other kids. They wanted to tack up a flyer for some church. I just took it down yesterday. Now where is that thing?"

He moved down the length of the counter and rifled through several sheets of paper that were under the cash register, finally grabbing one. He returned, handing it to me, and I read it.

**LOOKING TO DO GOD'S WORK IN THE
COMMUNITY WITH OTHERS YOUR OWN AGE?**
COME MEET OTHER 13-18 YEAR OLDS FOR BIBLE
STUDY AND COMMUNITY VOLUNTEER SERVICE
DURING THIS DIFFICULT TIME OF WAR.
CHRIST THE DIVINE LUTHERAN CHURCH
2334 MICHIGAN AVENUE
THURSDAY, APRIL 15 AT 7:00 P.M.

"Who was the guy the kids were with?" I asked.

He shrugged. "I don't know, but I figure he might be the pastor or something. Seemed like a nice fella. He bought the kids a Coca Cola, asked me if I would post that, and then they left." He laughed. "She acted decent and her face was washed when she came in with that group. I can keep an eye out for her and if ya come in again, I'll let ya know."

Joe asked me if there was anything else he could help me with as he returned the picture of Myrna Lou to me. I told him there was.

"Let me keep this flyer, and wrap this last burger to go for me," I said. "You might as well put another one on the grill, making it just like this one. I got a grandmother at home who loves these things."

Judith White

# Chapter Five

Thursday morning's weather was the complete opposite of Wednesdays. The sky was a beautiful blue with no clouds as far as my eye could see. There was a gentle breeze, and the thermometer that hung on the outside wall of the stone garage out back said it was sixty-eight degrees. I was sitting at the kitchen table with a cup of coffee, about to read the Detroit News, when I heard a truck stop and idle in front of the house, so I went into the living room and looked out onto the street. The milkman was delivering our weeks' worth of the dairy product, and I opened the door and met him on the porch.

"Morning," I greeted him. "You wouldn't happen to have any buttermilk on the truck today, would you?"

"I sure do," he said. "How many do you want?"

"Just one. Add it to the bill for the end of the month."

I carried the bottles back to the kitchen and refrigerated them. Gran would be surprised when she saw what I'd added to our order. She wanted to use it to bake buttermilk biscuits for the Easter Sunday dinner, but we couldn't find any at the market a couple of days ago. She'd come into my room early that morning, telling me her friend, Helen, was going to pick her up and they were going to Ben Franklin, the five and dime store on West Grand Boulevard. She wanted to buy herself a new apron for the holiday, and she asked me if I had any money she could have. Whatever I had had been sitting on my dresser. When I got up about twenty minutes later, I'd found half of it was gone. I now had eight dollars in cash to my name. I mentally made a note to stop by the bank to withdraw some money before the holiday weekend began, just in case.

I took my seat at the table once again and picked up the newspaper. I was shocked to see our former governor, Luren Dickinson, had suffered a heart attack, and the prognosis was grim. He was eighty-four. Throughout his terms in office, he'd been loudly and openly opposed to the sale of liquor, saying it caused all sorts of evils in society.

I read another article about Doolittle's Raiders, and how the Japs had executed some of the group who had fallen into their hands after their planes had crash-landed. I found myself getting angry and very sad all at once. I said a silent prayer for those brave men and their families, then pushed the paper aside. I didn't want to read any more bad news for the moment.

Finishing my coffee, I grabbed my keys, heading out the back door toward the garage. It was 11:30 a.m., and Grace would be expecting me soon.

****

The streets of Dearborn were much more populated today. I passed the White Castle and instinctively turned to look in the window. I saw Joe with his back to me, undoubtedly flipping burgers on the grill.

When I reached Johnny's house on Garrison, I pulled into the drive. A green tricycle was sitting on the lawn near the porch, and a doll was positioned on the seat of it, leaning to its right, in danger of falling to the ground. The oak front door to the house was open and only the screen door blocked direct access to the living room. I knocked on it, and Grace appeared almost immediately. She smiled and swung the door out, inviting me in.

"Sam, it's been so long. Good to see you...but I wish it weren't under these circumstances."

"Howdy, Grace."

Johnny's wife was a small woman standing about five feet two inches tall, with light brown hair that she kept short and neat, beautiful hazel eyes, and a warm smile. Grace was wearing a solid navy blue housedress with short sleeves, belted at her tiny waist.

I moved past her and into a small living room that was bright and cheery. White lace curtains hung from rods at the large front window. A blue and green floral print couch sat in front of it with round tables at each end. Two navy armchairs sat across from the sofa, and the cream-colored walls were partly covered with family photos. In the middle of one wall, under an arrangement of pictures, stood a newer floor model radio with a vase of fresh flowers sitting on top of it. I could smell their scent as it filled the room.

I removed my hat and sat in the chair closest to me, which had an ornate floor lamp next to it. As I lowered myself into the chair, I caught movement behind the other one. I turned to see a blond headed little girl, who smiled and quickly ducked back into hiding position. I laughed. Grace held out her hands.

"Come here, Bonnie. Come and meet Mr. Flanagan."

The child hesitantly showed herself, looking at me, ran to her mother, and then turned back toward me and smiled shyly. She hopped up onto her mother's lap, laid her head against Grace's chest, and then stuck her left thumb into her mouth and began to suck.

"You haven't met Bonnie yet, Sam," she said as she ran her fingers through her daughter's hair.

"No, I haven't. She's adorable, Grace."

Bonnie had very light blond hair falling in waves an inch or two beyond her shoulders. Her large eyes were dark brown and long, thick black lashes framed them. She had a button nose. She resembled Johnny when she smiled.

"How old is she now?" I asked.

"She just turned five at the beginning of the month. Did Johnny tell you about her?"

"Tell me about her? What do you mean?"

I was puzzled. I wasn't sure what Grace meant by the question. I'd never seen Bonnie; it had been that long since Johnny and I had connected, but I certainly knew of her existence and

Grace was aware of that. Silently, I vowed not to let that amount of time pass again before getting together with him and his family.

"She doesn't speak…or won't. We've had her to a handful of doctors who all say the same thing; that nothing is wrong physically. I can count the number of words she's said to us on both hands."

"No, Johnny didn't tell me. That's too bad, but I am sure she'll speak when she's ready. It might just be that once she starts she won't stop," I said, and we both started laughing.

Suddenly, Grace's laughter turned to tears. She tried to hide it by burying her face in Bonnie's hair. The child took on a look of bewilderment and fear, and soon she too started to cry. Bonnie looked at me, wondering what I had done to her mother to cause her to be so unhappy. Grace sensed this and tried to pull herself together.

"Shh," she said while stroking her daughter's hair. "It's okay, baby. Momma's alright." Looking at me she said, "Sorry, Sam. I guess I'm very emotional about Myrna Lou. I try to function as I normally would, but I feel as though I'm a zombie and I'm just going through the motions. I can't believe this is happening. I called Vivian last night and she was sleeping, but Bart answered and he wouldn't wake her. Can you *believe* that? I told him that Myrna Lou had taken off Monday and we haven't seen her since, but he said he would tell Viv when she woke up. He wasn't going to wake her because she'd come home exhausted from work and she needed the rest."

"You're kidding me! This Bart is her husband?"

Grace nodded.

"I guess this means that the girl didn't return home then, right?" I continued.

"Right," Grace said. "I called again this morning, but he told me Vivian had already left for work. She works at a small restaurant in Harrison. She manages the waitstaff while Bart does nothing in between the few jobs he's been able to get. He never lasts long at any one of them. I'm beginning to see why Johnny dislikes him so much. At first, I thought he was being a bit too hard on Bart, but after eight years of seeing the same old behavior...anyway, I asked him if he'd told her what I had called about last night and he told me no; that he didn't want to upset her before her shift; he'd wait until tonight. He's an imbecile!"

I had to agree; the man sounded like a good for nothing.

We got down to business when I took out a small spiral notebook and a pencil. Grace gave me the names of some of the teens that were in the youth group at the church, as well as the addresses and phone numbers of those she knew. She told me that Myrna Lou had talked about a girl at school named Marion when she first started going to the high school in Dearborn, but she hadn't spoken of her recently, and that her niece had never brought the girl home for the rest of the family to meet. Although she suspected that Myrna Lou was fond of boys, Grace didn't know of anyone she was interested in at the moment. Thinking back, Grace was frustrated by all she really didn't know about Myrna Lou's life in Dearborn.

"I had such high hopes for her. I thought once we got her going to the church and involved with the youth group there, she'd settle down a little and start doing what was right. She was going to go to youth camp for a few days next week while school is out and was looking forward to it, but suddenly, on Sunday night after we got home from church, she announced she didn't want to go. She wouldn't tell us why, but she seemed a little upset. I've been wracking my brain, trying to think of where she might have gone and why."

Bonnie slid off her mother's lap and climbed on the sofa next to Grace, leaning on the back and looking out the window. She turned to Grace and yanked on her dress sleeve, pointing out the window and across the street. We both turned to look at what the child was pointing at. An elderly man was out on his front lawn pushing his mower in what looked like its first cut of the season. With him was his large black Labrador, running in the yard and then disappearing behind a brown auto that was parked at the curb one house down. The dog appeared again, running in circles on the lawn while his master continued his yard work.

"What is it, hon? You see Buster, don't you? You can't go out right now to play with him, sweetie," Grace said, and then turning to me, "She loves that dog."

The little girl turned to her mother, tugging at her again and pointing. Grace picked her up and returned her to her lap. Bonnie wriggled to get free. She was successful and stood again to gaze out the window.

"How about some lunch, Sam? I've made tuna salad for sandwiches if you'd like to stay," Grace offered.

I declined, saying I'd like to swing by the high school to talk to the principal there. He might have more information on who Myrna Lou hung around. I figured I'd better get that done, seeing as how school wouldn't be in session in the coming week.

I picked up my hat and rose from the chair. Bonnie slid off the couch and made her way toward me. She tugged at the sleeve on my suit coat and pointed toward the window yet again. I gazed outside. The dog and his owner weren't there anymore. I smiled at her and patted her on the head.

****

Dearborn High School was located at the corner of Mason Street and Garrison Avenue, just a few short blocks from the Delbeck home. I pulled into the parking lot and cruised up and down the aisles looking for a spot. I finally found one at the outer edge of the area. It wasn't a very large building, but its grounds were nicely manicured, with attractive bushes lining the front of it.

I walked in and spotted the principal's office to the left. Two women were sitting behind desks when I entered. The younger of the two looked up and stared at me as I approached her. She couldn't have been more than twenty or twenty-one years old. Her long, thick black hair and light blue eyes were striking. The nameplate on her desk read Becky Timmons.

"Good afternoon. Can I help you?" she asked.

"I'm wondering if I could speak to the principal. I don't have an appointment, but I believe it's quite important. It concerns one of the students here."

"Can I give him the student's name?"

"Myrna Lou Stevic," I answered.

"Ah, yes," she said. "Are you her father?"

I shook my head no and she rose and softly knocked on a door leading to an inner office. She stuck her head inside and muttered something to the man behind the door. She backed out, looking at me, and held the entryway open wider.

"He'll see you now."

I walked into the office and heard the door shut behind me. The man sitting behind the desk looked up and then stood. He was a big man; not fat, but tall and very solid and muscular. His brown hair was speckled with some gray, and black framed glasses sat on his nose. The man wore gray trousers and a white shirt, with the sleeves rolled up to just below his elbows. His loosened tie was black and his suit jacket was resting on the back of his leather chair. A brass nameplate on his desk said "Vernon T. Wagner." He extended his hand and I leaned over the desk to shake it.

"This is about Myrna Lou, Mr...uh...?"

"Flanagan. Yes, I'm looking into her whereabouts. Her uncle is a friend of mine and they haven't seen her since early evening on Monday."

"Take a seat." He gestured to one of the chairs facing his desk. "Mrs. Delbeck called me Tuesday morning telling me the same thing and asking if Myrna Lou had shown up for classes. This is very disturbing, Mr. Flanagan. I can't imagine what happened to her, outside of her just walking away...and I don't doubt that would be something she would do. I don't think she's been very happy here at Dearborn High."

He sat and pulled his chair in closer to the desk. Mr. Wagner mindlessly picked up a pencil that had been lying in front of him and began tapping it against the wood.

"I thought maybe you could tell me which other students Myrna Lou has made friends with and maybe I could question them," I suggested. "Her aunt tells me she's heard the girl mention a Marion, but she doesn't know her last name."

"We have two students by that name here, but it has to be Marion Dombrano. She's a senior this year and the other girl is a freshman. I hate to admit this, but I'm not really sure who Myrna Lou got chummy with. Her teachers might know a little more than I would. Hold on," he said, and then rose from his chair and walked to the door, opening it.

"Miss Timmons, would you go down to the teacher's lounge and tell Mrs. Dade and Mr. Schramm that I'd like to see them in my office?"

He returned to his chair, unrolling his sleeves and fastening the buttons at his wrists. He tightened his tie and put his jacket on.

"I hate to rush out like this, but I'm taking the rest of the afternoon off because of personal business. Mrs. Dade and Mr. Schramm can probably tell you more of what you want to know. They are two of the girl's teachers. Will you please keep me abreast of this situation, Mr. Flanagan? Even though Myrna Lou wasn't a stellar student here, we care about all the young people who attend our school."

I assured him that I would. He leaned down to pick up a brown briefcase as the door to his office opened and the two faculty members entered. Before leaving for the day, he explained who I was and what I wanted.

After he left, the two teachers took seats, Mrs. Dade choosing a chair next to mine, and Mr. Schramm sitting behind the desk where Mr. Wagner had sat moments before.

"How can we help you, Mr. Flanagan?" Mrs. Dade asked.

She was a hard looking woman with steel gray hair combed severely away from her face and done up in a bun at the crown of her head. She wore no makeup, her nose was long and straight, ending with a point, and her mouth was small and tight. I pegged her to be in her mid to late fifties. She reminded me of some of the strict teachers I had had while growing up. I tried my best not to let her intimidate me and cause me to revert to the position of student.

"Well, I need to get a line on which students are friendly with Myrna Lou. At this point, we have no idea who her friends are. Maybe on Monday she went over to see one of them. I'm really starting from scratch here, but someone must know something."

"I'm afraid that Myrna Lou wasn't well liked here, by the students or teachers, Mr. Flanagan," she said.

"That's being rather harsh, isn't it, Agnes?" Mr. Schramm asked.

"The man needs answers, Tony. I'm not going to sugar coat the situation here with a lot of nonsense. I won't pussy foot around with him...I'm telling it like it is. Of course, you and I both know what kind of relationship *you* had with the girl!"

I turned to look at him. He was a good twenty-five years, or more, younger than his colleague. Tony Schramm wore his blond hair a bit too long over his ears and at the back of his collar. He was a very handsome young man, and I could see where adolescent girls would swoon over him being their teacher. His face took on a soft shade of red and he abruptly leaned forward and put both of his palms on the desk. He was angry.

"Just what do you mean by that? That's an unfair remark and you know it!"

"Oh really? Well, you forget that the second week that girl was here, I walked into your room and she was standing so close to you, you could probably feel her breath on your neck!"

Before he could object and defend himself, she turned to me and said, "That's how Myrna Lou is. She throws herself at boys and, obviously, at older men, too. The girl knows no shame. That's why very few of the other students—the female students, that is—tried to befriend her. And whatever brains the good Lord gave her, she doesn't use them academically. She isn't interested in learning."

"I need to know about a Marion Dombrano. I've heard that they're chummy, at least, to some degree."

"That much is true," Agnes Dade said. "Marion is a very nice young lady who goes out of her way to be friendly to everyone. But I get the idea that she's had enough, too. I believe Marion was seeing Arthur Gellert, who is a senior also, socially, and I get the feeling Myrna Lou was interfering with that relationship. I don't know this for sure; just my observation and intuition, you understand. I don't make it a practice to get involved with the personal lives of my students. I'm here to instruct them and nothing more. If they have something they want to talk about that is bothering them, there are counselors for that. I believe Richard Neller was quite friendly to Myrna Lou as well. I'm not sure of the nature of his intent, but he tried several times to engage her in conversation. But like I said, these are just idle observations on my part."

I jotted these names in my little notebook. I remembered Rick from the park that was adjacent to his house on Garrison Avenue. I looked up at Tony Schramm and noticed the look of disdain he wore as he stared at Agnes Dade. He tore his gaze away from her and looked at me.

"I teach general science," he said. "Myrna Lou's seat was next to Audrey Sweeney. You might want to talk to her. They talked sometimes in class, but I don't know if they ever saw each other after hours. You might want to speak to Louise Elliot and Rose Peterson. I've seen them sitting with her at lunch, but what Agnes says is true. She tended to alienate the girls in the school because of her flirtation with the boys. I truly didn't think she was having the kind of trouble at her aunt and uncle's where she would want to run away. She didn't give any evidence of that." He shrugged. "I don't know, maybe I'm wrong, though."

I asked them if they could give me addresses to go along with the names they'd given me and Tony Schramm extracted a large binder from the bottom drawer of the principal's desk. I wrote the corresponding addresses next to the names that I had jotted down. I rose, thanked them, and took my leave from the office. Out in the parking lot and half way to my car, I stopped and stuck a Lucky Strike between my lips. Drawing a pack of matches from my right jacket pocket, I lit the cigarette and took a long drag on it.

I heard running footsteps coming up behind me, and when I turned, I saw Tony Schramm approaching.

"Mr. Flanagan," he called. "Wait, I need to talk to you."

He was out of breath from running, and when he caught up to me he bent at the waist, drawing in oxygen. I waited for him to recover.

"What Agnes said in there was true; well, partly true. But she's got it all wrong. There was one day when Myrna Lou stayed behind after the bell had rung dismissing class. I thought she had a question about the assignment or something. But she came behind my desk and got too close. I tried to be discreet and back away from her, but I was so shocked to see she was flirting with me. I was dumbfounded. I swear nothing happened then or at any other time. My God, I'm thirty years old! What would I want with a seventeen year old?"

"Oh, I don't know," I said. "It's been known to happen before, Mr. Schramm. You tell me."

"Oh for God's sake; I'm telling you nothing happened. Look, look here. I want to show you something."

He reached in his back right pocket and brought out a black leather wallet. He flipped it open to a small photo he had of himself and a cute woman. She had blond hair and big eyes. They were both smiling in the picture, looking very happy.

"This is my wife. We've been married going on three years now. Why would I want Myrna Lou? If this gets out, and people take it the wrong way, it could ruin my career and my life! Agnes is nothing but a witch. The students call her dragon lady because she's so strict and righteous. I tell you, I'm not that way with the female students. I don't cross the line. Please don't think otherwise and go delving into this. There is nothing to find out."

"Look, Mr. Schramm, I'm not here to delve into what isn't my business. I just want to find the girl and take her back to the Delbeck's. If what you say is true, you have nothing to worry about."

He sighed with relief and turned away after thanking me, and I watched as he walked slowly back to the school entrance. Catching some movement, I looked up to a window on the second floor. Agnes Dade had been watching us. I waved but she didn't wave back. She moved away from the window and disappeared from sight. I headed for my car.

Judith White

# Chapter Six

Instead of leaving the school parking lot right away, I sat in the auto with my window down, smoking my cigarette. The breeze that entered the interior was wonderful. I sat there and contemplated all I was learning about this girl, Myrna Lou.

It wasn't turning out to be a pretty picture. It didn't appear that she was the type of young lady that was popular; at least not with members of her own sex. She had to be staying with *someone, somewhere.* I wondered if she had a girlfriend that she was closer to that no one else knew of. And why did she leave and stay away? No one had given me any indication that she was dissatisfied with staying at Johnny's. Then, what Grace said about her deciding all of a sudden not to attend youth camp surfaced in my mind. Grace said that after church on Sunday night, the girl seemed upset. I wondered what could've put her in a foul mood. Something must have happened at church to make her change her mind about going on the outing. But why punish Johnny and Grace by running away? It didn't seem that they had anything to do with the situation. I'd have to find out what that was all about.

I started the engine of the Chevy and thought about where I could go now. I pitched the butt of my cigarette out the window and looked at my watch. It was 2:10, and it would be another hour or so before school let out. I didn't really want to head back to Detroit and call it a day. What I really wanted was to find Myrna Lou on some street corner here in town and haul her rear end back to Johnny and Grace's and be treated as a hero; but somehow, I doubted that was going to happen; not today, anyway. The growling in my stomach told me there was only one place that I needed to go. I pulled out of the parking space and headed for the White Castle on Michigan Avenue.

****

"Well, whaddya know?" Joe said as I entered his eatery. "Back again, huh? I gotta tell ya, though; I haven't seen that girl, yet. You gotta give it a little time. I'm sure she'll show her face in here soon."

"Nah, I didn't figure you'd have any information for me, yet. But I'm hungry, Joe."

"Well, hop on up and I'll fix ya something," he said, turning to the grill.

I mounted a stool at the counter while he threw three balls of meat on the hot surface. Then he turned and filled a mug from the coffee pot. He set it in front of me and placed plastic bottles of mustard and ketchup off to the side. Turning his back to me again, he threw two handfuls of fries into the wire basket and lowered it into the crackling oil.

"So, how's the search going?" he asked over his right shoulder.

"I've at least got some names now," I said. "I figure I'll wait until school is out to talk to who I can. I just came from the principal's office at the high school."

"Would that happen to be Vernon Wagner?" he asked.

"One and the same," I said.

"He's a good guy. I got a nephew that'll go to that school starting in the fall. Vern comes in here with his wife and kids every once in a while. I imagine he's good at what he does, 'cause he sure cares about the students."

"Yeah, it seemed that way," I said.

Joe walked the length of the counter, pausing when he came to two elderly women sitting near the other end. He tore off the top sheet on his order pad and placed it between them.

Returning to me, he said, "I was thinking and I got an idea. Remember that flyer you took?"

I nodded that I did.

"Well, why don't you make one up asking for information about your friend's niece? I can tack it up on that side of the cash register. There isn't a day that goes by those kids from the high school don't come in here. I mean, what are you gonna do? Interview every one of them? Let them come to you."

I stared at him and smiled. He was a genius! He tore me off a piece of paper from a notebook he kept underneath his cash register and handed me a box of crayons, telling me he kept those, along with a couple of coloring books, for the little ones that came in with their folks. He resumed cooking my meal as I sat with the blank paper in front of me, wondering how I should word my plea. I thought this just might work if I offered a reward for the information. I ran that idea past Joe.

"Good thinking, Sam. But you'd better be careful what you say in that," he said, pointing at the sheet. "You'd better make sure their information really leads to something solid, or else you'll be paying out to every one of them."

He had a point.

**Reward of $5.00 being offered
to anyone with information
leading to the whereabouts of
Myrna Lou Stevic,
last seen on Monday, April 19
on Garrison Avenue, Dearborn.**

Joe placed my plate in front of me and picked up the flyer, reading it. He told me to put my phone number at the bottom and I did, thanking him for bringing the oversight to my attention. He nodded his head in approval, came around to the front, and taped it on the cash register.

"That oughta get ya some type of response," he said. "Sometimes these kids know more than they're willing to tell, but that five dollars should make 'em speak up."

I ate in silence as Joe first cashed out the ladies sitting down the counter from me, and then went into the back of the restaurant. While I devoured my food, Ernie came out in the front twice, smiling and waving to me both times. I had pushed my plate away and pulled out a cigarette, lighting it. I was running low on coffee, but I was sure Joe would be out in a moment.

A draft of mild air ran over me and I turned to see four teenagers enter…two boys and two girls. They glanced at the flyer and kept walking toward the opposite end of the counter. They took seats and I watched them as I puffed away. The young men sat at the outside of the girls and the girls, sitting side by side, were deep in conversation with each other.

Joe emerged into the front, wiping his hands on an already stained towel. He looked to his left and noticed the newly arrived customers.

"Hey there!" he greeted them as he walked over. "Art, your daddy still wanting to sell that tool set?"

"As far as I know," one of the young men answered.

"Well, tell him I'm interested. Now what can I get you?"

Joe threw french fries for four into the deep fryer and was pouring Coca Cola into four glasses when I asked if Art could possibly be Arthur Gellert. When Joe replied that he was, I left my seat and approached the young people.

"You're Arthur Gellert?" I asked.

The young man turned to me. He had dirty blond hair and a face that was slightly broken out. He turned a shade of red in embarrassment.

"No, I'm *Art* Gellert," he said. "Who wants to know?"

I directed my next comment to all of them.

"I noticed when you came in you saw the flyer at the register. I'm a private investigator helping the family to locate Myrna Lou Stevic. Have any of you seen her since Monday?"

They all shook their heads, so I directed my next question to the girl sitting next to Art.

"Are you Marion Dombrano?"

She sighed exaggeratedly and rolled her eyes. She appeared to be offended.

"No, I am not!" she said, and turned away from me.

I didn't seem to be making a good impression with this group of young people. I asked if any of them knew Myrna Lou. The other girl told me that they knew who I was talking about, but they, excluding Art, were in tenth grade and didn't know her. Art admitted to knowing her and having two classes with her. Now we were getting somewhere. I asked if I could speak to him privately, and he followed me to where I had been sitting. I returned to a full cup of coffee, and I took a sip when I sat down.

"Look, Art, sorry for being a bit awkward back there, but this is serious stuff. Myrna Lou hasn't been seen since Monday evening and she's got to be found. Now, someone told me that maybe there was a thing between you and Marion, but maybe Myrna Lou was upsetting that relationship. Is that true?"

"Who told you that?" he asked.

"I'd rather not say. Besides, that's not important. I want to know if you've been close to Myrna Lou and know where she might have gone."

"I don't know nothin'," he said. "And Marion and me didn't have anything going, either. I saw her in here one night and asked her to the movies. We went to the movies and that was it. She's a nice gal and all, but I found she wasn't really my type. I think she thought it was more than it was, but it wasn't. As far as Myrna Lou is concerned, yeah, she was comin' on to me. But she came on to half the senior class. I might've flirted a little, but that was all. Marion flipped out like she owned me or something. Ever since then, I stay away from them both. That was well over a month ago."

"So you can't give me any information about where Myrna Lou might've gone?" I asked.

He shook his head. "Nope, I didn't know her that well where she would tell me her plans. I haven't seen her."

I thanked him and pulled out another cigarette while Art returned to his seat. When he hopped up on the stool, the young lady he was with gave him a dirty look and then turned away from him. Gee, I'd messed up his evening, that was for sure.

About ten minutes later, three girls entered White Castle. They looked too young to be in high school...I would've guessed them to be in junior high. They stopped when they saw the sheet telling of the reward, and took their time in reading it. I watched as the shortest girl of the three suddenly yanked the flyer from the register, tore it into several pieces, and threw them into the air...from there they floated to the floor like confetti. Her friends were surprised at her behavior and I heard them ask her, "Who is she?" indicating they'd never heard of Myrna Lou. I furrowed my eyebrows.

"Hey!" Joe yelled. "Now you pick every piece of that up and throw it in the trash container."

She did as she was told. As they neared me, I asked why she had done it. One of her friends told her she didn't have to speak to me, that it was none of my business.

"That's not actually true," I said. "I'm Detective Flanagan."

I knew I was giving them the impression I was a police officer, but too bad; it worked. The two she had come in with quickly hopped on a stool far away from me and left her alone to deal with this. Her eyes grew wide with fear.

"What's your name?" I asked, using a tone of authority.

"Kay," she said, barely above a whisper.

"Kay what?"

"Dombrano."

"Well, Kay Dombrano, why did you rip that down?"

# Chapter Seven

*Poor kid*, I thought as I neared St. Aubin, the street I lived on in Detroit. I had laughed several times to myself during my ride back home. Kay Dombrano had been scared out of her mind when she thought I was with the Dearborn Police Department and realized I had just witnessed her destroying my flyer back at the White Castle. She had been close to tears as I questioned her.

The information I'd gotten out of her didn't amount to much. Her older sister, Marion, had a crush on Art Gellert some time back. When Marion thought Myrna Lou was stealing him from her, she had lain on her bed and shed a whole lot of tears over it, causing Kay to feel protective of her and to hate her sister's nemesis. I'd forgotten how it was to hurt with young love; or with any love, for that matter.

Back at the eatery, I posted a new flyer which said the same thing and re-taped it at the register. I left Dearborn at approximately 5:00. My plan had been to swing by the Dombrano home, since I now had Marion's address, but I found myself developing a bit of heartburn. I decided the latest round of Joe's burgers were a bit too greasy for me.

I did swing by Johnny Delbeck's house again, though. I wanted to talk to his older children, Jake and Susan. It was as Johnny had told me though; Jake had been at baseball practice and Susan was so intent on doing research for her report that she didn't hear a thing. Neither could tell me anything pertinent to the whereabouts of their cousin.

When I arrived home, I found my grandmother and her friend, Helen, sitting at the dining room table immersed in a card game of Old Maid. She told me that they'd already eaten, but there were leftovers in the refrigerator. This was a good thing, because my stomach couldn't handle anything right then. I went to my room to lie down, shutting the door so I wouldn't be disturbed…I wanted to be alone with my thoughts.

To tell the truth, I was getting a bit anxious over Myrna Lou's disappearance. I hated to even use that term: *disappearance*. But to all of us, she had disappeared off the face of the earth; sitting on the porch steps one moment and in the next moment, she was gone.

Myrna Lou, on the other hand, knew exactly where she was. She had been gone away from her aunt and uncle's for three nights and this was going to be the fourth, unless she suddenly returned home this evening. But what were the chances of that? If she was staying with a friend, what kind of parents did this friend have to keep her all this time? She obviously wasn't attending school. Where did she go during the day if that was the case?

No, I had to admit, I was getting worried. I was truly glad that Joe came up with the idea of a flyer, because there was work to do around the house with the approach of Sunday. I couldn't leave Gran to do it all by herself. We were expecting company and things needed to get done in the next two days. I would feel less guilty knowing that, while I wasn't out searching the area for the girl every moment, people with any information could still contact me. I closed my eyes and turned over on my side, drawing my knees up closer to my chest. Yep, I had heartburn, alright. I could feel myself sinking into a drowsy state and I allowed sleep to overtake me.

****

When I woke, I was a bit disoriented. It was pitch black in my room and I heard no noises from beyond my door. What day was it? What time was it? Leaning toward my bedside table, I strained to make out the hands on the clock. I thought it said 9:30, but I couldn't be positive. Surely if it was 9:30 in the morning, some light would be filtering in through my drawn curtains. I swung my legs over the side of the bed and sat for a moment, trying to let the fuzziness clear. Rubbing the back of my neck, I realized, with gratefulness, that my heartburn was gone. I rose from the bed, flipped on the light, and found I was right; it was 9:30 p.m.

Opening my door, I was met with darkness throughout the house. From the light streaming out of my bedroom, I could see the deck of cards still sitting on the dining room table. Had Gran gone to bed already? I moved through the dining room and into the living room. Our front door was open wide, allowing a soft, still mild breeze to flow through the screen. What the heck? Gran wouldn't just leave the door open, would she? Had she forgotten to shut it?

I moved toward the door and gazed outside. There she was, sitting on the top step of the porch, alone. Helen must've gone to her own home.

"Gran, what are you doing?" I asked.

She turned around, and then I could see that she was holding a glass filled with something that had froth at the top. She was drinking a beer and gazing at the stars in the sky.

"Just sitting here; it's such a nice night out, dear. Why don't you join me?" She hesitated and then said, "Don't you feel well? You slept for an awfully long time."

"No, I'm fine. I'll be out in a minute."

I made my way back to the bathroom. After relieving myself and washing my hands I got a glass of water, then took it with me back to the porch and eased myself down next to my grandmother. I looked up, too. The sky was incredible, with millions of twinkling lights. It truly was a beautiful night.

"Tell me about this case you're working on," Gran said. "Tell me about Johnny Delbeck. Did he mention his mother?"

She listened wordlessly as I told her the story of Myrna Lou and all that I'd learned from Johnny and Grace. I told her about visiting the school, and how I'd talked to the principal, a couple of her teachers, and the kids at White Castle.

"I have this fear that I'm not going to be able to find her, Gran. How can I let Johnny down? I want to be able to take her back to where she's staying and make everything alright again."

I took a drink of my water and Gran sipped at her beer. She looked into the heavens once again and sighed. Without looking at me, she started to speak.

"Oh, you'll find her, dear. I have faith in you. You're a good detective and you'll get the job done. But I think what's really worrying you is that you might find her in a different condition than what you'd like. I'll say a special prayer for that dear child tonight."

She used the porch railing to pull herself up, and then she leaned over and kissed me on the top of my head. Yawning, she told me she thought she'd hit the hay; there was a lot she had to do the next day. And then she was gone, leaving the blanket of stars to cover me, alone.

I was astounded. Even though these moments were few and far between, Ruby Flanagan could be extremely lucid in her reasoning. Gran was right. I hadn't allowed myself to think too much about it until now, but I wanted to find Myrna Lou safe, sound, whole, healthy, and happy, and there was a creeping fear inside of me that told me that might not be the case. I'd say a special prayer for Myrna Lou that night, too.

# Chapter Eight

I called the Delbeck home at 10:00 on Friday morning; Grace answered after the second ring. I caught her up to date with what I had learned. Leaving out most of the opinions of people toward her niece, I told her I had obtained a few names and addresses that I would be checking up on. Sadly, I realized how little I really had to tell her in the day and a half I'd been searching for Myrna Lou, and I somehow felt a great guilt build inside of me. She seemed to sense this.

"I appreciate everything you're doing, Sam. I've done a lot of thinking, and I've come to realize none of us are to blame for this. Johnny and I did our best for her, and when you get right down to it, you can't control what someone else does, no matter how much you want to. She has to take responsibility for her actions. And I'm ashamed to say that I'm starting to get angry now."

She paused and I thought I could hear her trying to hold back tears. I allowed her the silence for a few moments. Finally, she found her strength again.

"The children and I are going to a special service today at church. Johnny is working, like always. I so wanted Myrna Lou to be with us for the holiday," she said. And then after a few moments, she hesitantly asked, "Do you think that's even possible, Sam?"

"We're going to do our best, Grace. Keep your chin up. Gran is praying, I'm praying; and you know the power of prayer."

"Yes, I do. The pastor and some others at Christ the Divine are praying, too, and that's a whole lot of voices being sent heavenward," she said.

"What time is the service, Grace? And how long does it last?"

****

Two days ago, I'd gotten most of the inside windows cleaned, but the outsides still needed to be done. At breakfast that morning, Gran had also voiced her desire to move the living room furniture into a different arrangement. I couldn't let her attempt it by herself, so prior to making my call to Grace, I moved the heavy items as Gran waxed the tables and ran the sweeper over the area rug. I now could hear my grandmother singing "Oh Danny Boy" as she bathed behind a locked bathroom door. She often spoke of the "gifts" the Lord had bestowed upon each of us, and believe me, He hadn't bestowed the gift of song on her. She sounded horrible.

I looked over at the dishes sitting in the dish drainer. I had washed them after our morning meal and now I needed to make sure they were dry and placed back in the cupboard, but with the screeching that was reaching my ears, I decided to grab my Lucky Strikes and head for the front porch. Easing down on the top step, I lit my cigarette. The day was sunny and a warm breeze floated through the air. It had to be a few degrees warmer than it was yesterday.

The boys next door, Albie and his younger brother Bobby, were outdoors playing kick the can with two other boys, but instead of a can, they were using a milk crate. I watched them play their game as I smoked my cigarette. An idea was forming in my mind, and I waited until they were finished before calling Albie over. He came running when I called, leaving the others behind. The boy was twelve, four years older than his brother, and seemed to have gone through a growth spurt of late, because he appeared to be a couple of inches taller than he was even a few months ago. His trousers were too short and ripped at the knees, and he needed a haircut.

"Have you ever washed windows for your mom?" I asked him.

"I've washed the window in the back door before," he answered.

"Well, I was thinking of hiring you to wash the outside of these front windows; maybe the ones in the back of the house also."

He leaned to the left, craning his neck to view the glass on the house. He shrugged.

"I guess I could do that. When do you want this done and what's the pay?"

"How about sometime today?"

"I've got company right now." He pointed toward the boys in his front yard. "Those are my cousins. But they'll be leaving soon. I won't be able to start the job until after 3:00. Ma is gonna make us go in the house at noon and do nothin' for three hours on account of it being Good Friday. I guess if I don't finish it today, I can always spend time on 'em tomorrow, too."

"That sounds good. Now about your wage; I was thinking fifty cents."

"I was thinking more like a dollar."

I shook my head.

"Well, you gotta figure," he continued, "it *is* a holiday and I should get extra for that. *And* I'll need a ladder, and it might be kinda dangerous climbing up to reach the top."

He was a slick one, alright. But he did have a point.

"Okay," I said. "I'll tell you what. I'll go as high as seventy-five cents."

He shook his head.

"Nope, I'm still thinkin' that dollar would be better."

I took another cigarette out of my pack and lit it. I inhaled and exhaled, and then waved my hand in the air.

"Eh, never mind. I guess the windows don't look that bad after all. I'll just wait until I have time to do them," I said.

He stared up at the front picture window and rubbed his chin, appearing deep in thought.

"Your gramma want them done for Easter?" he asked.

"Well, she did, but I'm just going to have to disappoint her this time."

"I'll tell ya what I'm gonna do, Mr. Flanagan," he said, still rubbing his chin. "I'm gonna do the job for the seventy-five cents. We can't have an old lady like herself feelin' bad over the holiday. I'll be here a little after three."

I had to laugh inwardly, but told him that was a fine thing he was going to do for Mrs. Flanagan, and that he could find a ladder in the garage when he was ready to wash the windows. He ran back to his brother and cousins and proceeded to play another game of kick the can.

When I re-entered the house, I found Gran coming out of her bedroom wearing her silk slip and seeming to be in a bit of a panic. I could see through the sheer material that she was wearing her garter, which was hooked up to her mock nylons. Her stockings were a bit thicker than actual nylon, which was very difficult to find nowadays.

"What's wrong?" I asked her.

"Oh, I can't find my dern pearls, and Helen's gonna pick me up for the noon church service in a half hour." she whined.

"Well, you wore them Tuesday when we went to Baker's Keyboard Lounge," I informed her.

"I did?" She stopped in the middle of the dining room and softly tapped at her forehead with a closed fist. "Oh, think, think," she muttered.

"Okay, what did you do when we got home that night? Can you remember getting ready for bed? What hiding spot did you choose to put the pearls in this time?"

She stood motionless, face tilted toward the ceiling, eyes closed tight. She was concentrating, trying to envision her last moments that Tuesday night. The string of pearls her husband had given her for the Christmas of 1923 was her most prized possession. She had told me that my grandfather said that when she wore the pearls around her neck and resting on her chest, it would be his way of always being close to her heart. He would be gone from this earth six months later. After wearing them, she would hide them each time in a different location, making sure no intruder would ever find them. The wooden jewelry box sitting on her dresser held numerous cheap baubles, but the pearls never saw the inside of it.

"What were you thinking of when you got undressed for the night?" I asked.

"I was thinking of *something*," she muttered, eyes still closed.

"Yeah, but what?"

"*Shh!*" She cautioned me. "Oh, I know!"

Her head came forward and her eyes grew wide.

"I was thinking of what a pretty name that beer had; Champagne Velvet."

On the move, I headed for the icebox. I opened the door and searched the shelves, moving the two remaining bottles of beer she had. Hearing a noise behind me, I looked to see my grandmother sticking her hand inside the cookie jar. When she pulled it out, she had the pearls in her palm. I let the door to the refrigerator close.

"Now, what does the cookie jar have to do with beer?" I asked.

"Nothing, but when I was drinking the beer, I was talking to that sweet wife of your friend's. She's such a sweet woman. Sweet, cookies, get it? Now come here and hook these for me."

I rolled my eyes and did as she asked. She emerged from her bedroom fifteen minutes later wearing a light blue dress that hung to just below mid calf. It had white butterflies spattered across the material. I'd never seen it before.

"New dress?"

"It is to me. Helen's neighbor was getting rid of it, and it's way too big for Helen, so she saved it for me. It's got a hole in the armpit. Can you tell?"

I looked and told her honestly that I couldn't. A horn honked from outside and Gran hurried to the dining room table and picked up the Bible that was laying there. She handed it to me.

"What are you giving this to me for?" I asked.

"That's for you to read from noon until three. You need to spend time with the Lord if you aren't going with us to hear Pastor Ferron's message. I've got my other one in my bag."

She patted her purse, gave me a quick peck on the cheek, and was out the door. I watched from the front window as Helen backed up and jumped the curb across the street before shifting into drive and pulling off down St. Aubin. Thank God no vehicle had been parked there today. I looked toward heaven and said a silent prayer that my grandmother and her friend would make it to their destination and then back home safely. When they were in the car with Helen behind the wheel, it was all in God's hands.

# Chapter Nine

I pulled into the lot of Christ the Divine Lutheran Church at 1:18 p.m. I drove until I found one lone empty parking space and filled it. Until I spied people starting to exit the church, I relaxed in the Chevy.

Grace passed through the double glass doors holding Bonnie's hand and I got out of the car. I waited until they descended the steps and then walked toward them. Johnny's wife was looking sharp in a figure fitting lavender skirt, white lacey blouse, and white heels. Bonnie was adorable decked out in her pastel pink dress, solid on top and white horizontal stripes circling the skirt portion. She kept looking down at her new black patent leather shoes, apparently marveling at the sound they made as she walked.

Grace spotted me and waved as I made my way through the autos. A young couple was walking closely behind her and Bonnie. When Grace stopped to speak to me, they stopped in back of her.

"Sam, are you here to work on the case?"

I nodded and then stretched my hand out to rustle Bonnie's hair. The child looked up at me, squinting because of the brightness of the sun, and smiled. Grace faced the couple behind her.

"Sam, this is Jim and Karen Wieboldt. They live across the street from us. If it weren't for them, we wouldn't have been able to attend today. They gave us a ride."

I nodded, and Jim extended his hand toward mine. I shook it and uttered a hello. The two looked to be in their mid-twenties, with the good looks of youth on their side. Mrs. Wieboldt was expecting, and it appeared as though she might give birth any day. They excused themselves and said they would round up Jake and Susan and meet Grace back at the car. I waited until they left.

"I thought I would talk to the pastor. Maybe he knows something we don't." I shrugged. "It's worth a shot."

"I can't imagine what he could tell you that he didn't tell me," Grace said. "But, like you say, it couldn't hurt. His name is Bertram Mayhew. He's probably in his office. Go through the doors and down the hall, then turn left. It's right around the corner."

I nodded and then looked down when Bonnie got hold of my sleeve and began pointing to something behind me. I turned to look. A man and a child of about Bonnie's age were between two brown cars, obviously heading to their own auto. The man had hold of the young boy's wrist and was pulling him roughly. The child's wails could be heard throughout the parking lot.

"*Come on!*" the man yelled. "If you don't stop, I'll give you something to cry about, *mister!*"

I didn't know what to say, but turned back to Bonnie and shook my head. She tugged again on my sleeve and pointed. She startled Grace and me when she suddenly said in frustration, "*No!*" still pointing. I turned and looked again. The man and boy were no longer in sight. I couldn't figure out what it was that had affected her. Grace squatted and looked into Bonnie's face.

"What is it, baby? Did that man scare you?"

Bonnie moved close into her mother's arms and began to cry. Grace hugged her daughter and looked up at me.

"I'd better get her home, Sam. She might just be over tired. Let us know what you find out."

I assured Grace that I would, and watched as she made her way toward the Wieboldt's car.

****

The interior of the church smelled like lemon oil. An expanse of red carpeting covered the floor. Rods with hangers lined the wall near where I entered, but only one lightweight white sweater hung there. Organ music reverberated throughout the church. As I passed the door leading into the chapel, I saw a woman with stark white hair sitting behind the instrument, playing a hymn.

I kept walking, and following Grace's directions, turned left when I came to the end of the hallway. About ten feet ahead of me was a slightly ajar door on the right leading to an office. The pastor's name was etched in a plate attached to the outside of it. I gave two raps on the door and stuck my head in. The man behind the desk looked up. He'd been writing in some type of notebook. The expression on his face told me he was trying to figure out if he should know me or not.

"Pastor Mayhew?"

"Yes?"

He rose from his seat. The man was big…not so much fat, but thick and burly. He still wore his buttoned black suit coat, which looked expensive. His thick salt and pepper wavy hair was slightly parted on the side. Having a face that was clean-shaven, he wore round, wire- rimmed glasses. I pegged him to be in his mid-sixties. After extending his hand in greeting, he gestured to one of three burgundy leather chairs that sat opposite him. As I eased myself into it, he still stood.

"Are you looking for a church home, son? Should I be embarrassed not to have noticed you during our Good Friday sermon?"

"No, no, nothing like that," I replied.

He looked disappointed, but delved right into conversation as he seated himself in his massive chair.

"Do you know the Lord, Jesus Christ?"

I was taken aback at his abruptness, but recovered nicely.

"I think I do, sir."

"Thinking isn't as good as knowing," he said. "We live in perilous times. Evil is fighting fervently for victory over our souls. You need to be sure. God awaits your decision."

His voice was very deep. I pictured him behind the pulpit spewing hell, fire, and brimstone, and the imagery made me feel uncomfortable. He placed his elbows on his desk and intertwined his fingers, placing his chin on top of them. I sighed louder than I should have and tried to cover it by diving right into the reason for my visit.

"Pastor Mayhew, I'm a private detective the Delbeck's hired to look into Myrna Lou Stevic's whereabouts. I came here today hoping you could tell me anything you know of the girl. I know she's involved in the youth group here."

"Ah," he said, easing back, resting his right elbow on the arm of his chair. "Yes, that *is* rather tragic. Grace has voiced her concerns about the girl to me. I can't even imagine the anguish they are going through. I have a daughter of my own, and I would be beside myself with worry if I didn't know where she was."

His eyes traveled to a framed picture sitting on top of his desk. My gaze followed and I saw the lovely face of a young lady staring back at me. She wore a solid plum colored sweater, and her dark blond hair fell in front of her shoulders in waves. It was held to one side with a dark barrette. Her eyes appeared gray and her smile revealed straight, white teeth. A dark mole sat at the left corner of her mouth and was actually quite attractive. She wore a silver chain around her neck that held a small cross.

"She's very beautiful," I said. "You and your wife must be very proud."

He picked up the picture, turning it toward himself. He stared at it lovingly for a moment in silence, and then returned it to where it had sat. Looking at me, he began to speak again.

"Frances never got the chance to know her daughter. You see, Mr.....uh, I'm so sorry. I don't believe I caught your name."

"I never said it. It's Flanagan, Pastor. My name is Sam Flanagan."

"You see, Mr. Flanagan, my wife and I were unsuccessful in producing offspring until twenty some years into our marriage. Imagine yourself at forty-four finding you were going to be a first time father." He laughed. "I was beside myself with excitement, but my wife was just a year behind me, and we knew the risks. I'm sorry to say Frances died giving birth to Sheila."

"I'm so sorry," was all I could think of to say.

"Well, the Lord has His reasons, Mr. Flanagan. We won't know what those are until we meet Him face to face. There is nothing I wouldn't do for the girl...*nothing*. She is my pride and joy. Do you have children?"

"No, I'm not married," I said.

We were silent for some seconds; me, thinking of what could've been with Dee Dee, and him with whatever consumed his thoughts. He came forward in his chair and cleared his throat. His face took on a look of pain and sadness.

"I've been doing a lot of praying over this situation throughout the week," he said. "I'm probably not the best one to question concerning the girl, but I can tell you my observations since she graced our church with her presence. I found her to be a lost soul needing love and acceptance. I guess I still do. I don't know whether I should use this word—and I certainly wouldn't to Grace or Mr. Delbeck—but promiscuous comes to mind. But that might be too strong. Maybe she's just extremely flirtatious. I can't help but wonder what the girl's relationship with her own father was or is. I know that she and her stepfather are at odds most of the time; Grace has told me that much. So, I'm wondering if there isn't a void that needs to be filled in her life, causing her to act inappropriately around members of the opposite sex. Please forgive me for saying this, but she wasn't an attractive young lady, not in appearance or personality. Of late, she started to come to church with her face done up in loud make up. I asked our youth pastor to speak to her about it, and the last couple of times I saw her, she wasn't wearing any. I believe Jake Delbeck is about fifteen now. He didn't seem to pay any attention to her. But Susan; well, that was a different matter."

He paused and lifted a glass of water, which was sitting to the left of him, to his mouth and drank. After doing so, he gestured toward me.

"I'm so sorry," he said. "Can I offer you anything?"

I shook my head to indicate no and urged him to go on. I wondered what he was going to say about Susan Delbeck, Johnny's daughter. He continued.

73

"Ah, yes. Well, I was concerned about Susan. She's thirteen and very impressionable; I worried that she would look up to Myrna Lou and want to emulate her. I thankfully haven't seen any evidence of that so far. Grace and her husband are very good parents and have brought up their children in the ways of the Lord. Obviously, Grace's sister didn't do the same. I don't see Johnny too many Sundays, but from what I know of him; well, he seems to be a fine man and one who believes."

"Do you think you could tell me if Myrna Lou was friendly with anyone in particular in the church? Any girl she gravitated to, or any young man she might be interested in?"

He chuckled and then rubbed his forehead with his right hand while his right elbow rested on his desk.

I was not sure what he thought was so funny, but I felt myself growing agitated at his manner. What was it about this man that I didn't like? I couldn't put my finger on it. Maybe it wasn't him at all. Maybe I was tired of hearing how no one liked this seventeen-year-old girl…that was a bit unfair. I was beginning to feel very protective of her. I wanted to find Myrna Lou, and I wanted her to turn into a stunning beauty within the next couple of years. I wanted her to find happiness and confidence, be successful in life, and tell all these people she'd met in Dearborn to go to hell.

"I believe she drove most of the young females at Christ the Divine away. I guess I just feel she was competing with them for something and they grew tired of that. There *is* a boy who seemed quite interested at first. This is just my perception, you understand. His name is Lonnie Orwick. I have no idea what Myrna Lou felt about him, though. He attends occasionally, but not with his family. I believe his home life is rather suspect…not a very good environment for the boy. There are about thirty-five children we pick up at their homes for Sunday school…he's one of them. I can't give you his address, but our youth pastor must surely have it. Perhaps you'd find more success in speaking to him."

I rose from my seat and asked where I could find this youth pastor.

"Actually, we have adjoining offices," he said, looking to his right at a door that led to another room. "If you go back out into the hall and turn right, it's the first door you come to."

I'd almost reached the door when he called me back. I turned and saw he was standing and holding out a pamphlet.

"Mr. Flanagan, please take this with you and read it at your convenience. We can help you in your search for the Lord."

I doubled back and accepted his offering. When I got into the hall, I glanced at it. It was a pamphlet written by Pastor Bertram Mayhew. Its title was "Accepting Jesus Christ and the Assurance of A Place In Heaven." I crammed it in my suit coat pocket and headed for the office next to Pastor Mayhew's.

Judith White

# Chapter Ten

The door to the office next to the pastor's was wide open. It was a larger room than the one I had just come from, and it housed two desks. One sat empty, but there was a young man seated behind the one straight across from the entrance. He sensed me in the doorway before I got a chance to knock. Upon seeing me, he jumped up from his chair and came toward me, extending his hand. We greeted one another with a shake.

"Ah, Mr. Jacobi; after speaking with you so many times on the phone, it's finally good to see you in person."

He turned back to his desk and picked up a sheet of paper.

"We're going to try to stick to the departure time of 8:00 a.m. on Monday morning. What a Godsend you are to us to agree to go with us," he said.

This young man didn't appear to be any older than twenty-two. His hair was auburn and curly, and very disheveled. His faced was spattered with freckles. He wore denim pants and a red polo shirt that hung below his hips, and his sneakers made a squeaking sound on the wooden floor when he walked. I cleared my throat while twirling my fedora in my hand.

"I see you're expecting someone, but it isn't me. I'm not Mr. Jacobi. The name is Sam Flanagan, and I wondered if I could take a few moments of your time for something entirely different?"

He said nothing for some seconds, trying to take in what I'd just told him. He ran his fingers through his hair and laughed.

"Oops," he said. "I guess I goofed there. I was expecting the husband of one of our congregants. He's graciously offered to accompany us to Camp Arcadia with the teen group next week. Was it me you wanted to speak to, Mr. Flanagan?"

"If you're the youth pastor, I do," I said.

"The actual youth pastor is Matthew Coady. You just missed him…he was here until about ten minutes ago. Sorry to say he's gone for the day. I'm sort of the assistant youth pastor. The name is Duane Whelan. Can *I* help you with anything?"

He made no move to return to his seat behind the desk, nor did he offer me the one wooden chair facing it. I told him what I wanted to learn from him; who was Myrna Lou close to? Who could she possibly be staying with? I told him she'd last been seen in front of her aunt and uncle's house about 4:15 p.m. on Monday. He looked stunned.

"Are you kidding me? No one even told me of this! I can't believe Matt didn't share this with me. Come to think of it, I wonder if he even *knows*. Is Pastor Mayhew aware of this?"

"Yes, I just came from speaking with him in his office," I said, gesturing with my hat toward the adjoining door.

My eyes stayed focused on the door. I could've sworn when I was in Pastor Mayhew's office that the door leading to where I now stood had been shut. Now it stood open an inch or so. I found this curious.

"Wow," he said, shaking his head. "I guess you'd better wait until you can speak to Matt. I really don't know anything about the girl."

My face must've showed my confusion.

"Let me explain," he said. "I'm actually a student. I attend Bethany College in Kansas in their theology department. This is sort of an internship for me, Mr. Flanagan. I'm going to be working with the youth program here for the summer. I wanted to return to Michigan to do this, to be close to home. Hopefully, when I graduate in December, they can find a permanent place for me here at Christ the Divine. I think I know who Myrna Lou is, but I know so little of the teens at this point. I started here only two weeks ago. That's why I'm so looking forward to our going to Camp Arcadia for the four nights. I can get a real feel for who they are and what their walk with God has been in that close environment."

"So this is what you want your life's work to be, huh?" I questioned him.

I noticed that each time I spoke to the young man, he turned his head slightly to the left. I was always aiming my words at the right side of his face.

"Well, it wasn't my first choice," he said. "I actually wanted to join the United States Navy in the worst way. I wanted to enter the fighting and kick some butt." He laughed and shook his head. "But they wouldn't have me. I'm deaf in my left ear due to an accident when I was eleven; can't hear a thing out of it. So, I guess the Lord led me in this direction."

I told him that he could mention my visit to Matthew Coady and that I would be back at some point. He nodded and then looked past me toward the open door leading to the hallway. I turned to see what he was staring at. A man had entered, but stood just inside and removed his black fedora.

"Mr. Jacobi? So nice to finally connect," Duane said.

The man shook his head.

"No, I'm Wilbur Jenkins. I'm here to pay for my daughters' trip to camp," he said.

Duane Whelan shrugged and rolled his eyes at me before gesturing his newly arrived guest inside the office.

Outside in the Chevy, I looked at my watch. It was 2:50. I could go straight home; in fact, that's what I *really* wanted to do. Or I could check up on some of these kids whose addresses I had. I knew that's what I *needed* to do.

I opened the small notebook I'd recorded the information in. Marion Dombrano was the name that jumped out at me. She lived at 46 Morley Avenue, and I headed that way. Less than five minutes later, I parked across the street from her house. I saw Marion's younger sister Kay pull up on her bike and look at my car. When I exited the vehicle and she realized who I was, she straightened and got a look of panic on her face, letting the bicycle fall to the ground. She ran around to the back yard and disappeared.

I approached the house with an inward chuckle. *The poor kid*, I thought. *She's afraid I'm here to arrest her.* I climbed the three steps that led to the porch and gave four raps on the front door. A man in his late thirties answered my knock. He wore a sharp brown suit and his speech was that of one who possessed intelligence.

"Hello, may I help you?"

"Are you Mr. Dombrano?" I asked.

"Yes, that's right. Should I know you, sir?"

"No, but I'd like to speak to your daughter, if I may. I'm a private investigator who is trying to find out what happened to one of her classmates. The girl in question disappeared early Monday evening."

"Oh my goodness," he said. "Which daughter would you like to speak to? I have three of them; Marion, Kay, or Ann?"

"Marion," I clarified.

He turned his head to the right and called out the girl's name in a loud tone. Instead of Marion appearing, a woman of about his age came to the door.

"What is it, Leonard?" she asked.

"This gentleman would like to speak to Marion. It seems one of her classmates has disappeared. I'm sure he wants to find out if Marion can give him any pertinent information about that."

"I'll get her," the woman said. "She's in her room."

Mrs. Dombrano walked away and Mr. Dombrano left me standing on the porch while we waited. Finally, he turned to me asking which classmate had gone missing.

"A girl named Myrna Lou Stevic," I replied through the screen.

"Oh my!" he gasped. "I believe she's been an overnight guest here. I wish you success with finding her, sir."

I nodded my thanks and we waited another thirty seconds or so until the girl appeared.

"Marion, this gentleman would like to talk to you. It seems your friend, Myrna Lou, hasn't been seen since Monday. Would you like me to stay? Or would you like to speak to him alone?"

"I'll be okay, Daddy," she said.

"Alright, but call me if you need anything."

He retreated farther inside the house, leaving Marion and I alone. She faced me through the screen door with a questioning look.

"Myrna Lou is missing?" she asked.

She opened the door and stepped out onto the porch. I nodded in reply to her question.

"She was last seen on the porch of her aunt and uncle's on Monday. Do you happen to know where she might be?" I asked.

"No, I don't have a clue," she said, shaking her head.

"Do you have any idea at all who she might have gone to see *if* she voluntarily went to see someone, Marion?"

Again, she shook her head and answered in the negative. After a moment, I noticed her face color slightly.

"You see, I don't really talk to her all that much anymore. We sort of had a falling out. When Myrna Lou first came to Dearborn, I thought we could be great friends, but she did something that hurt my feelings pretty badly and, well, let's just say I try to stay away from her now."

"I've talked to quite a few people who have said they don't really care for her. Do you know of anyone who might want to hurt her in any way?"

"Hurt her? Like how?"

"Oh, I don't know. Was anyone angry enough at her to maybe take her somewhere? Would she just go with someone she knew, thinking that it was alright and then...?"

I trailed off. I didn't even want to utter the possibility that harm had come to the girl.

"Gee, I don't think so. I haven't heard of *anyone* disliking her *that* much. I mean, she may have gotten on a lot of people's nerves, but no one would want to do anything bad to her. At least *I* didn't feel that way."

"Do you know if she was involved with someone; maybe some boy at school?"

"I don't think so, but a couple of weeks ago we heard her boasting about some guy she said was in love with her. She told us girls at lunchtime that she would probably be married before the year was out. No one believed her, though. She's always laying it on thick, trying to make out like her life is more exciting than ours are."

I felt an inner fear creep up my spine. Was there someone no one knew anything about who Myrna Lou was sneaking to see?

"Does this guy have a name?" I asked.

"I don't think she said who it was. If she did, I don't remember it."

"Who were the other girls sitting at the lunch table when she said this?"

"Just one other girl, really. I was sitting with Carlene Gilbert, eating lunch, and then Myrna Lou joined us. That's when she kind of leaned in and told us about maybe getting married. I think she said it so we would be jealous. But we didn't believe her. Gee, we haven't even *seen* her with anyone."

Carlene Gilbert—the name sounded familiar and I didn't know why. I asked Marion if she knew where Carlene lived, and she told me she'd never gone to the girl's house, but it was on the south side of Michigan Avenue; of that, she was sure.

I thanked Marion and told her to give me a call if she remembered anything else. She waited while I ran to my car to get a piece of paper on which to write my home phone number. Having done this and after handing it to the girl, I got back in the Chevy and started the engine.

Pulling away from the curb, I thought that the English teacher, Agnes Dade, had it right; Marion Dombrano *was* a friendly girl. And then I considered this new angle to the case. *Hmm*, I thought, *very interesting*. I was thinking about the possibility of Myrna Lou being picked up at Johnny's house and riding away, voluntarily, with her love interest. Would she be stupid enough to just take off and marry this guy, whoever he was? Would she be that cruel to

Grace and Johnny and her own mother? If what Pastor Mayhew voiced was true—that this girl needed to fill a void in her life with love and acceptance—she might do just that. But who was it? A boy from the school; a boy from the church? This was a whole new angle to worry about.

I came up to Michigan Avenue and had to stop for the red light. While sitting there, I picked up my small notebook and glanced through the names once again, and there it was… Carlene Gilbert! Grace had named her as one of the girls who attended Christ the Divine Lutheran Church.

I glanced at the address. She lived at 302 Park Street. Marion had said it was south of Michigan Avenue, so when the light changed, I crossed the main thoroughfare and began to check the street signs. It took me awhile, but I finally found it.

I parked across the street from the address Grace had given me, a small red brick bungalow that had a red awning covering its front porch. The front lawn had recently been mowed, and a row of neatly trimmed bushes lined the left side of the porch under what I assumed were two bedroom windows.

I got out of the car and crossed the street. After climbing the steps to the front porch, I knocked on the door. A girl of about ten years old answered. Her long light brown hair was braided on both sides of her head. She stared through the screen at me with questioning eyes.

"Is this the Gilbert residence?" I asked.

"Yeah," she answered.

"I'd like to speak to Carlene if she's home."

She sighed and said, "Just a minute," like I was greatly bothering her. She disappeared from view, but I could hear her yell out, "Carlene, some old guy is here for you!"

This would've been funny had I not been so sensitive about turning forty that summer. Cringing inwardly, I waited, but it wasn't long before Carlene came to the door with her mother right behind her. The woman was on the heavy side and stood with her hands on her daughter's shoulders. It was she who spoke.

"Yes? What is this about?"

"Mrs. Gilbert?"

"Yes?"

"My name is Sam Flanagan, and I'm helping the Delbeck's locate their niece, Myrna Lou. May I speak to your daughter, please?"

"Oh, yes! Yes, Grace told me someone was helping them to look for the girl. Please do come in, Mr. Flanagan."

She gently shoved Carlene to the side and held the door open for me. I walked into a very attractive living room. The Gilbert's had wall to wall dark green carpeting, on which sat a huge solid slate gray sofa. The child who had first answered the door was sprawled across it, immersed in a book. I noted the title: *The Boxcar Children* by Gertrude Chandler Warner; a book I'd bought for my niece—Eva's daughter, Catherine—some fifteen years ago or more.

I was directed by Mrs. Gilbert to sit in a wooden rocking chair. She then sat in a chair matching the sofa and Carlene sat at the end of the sofa, just missing sitting on her sister's feet.

"What's this about them not being able to find Myrna Lou, Mom?" Carlene asked, looking at her mother.

"Yeah, geez, no one tells us anything!" Carlene's younger sister said from behind her book.

The older woman rubbed her right temple and sighed.

"I didn't want to worry you girls," she said. "And Marjorie, sit up like a young lady!"

The ten year old sat upright on the sofa begrudgingly, pulling the hem of her skirt down to cover her knees. She folded her arms across her chest and looked me straight in the eye.

"So where did she go?" she asked me.

"That's what I'm here to find out. No one I've talked to so far has any idea where she could've gone. No one seems to be close enough to her to know anything."

"I'm close to her," Marjorie said.

Carlene shot her little sister a look and rolled her eyes.

"Oh you are *not*, liar! You're ten and she's like seventeen, so you're gonna tell me that the two of you are *best of friends*?"

Marjorie shrugged, "Something like that."

"Oh brother!"

"Girls, please! Mr. Flanagan needs help in finding this young woman. He didn't come here to listen to the two of you argue."

I looked at the older girl. "Carlene is there anything—anything at all—you can tell me about where I might find Myrna Lou? However small it might seem, I'd like to hear anything at all about her."

The girl looked up at the ceiling, as if deep in thought. She sighed and then looked back at me.

"It's so hard because none of us are really close to her. Some of us tried, but she always has to act like she's better than all of us. It's like she makes stuff up to make us think she's wonderful...like she thinks we won't like her if she just acts like herself. It's hard to really like someone when they behave like that."

"She's herself with *me*," Marjorie said.

Carlene turned to her. "Oh, would you just *shut up*? You don't know *what* you're talking about! She isn't *your* friend!"

"Yes she is. She told me we were secret friends," she said, looking to the right at her sister while swinging her feet, which were dangling over the front of the couch.

Marjorie had my attention. Something she said...or maybe it was in the way she said it...made me think she was telling the truth on some level. As Carlene rolled her eyes, I asked the younger girl to tell me about the secret friendship she had with Myrna Lou.

"Well, I talk to her sometimes at church," she began.

Then she told me the story of how she and Myrna Lou had talked at one of the church breakfasts right before Sunday school. She told me how she was feeling ugly because she had two toes on her right foot that were joined together, and she confided this embarrassing fact to the older girl. Marjorie took off her white anklet and lifted up her foot, showing two toes that were connected by thick skin.

"See? Isn't that strange?" she asked me.

Her mother snickered softly as she sat in her chair to the right of me.

"Well, Myrna Lou said we could be secret friends from now on; almost like blood sisters, 'cause she pulled her sweater down and showed me this big old purple mark right on her back behind her shoulder."

Marjorie took her left hand and patted behind her right shoulder, indicating where the mark was on Myrna Lou, and then she continued.

"She told me neither my foot nor her birthmark was ugly; they were unique, and that made us special. That God wanted to mark the special ones in some way."

She smiled and raised her head in defiance.

"So, what do you think of that, Mr. Flanagan? I am closer to her than anybody else."

"You're such a jerk!" Carlene injected.

"I think you're right, Marjorie. I have never seen anything like that before in my life," I said, pointing to her foot. "And I think that's the neatest thing ever. I believe Myrna Lou is right; the two of you are special."

The young girl smiled and Carlene cleared her throat.

"Well, I know something none of you know! I happen to know that Myrna Lou is *not* lost, but I bet she ran away to get married."

Mrs. Gilbert gasped and turned toward her daughter, giving her a stern look.

"Carlene! How can you say such a thing?"

"Well, *I* didn't say it, Mom; Myrna Lou talked about it. She said some guy was madly in love with her and they were going to get married soon...or something like that. Marion and I didn't believe her at first, but gee," she shrugged. "Who knows?"

"Do you know who she was referring to?" I asked.

Shaking her head, she said she didn't have a clue, and when they'd asked Myrna Lou who it was, she got all secretive. She said that Myrna Lou flirted with so many of the boys at school and church that it could be anyone. Carlene *did* mention that she thought Rick Neller liked her for a while, but added that *no one* would want to marry him because he acted nuts sometimes.

"So, you believe it's possible that she ran away with some young man on Monday, and they planned to find someone to marry them?" I asked.

Before Carlene could answer, Marjorie held up a hand.

"Wait, did you say Monday? She's been gone since Monday?"

"Yes," I said and nodded.

"Well, that can't be," she said.

"And why is that?" I asked.

"Because I saw her on Wednesday."

Mrs. Gilbert, Carlene and I turned and stared at the young girl.

Judith White

# Chapter Eleven

It was fifteen minutes past six o'clock when I arrived home. I pulled into the garage and found the ladder right where it had been when I left. *Darn that Albie*, I thought. If he didn't show up to do the windows tomorrow, he obviously wasn't getting his money. But what put me in a foul mood was the prospect that *I* was going to have to do them. I entered the house through the back door and found my grandmother sitting at the kitchen table in her nightgown and robe peeling hard-boiled eggs. I reached into the bowl she'd been putting them in after they'd been shed of their shell. As I picked one up, she reached out and slapped the back of my hand, causing me to lose my grip on it and making it fall back to where it had been in the first place.

"Stay away from those! Those are for my deviled eggs and macaroni salad I'm going to be making tomorrow."

"Well, I'm hungry," I complained.

"There's leftover meatloaf in the icebox from the other night. Make yourself a sandwich."

I got the bread and the meatloaf out and made two sandwiches, lathering each of them with a good layer of mustard, and poured myself a large glass of milk. Taking a seat opposite my grandmother, I ate and watched her peel the eggs.

"Why are you dressed for bed already?" I asked.

"Because when Helen was bringing me home, we were laughing so hard about something that I wet myself," she said.

I rolled my eyes and quit chewing.

"Gran, you really don't have to tell me these things, you know."

"Well, you asked, didn't you? And it's strange, but now I don't even remember what was so funny. Ah, well," she sighed. "You're going to have to do the windows tomorrow, dear," she said.

"Yeah, I know," I said with disgust. "I hired Albie to do them, but the little rat didn't show."

She looked up at me in surprise.

"Of course he showed. Who do you think did the outside of the windows? He was here when I got home, just finishing up. After church, I went back to Helen's and then we decided to go to the diner to get something to eat. Helen didn't bring me home until a few minutes after five. And there he was, replacing the ladder. That boy and his brother, Bobby, are so sweet. They did a nice job."

I felt a lump of meatloaf go down the wrong pipe and started coughing. I grabbed my glass of milk and chugged it. When I recovered, I looked at her.

"Wait a minute; *they*?"

"The two boys," she answered.

"Hey, I only hired *Albie*, not his *brother*, too!"

She nodded her head. "Yes, he told me that. But he made a good point when he said he needed an extra pair of hands to hand him the sponge and hold the bucket while he was on the ladder. He told me to tell you that they could wait for their money until tomorrow or the next day. But he and his brother are thinking of going to the movies one day next week, so they'll need their seventy-five cents by then."

"*Each*?"

"That's what it sounded like to me, dear."

I threw the rest of my second sandwich to the table and leaned back. I was angry.

"That kid thinks money falls out of my ears!" I said.

My grandmother rose from the table, lifted the bowl, and moved it to the inside of the refrigerator. As she bent over to slide it back on the shelf, she reacted to my outburst.

"Oh, don't be so silly, dear. He thinks nothing of the kind. Albie is smart enough to realize that money doesn't come from people's ears. He knows it's stored in banks."

"Well, okay," I said. "Let me ask you something then. Why do I have to do the windows tomorrow if he already did them today?"

She straightened as the refrigerator door closed.

"Because he did such a good job that now all the streaks you created on the inside are showing. You can redo them tomorrow."

She turned and walked out of the kitchen, heading to the dining room where the radio sat, but turned back to say something more.

"Oh, and did I tell you that you owe Helen ninety cents?"

"*For what?*"

"My dinner tonight. After I put money in the offering at church, I didn't have any more. My dinner cost seventy-four cents, and then there's the dime tip. She said you could just round it off to ninety since she hates those steel pennies the government came out with."

I rubbed my temples. I was getting a headache, no doubt due to a rise in my blood pressure.

"Gran, if your dinner was eighty-four cents, why can't I give her eighty-five? Why ninety?"

My grandmother shrugged and said, "Maybe she doesn't like nickels, either."

****

I lay in bed with my window cracked, allowing a flow of cool air to enter the room. Sleep was eluding me. I kept thinking about the new information I had been given by Marion Dombrano and Carlene and Marjorie Gilbert. I had to admit, the news of Marjorie seeing Myrna Lou on Wednesday gave me a great lift in spirit. But I had to be cautious. I'd thought about coming straight home and calling Johnny and Grace and telling them the good news, but thought better of it. Tomorrow I would have to check this out.

Marjorie said she was positive it was Wednesday, April 21st, when she had seen Myrna Lou entering a dress shop on Michigan Avenue, because that was the day that it rained all afternoon, and Mr. Gilbert had cut his work day short when he knew he had to come home and take his young daughter to the dentist. She had a tooth removed and proved it to me by pulling back the corner of her mouth and opening wide to display a hole where a molar had once been. When they were just about to go in the office building to have the procedure done, she'd spied Myrna Lou going into a dress shop with her "grandmother" a few doors down. She called out to her, but the girl didn't respond. There had been a loud truck passing by in the area and Marjorie just figured the older girl hadn't heard her.

What puzzled me about this story was that Myrna Lou's grandmother passed away almost eight years ago. I knew that for a fact because when Grace's mother died, I had gone to the funeral. I'd questioned Marjorie about that. How did she know it was her grandmother? *Because she was old.* How did she know the woman was old? *Because she had gray hair.* I wondered if her paternal grandmother was living in the area and she had just decided to go and stay with her. I also wondered if she was close to her stepfather's mother. Was *she* living in this area? There were so many unanswered questions floating through my mind. And who was this boy she was supposed to be thinking of marrying? This seemed highly unlikely to me. I was more apt to believe Myrna Lou had been lying that day in the cafeteria, just to impress the other girls. I was beginning to see a vivid picture of Grace's niece. Lying to receive admiration was something the girl would do. Pastor Mayhew was right. She needed love and affection in the worst way. I fell asleep with a heavy heart, praying that poor girl was alright.

# Chapter Twelve

I saw her through a film of hazy fog. She had long, dark hair and wore only a sheer white gown. I kept trying to get closer, but each time I advanced toward her, she floated farther away. She softly called out my name, and somehow, her hand spanned the distance and gently shook my shoulder.

"Sam...Sam...."

I groaned and reached out for the hand that touched me. This woman was beautiful and I didn't want her escaping my sight.

"Sam, are you going to sleep all day?"

I pried my eyes open and found myself clutching onto my grandmother's wrist. Her face was just inches from mine. Quickly, I let go and turned to the clock that sat on my bedside table. *My God*! It was 11:20! How could I have slept so late?

My grandmother straightened and stepped back as I suddenly sat up in bed. She told me there was hot coffee on the stove and she left the room. I jumped out of bed and stretched while yawning, then headed for the kitchen. As soon as I stepped from my room and into the dining room, I heard someone call my name in greeting.

"Well, hey there, Mr. Flanagan! Good mornin'! You musta been mighty tired to have slept it away."

Turning to my right, I saw Albie in the living room, standing at the window with a sponge in hand. A bucket of sudsy water was at his feet. I nodded and continued on to pour a cup of coffee for myself.

The aroma that hit me was wonderful. My grandmother had baked blueberry muffins while I slept. There must've been three dozen of them sitting in a wicker basket that was lined with a white cloth napkin.

"Boy, those look good!" I said.

"Well, you can't have any," my grandmother told me.

"Why not?"

"They're for tomorrow."

"All those for *nine* people?"

She nodded without looking up at me. She was cutting celery into small pieces and throwing it in a bowl which contained cooked elbow macaroni. Sitting across from her, I gestured toward the living room.

"What's *he* doing here? I thought *I* was going to do the windows."

"I tried to wake you at nine and then again at nine-thirty, but you wouldn't get up, so I walked next door and told Albie he had another job if he wanted. It's only going to cost you another dime. I did some negotiating," she said.

Actually, this might not be such a bad idea. This would free me up to go back into Dearborn. I wanted to go to the dress shop that Marjorie saw Myrna Lou walk into and see if I could find out the woman's name she was with. I took a couple of sips of coffee and then headed for the bathroom. The door was shut and locked when I went to open it. I was puzzled.

"Gran, this door is locked. Did you accidentally lock us out?"

"No, Bobby's in there," she said, still cutting celery.

"Bobby? I suppose I'm going to owe *him* another dime, too?"

"Of course," she said.

I sighed and gave the door a few hard pounds.

"Hurry it up in there!" I yelled. "I want to take a shower!"

\*\*\*\*

After taking a hot shower and shaving, I felt fully awake and energized. It was 12:15. I grabbed my keys off my dresser in the bedroom. Emerging from my room, I picked up my brown fedora from the dining room table. On my way out to the garage, I found

Albie and Bobby sitting at the kitchen table, each eating a blueberry muffin and drinking a large glass of milk while my grandmother made her macaroni salad. I stopped.

"Hey, I thought those were for tomorrow," I said, feeling jealous of the two young kids.

Gran sighed and said, "Sam, please don't be such a baby. The muffin and milk were part of the negotiation. You pay them each eighty-five cents and I give them milk and a muffin."

"Gran, what is *that*?" I suddenly asked, pointing out the window that was behind her with urgency.

She turned quickly in her chair and I grabbed a muffin, hiding it behind my back.

"What, dear? I don't see anything," she said, and then turned back to her salad.

The two boys looked up at me and snickered. I put a forefinger to my lips, telling them silently this would be our secret, and then headed out to the Chevy with a smile on my face. Once inside the car, I bit into the small cake and found the blueberries were still warm.

\*\*\*\*

The day was mild with big billowy clouds floating through the sky, and a light breeze was blowing in from the west. If this weather kept up, it was going to be a very nice Easter. Traffic was on the heavy side from people out doing last minute shopping for the holiday. I drove past Patti Ann's Boutique twice before I found a parking spot on Michigan Avenue.

As I entered the shop a bell chimed, signaling the staff that they had a potential customer. Three women were in the shop. One, obviously a shopper who appeared to be in her sixties, was standing in front of a full length mirror while a young employee stooped to pin a new hem into the dress she was trying on. Another woman who worked in the boutique was speaking to the older woman. Possibly this was Patti Ann?

"But Mrs. Gilford, the dress lengths are a bit shorter today."

"I don't care *what* they're wearing now, Patti! I *know* what I'm comfortable in and I want this hem lengthened!"

"Just fix it the way she wants, Lucy," Patti Ann said, rubbing her temple.

"Certainly," muttered Lucy.

The one called Patti Ann looked my way and smiled.

"Hello, I'll be with you in a few moments. Feel free to browse until I can get to you."

Nodding, I did just that. I went to a rack of women's suits. One that was solid light brown resembled the garment Patti Ann was now wearing. The skirt was straight with a small slit in the back bottom. The jacket had shoulder padding and two huge buttons on the lower front. I took hold of the price tag and gave it a glance, whistling softly. The suit cost twenty-four dollars and ninety-five cents!

Next, I moved to a display of hats. My favorite among them was a tan number with netting that cascaded over the face. The price tag read three dollars! Again, a soft whistle escaped my lips. This place was not cheap. I meandered around the shop for about another fifteen minutes, giving Patti Ann the time to deal with and check out her client at the cash register.

"The dress will be ready by Tuesday, Mrs. Gilford," she said. "Anytime after noon."

"I'll be here," the older woman said stiffly. The chimes sounded again as she made her departure.

I approached the owner at the counter. Her eyes were still on the older woman as she strutted down Michigan Avenue. Finally she turned to me, rubbing at her temple again.

"I'm so sorry you had to wait so long. Thank you for your patience. Some of my clients are easier to please than others, and we have to go way out of our way to please Mrs. Gilford. But it's worth it to us; *most* days, that is."

She broke out into a wide smile, showing a nice set of white teeth framed by peach colored lips. Her hair was light blond and she wore it in a twist at the back of her head with a sparse amount of bangs feathering her forehead. Her makeup was expertly applied; she was extremely attractive. I found myself staring into her deep brown eyes. They were beautiful, with a soft fanning of dark black lashes outlining them. She looked to be somewhere between thirty and thirty-five years of age. I glanced at her left hand. She wore no wedding ring. I was brought down to earth by what she said next.

"Is there something I can show you for the wife? Or perhaps a girlfriend?" she asked.

I shook my head. "No, sorry to disappoint you, but I've come in to ask a question."

Her eyebrows furrowed.

"You were open this past Wednesday?"

She looked surprised.

"Of course we were. Is that what you wanted to know?" She broke out into soft laughter. "All you have to do is read our hours on the door," she said while pointing to the front of the store. "We're open until five every day of the week except Fridays and Saturdays. Fridays we are open until six, and we close on Saturdays at three. Of course, we're closed on Sundays."

"No, no; that isn't exactly my question," I said, feeling flustered in the presence of this woman. "Let me begin again. My name is Sam Flanagan and I'm a private detective. I'm looking for a young lady who hasn't been seen since Monday. The girl in question might have been seen walking into this dress shop late Wednesday afternoon with an older woman; a woman with gray hair; possibly her grandmother. I need to know if you remember such a woman and young girl in here on that day."

She looked beyond my left shoulder, staring at nothing, but trying to think back to that day. I said nothing to interrupt her train of thought. I was a bit miffed when Lucy came out of the back room with a measuring tape draped around her neck. She walked behind the counter and opened a drawer that was next to Patti Ann and started rummaging for something. The owner ignored her.

"The only more mature woman who came in here on Wednesday was Thora Sutcliffe. She's old enough to have grandchildren, but she came in just before noon, and she doesn't have gray hair. She dyes it brown. And she was alone."

"Are you sure? It was told to me that this would've been close to 4:00 when the couple of them came in here."

Patti Ann turned to Lucy and impatiently asked, "What are you looking for?"

"I was looking for the scissors. I could swear I'd left them in this drawer."

Patti Ann turned to her left and opened a drawer.

"No, they were lying on the counter and I put them in this one."

She handed the girl the scissors and then turned back to me.

"I can assure you no one by that description came in at 4:00, Mr. Flanagan. I vividly remember that my last customer came in at around 2:30."

"Did you say Wednesday? This past Wednesday?" Lucy chimed in.

We both turned our heads in the direction of the young seamstress and waited for her to continue.

"Well, someone *did* come in about that time. She said she'd bought a dress here last week and when she got it home it had a flaw in it. There was a small rip in the seam. I told her it was nothing to worry about and that I could fix it for her within a few moments. She waited and I handed her back the dress. She had gray hair."

"What? Why wasn't I aware of this? I would've known if someone had come in. Where was I?" Patti Ann asked.

"Don't you remember? You left early that day," Lucy said. "You went to the airport."

"Oh! How could I be so stupid?" Patti Ann gently smacked her forehead with her right hand. "That was the day Walter returned from New York and I picked him up from his flight."

I didn't know why, but this revelation affected me. Patti Ann wore no wedding ring, but there was a Walter in her life. I felt my heart go south. I shoved any diversion and emotion away.

"Did she have a young girl with her? Say about seventeen years old? Brown hair?"

I felt my heartbeat picking up speed.

"Yes."

"Do you know who this woman was, Lucy?" I asked.

"Well, I wrote it in the book."

Patti Ann turned the pages on her personal client book.

"Oh yes," she said. "She doesn't come in here often. Her financial status doesn't allow for that, but when she needs something new for work, she comes to me. She's a teacher in the area. Her name is Agnes Dade."

Judith White

# Chapter Thirteen

*Agnes Dade*? I was dumbfounded. I wasted no time in asking for Mrs. Dade's address. Patti Ann seemed hesitant to give it to me, but she could see the urgency on my face and knew I felt the situation was dire. She finally rattled it off to me and I committed it to memory...278 Eugene Street. I thanked her and quickly headed for the door. I decided to throw caution to the wind, and turned back to Patti Ann as I reached out for the handle.

"Patti Ann, I noticed you don't wear a ring on that left hand of yours, but you broke my heart when you mentioned a Walter in your life."

She didn't miss a beat when she replied, "Mr. Flanagan, I noticed *you* don't wear a wedding ring, either. And you're right; Walter is a permanent part of my life and always will be. He's my father."

I let my smile grow to its widest boundary while she tried to hide hers.

Out on the street, I had to ask passersby if they knew where Eugene Street was. I hit pay dirt with the third man I asked. He told me it was on the eastern side of Dearborn and gave me exact directions. It was going to be easy to find; it intersected with Michigan Avenue and was the street before Wyoming Avenue, a busy thoroughfare.

By the time I reached the '38 Chevy, I had to calm myself. I entered the car and rolled my window down all the way. Reaching into my pocket, I took out a Lucky Strike and lit it, taking a deep puff. I still couldn't get over the fact that it was *Agnes Dade* who Myrna Lou had been seen with! What the hell was going on? What reason would Mrs. Dade, English teacher, have for taking Myrna Lou home with her? What reason would Myrna Lou have for going along with her instructor? It just didn't figure. What was I missing? The Dearborn High School teacher certainly gave me the impression that she didn't like the girl at all. Was she keeping her against her will for some reason? None of these questions were going to be answered by my sitting there asking them to no one. I needed to head on over to the east part of Dearborn.

I pulled up to the house, a two-story brown brick structure, at 2:48 p.m. The front yard needed cutting and the left side of the chain link gate leading to the back yard was hanging awkwardly on its hinges. When I exited the car, I could hear the loud continuous barking of a large dog from several houses down.

Approaching the house, I noticed the front drapes were drawn and the inside door was shut to the nice breeze and sunshine. I rang the doorbell once, assuming no one was home. On the other hand, it occurred to me maybe someone was trying to keep something or *someone* inside and hidden from view.

I was about to give a second ring when the door was jerked open. Agnes Dade stood there with a wet cloth in her hand, dressed in baggy faded black pants and an oversized white shirt. Her face showed great surprise at seeing me. I could tell it wasn't a good surprise to her. I caught a whiff of lemon wax coming from the cloth and assumed I'd caught her in the middle of cleaning.

"Hello, Mrs. Dade," I said. "May I step in for a moment?"

Her eyebrows furrowed and her face took on a look of defiance.

"You certainly may *not*! What are you doing coming to my home?"

"I came to check something out. Someone said they saw you enter a boutique on Michigan Avenue just this past Wednesday."

Before I could continue, she interrupted me with anger in her voice.

"And what business is that of yours? How dare you track my movements! And who gave you this address? I'll have their hide when I find out!"

"No one gave it to me. It's in the book, right?"

I prayed it was in the book. Her expression told me that I was right.

"I was told that when you entered the dress shop, a girl was with you who fit Myrna Lou Stevic's description." I said nothing more. I wanted that to sink in. Her face turned a rosy shade and she gasped.

"Are you implying that *I* know where that girl is? That maybe I have her tucked away somewhere? How dare you, Mr. Flanagan! I'll sue you for libel! How dare you come here and accuse me of—"

I cut her off before she could continue with her rant. I held up my hand, stopping her flow of words.

"Wait a minute! I'm investigating the disappearance of one of your students. I would've thought you cared about that. I would've thought you had more concern for her than this. Okay, so she's not *your* kind of student. Okay, so she's not the young lady *you* would have liked her to be. But the fact is she's missing, and I would've thought you cared about that. I see you don't. But I'll tell you, lady, she's out there somewhere, and she might not be in good condition or in a good situation. Now, if you don't want to tell me who you were with, I'll go and get a squad car, and they'll come here and search your home whether you want them to or not!"

She quietly stared at me as her face took on color again, obviously making an attempt to calm herself. Finally, she spoke. Her voice was fainter and filled with less venom.

"Fine, I'll satisfy your curiosity. But know this Mr. Flanagan; once it's satisfied, don't you ever come back here again uninvited. And believe me, you will never *be* invited."

"It's a deal," I said.

She backed away from the door and went to the bottom of a staircase that led to the second floor. Right beyond her, I could see a doorway that I assumed led to the kitchen. She looked up to the top of the stairs.

"Jeanette! Jeanette? Come down here, please," she called out.

I heard movement on the stairs. A young woman came into view, but it was hard to get a good glimpse of her through the screen until she came closer. Mrs. Dade walked with the girl to where I was standing, and without opening the door introduced me to her granddaughter. From that vantage point, I could see the girl may have been seventeen or a year or two older.

"She's been staying with me for the last two weeks. My son and his wife are moving back from California, and are finalizing the sale of their home out there. Are you satisfied?" she asked tightly.

I'd been studying the girl closely. She had medium brown hair, about the same length as Myrna Lou's in the picture. Unlike Myrna Lou's deep brown eyes, though, this girl had eyes that were a pretty shade of green. She was a very cute girl of medium height, but lanky like her grandmother. When she smiled, there was no chip in her tooth, and most importantly, she admitted to being Jeanette Dade.

My hopes had been dashed. I so wanted to find Grace's niece, no matter what the situation was at Agnes Dade's house. I could've apologized to the English teacher, but I didn't. I figured she didn't deserve an apology. In the presence of her granddaughter, I made one final comment.

"If I find anything else suspicious involving you, I'll be back."

I turned to descend the porch steps and heard the door slam behind me.

Back out on Michigan Avenue, I headed west. I thought about Marjorie's assertions that she had seen Myrna Lou on Wednesday, and I could understand the mistake. From behind, Jeanette probably *did* look like Myrna Lou. And besides, Marjorie was only ten years old. I wasn't angry at the child, I was just very disappointed.

Now, I was going to do something that should've been done right from the beginning. As I drove, my anxiety about Myrna

Lou's whereabouts grew. I knew *someone* had to know *something*, but I hadn't connected with that person yet. My ex-partner, Bill McPherson, had been right; time was of the essence. Maybe too much time had been wasted.

I pulled into Johnny's drive, right behind his car, and parked. Getting out, I climbed onto the porch, and could hear voices from within. I gave the screen a rap. Johnny came to the door, looking hopeful. He swung the screen out for me and I entered.

"Care to go for a ride?" I asked him.

He looked confused and then I looked past him. Grace was sitting on the couch with another woman; it was obviously her sister, an older and more worn out version of Johnny's wife. A man stood in the middle of the living room, wearing dark gray trousers that were held up with red suspenders over a stained white shirt. His belly protruded, separating the suspenders farther than they should've been. He looked like he hadn't washed or combed his hair in days, and he needed a shave.

Johnny turned to the couple and said, "Sam, this is Myrna Lou's mother and her husband. They just drove into town this afternoon."

"Myrna Lou's *stepfather*," the guy corrected, and Johnny sighed loudly.

"Do you have word of my baby?" Vivian asked with pain in her voice.

I looked down at the hat in my hand and shook my head. I suddenly felt inept in the presence of this woman.

"I don't, ma'am. In fact, I'm here to take Johnny with me down to the Dearborn Police Department." I turned back to my friend. "I'll keep on with the case, but we need them. They have resources I just don't have. They have communication with other area departments, so the search will be more widespread. We need their help."

Vivian leaned against Grace and burst into tears. Grace held her sister, and I could see her own eyes were watering. Bart, Vivian's husband, turned to us, his thumbs inserted in his suspenders.

"I'll just stay here to care for the women," he said, while Johnny again rolled his eyes at me.

My friend's face was filled with fear as we crossed the lawn to my vehicle. I thought I could see him shaking slightly out of nervousness. At the sound of the screen door opening, I glanced back.

"Hey, Johnny," Bart shouted. "You got any beer in the icebox?"

Johnny never looked his way and never answered him. He just opened the Chevy door and climbed in.

# Chapter Fourteen

It was Easter Sunday, April 25, 1943, and Myrna Lou Stevic had last been seen six days earlier. When Johnny had first approached me to ask for my help in finding her, I thought it would be a short case. I had truly figured we would find her at a girlfriend's house or sitting in a nearby park. Never did I think we would find her to be in danger. Although I didn't know for sure that that was the case at the moment, I knew from being in my line of work that the longer a person stayed missing, the greater the chance that the ending wasn't going to be a good one.

I was feeling a bit guilty at not being more forceful in suggesting Johnny go straight to the Dearborn police to report her disappearance. I'd done what I could, such as contacting people I knew she was associated with—in fact, there were still others I needed to contact—but I somehow felt that their stories would be no different from the others. The story that kept repeating was they weren't close to her because they didn't care for her, and therefore, knew nothing of where she might have gone or might be now.

As I'd constantly thought throughout the week, *someone* had to know *something*. I just hadn't crossed paths with that someone yet. Either that, or someone I'd already spoken to hadn't been completely honest. If that were the case, I couldn't think who that could be.

At any rate, a huge burden had been lifted when Johnny Delbeck and I had entered the police station the previous afternoon. The desk sergeant showed us to the desk of Detective

Pete Levasser, who was filing a report on some minor crime that had happened in the city during the wee hours of the morning. When he looked up, I found him to be an extremely odd person in physical appearance. His black hair was short and combed completely forward from the crown of his head, ending in full bangs that spanned his wide forehead. He reminded me of what Julius Caesar might have looked like. His black eyebrows were bushy and wild, outlining close set gray eyes. The nose on his face was smaller than I had ever seen on any man. He may have been my age or a little younger. When he stood to greet us, he appeared to be about five feet six inches tall and was slightly built. I knew it was shallow of me, but I found him to be so strange looking that I glanced at his wedding ring finger to see if he was married. He was, by all appearances. Pete Levasser wore a plain silver band on his left hand.

He listened to Johnny's story without interruption. When the story was told, he asked all the usual questions, questions I'd asked when Johnny first told me about Myrna Lou. The Dearborn detective had a way about him that put people at ease. I could see my friend physically relax while telling the situation he was facing. Pete Levasser inspired confidence and hope. He told Johnny that even though almost a week had elapsed, many young kids showed up after having run away from home out of their general confusion and discontent. He assured Johnny that he'd seen this all too often and that it wasn't at the stage where he needed to worry…yet.

While he spoke, I suddenly remembered the picture I had of the girl, so I reached into my back pocket and withdrew my wallet. He took the picture and asked to keep it while they searched for the girl. Then he turned his swivel chair slightly to his left and toward me.

"And what's your involvement in all of this?" he had asked.

I told him. I told him everyone I'd talked to and what they had said, holding nothing back. Out of the corner of my eye, I saw Johnny's flinch and sudden head movement toward me. He was surprised at hearing how many people had disliked Grace's niece.

He may have been stunned at hearing this, but now wasn't the time to hold back. This detective needed to hear the whole story.

"Will you continue to work on the case, Mr. Flanagan?" Levasser asked, and I nodded. "That's fine, but do be cautious of stepping on our toes during this investigation. And of course, we want to hear anything new you find out immediately after finding it out."

I nodded again; I understood. When we left the station, even *my* fears had been diminished. But now, as I placed the ham in the oven while my grandmother attended an early morning service at church, they came flooding back. Pete Levasser may have been successful in calming Johnny, but having my own agency for the last six years or so told me a different story. I prayed the Dearborn detective was right.

By a quarter of two in the afternoon, Gran was finishing mashing the potatoes and I'd just set the last glass at the table. Everything was ready for our guests, who were to arrive on the hour. I had inserted a leaf in the dining room table which made it possible to seat up to ten people; four on each side and one on each end.

While positioning the chairs, I heard a rap at the front door. It was Helen, Gran's friend of umpteen years. She had a huge purse with her and I could see a red bottle top sticking ever so slightly out of the opening of it. *Oh my God!* I thought. *She's brought her vodka, and if my Aunt Pearl ever gets wind of the fact she's drinking....*

"Hey, Helen," I greeted her. "Happy Easter."

I opened the screen door and moved back so she could enter. She passed me in a flash and made a beeline for the kitchen. She called back to me over her shoulder.

"The coleslaw is in the car. Get it!"

"Well, nice to see you, too," I muttered under my breath as I stepped out onto the porch.

"Hey, Mr. Flanagan! Happy Easter! You able to pay us for doin' the windows now?"

I looked over and there were Albie and Bobby about to get into their father's car, dressed in hand me down suits that had seen better days. Each wore a bow tie at the base of their necks. Obviously, they were heading out for the day. I waved to their parents and they waved back. I told Albie to come get it; I had it with me now. As I was reaching in my pocket, he called back, telling me he would stop over after they got back from their aunt and uncle's. I waved again as the car cruised on down St. Aubin.

**\*\*\*\***

Great Uncle Derwood was saying the blessing as we sat around the table with heads bent. He sat at the head of the table with his back to my bedroom door. Gran sat to his left with Helen next to her. I was next to Helen and to my left was Gloria. Gloria was Dillard's wife, and Dillard was the grandson of Pearl and Derwood. They had two children…a boy of about six or seven and a beautiful little girl who was five. On the other side of the table were Pearl, Dillard, Celia, and Randall.

The surface of the dining room table was covered with bowls and platters of food; ham, mashed potatoes, ham gravy, macaroni salad, coleslaw, green beans, butternut squash, deviled eggs, cheese cubes, and buttermilk biscuits. Pearl's pies sat on the counter in the kitchen, along with the blueberry muffins. When Derwood said "Amen" and raised his head, we started to pass the dishes to each other.

"Wait," my grandmother said. "I'd like to say something special."

She bowed her head again and brought her hands together in front of her. We all did the same.

"God, we don't know where that young girl is, but you do. Keep her safe and make sure she gets fed. Amen."

"Amen," we all said.

"What young lass might that be, Ruby?" asked Derwood in his thick Irish brogue.

As she began to tell all about the case that I was currently working on, as if she'd actively been working on it with me, I noticed young Celia, who was sitting directly across from me. As she filled herself with mashed potatoes, her eyes never left me. She ate with an open mouth and I could see the fluffy white substance rolling over her tongue. I remembered something my grandfather and Uncle Derwood used to do, without fail, at each holiday gathering when I was just a young lad, so I tried it out on her. I put a forefinger to the tip of my nose and pushed. Out popped my tongue. I pulled on my right ear lobe and my tongue moved to the far right corner of my mouth. I pulled on my left lobe and the tongue quickly shot over to the left side of my mouth. I pressed on my chin and the tongue returned to the middle, sticking out straight ahead. I pushed on my nose again, and the tongue disappeared inside. She shyly lowered her gaze to her plate and then raised her eyes again with a big smile on her face. I repeated my little performance and she started to giggle softly as she ate. Still, she stared at me.

I was at the beginning of a second replay when her brother, Randall, who was sitting next to her, suddenly belted out in a loud voice, "*Dad, that guy over there keeps making faces at Celia!*" He was pointing his finger at me. Dillard looked up at me, got a scowl on his face, and threw his fork back onto his plate. He reached to his right, pulling his daughter roughly toward him where she ended up resting under his armpit, causing the piece of ham she'd just put in her mouth to go flying and disappear under the dining room table. The sudden movement of her father startled her and caused her to cry in loud shrieks.

"That's okay, baby. Daddy is here." Then he looked at me again. "Aw, Sam; what ya gotta do that for? Ya always gotta cause trouble!"

"Hey," I said. "I wasn't *doing* anything to her. She liked it."

Dillard turned to my grandmother.

"Aunt Ruby, can't you *do* something with him?"

Gran shrugged and continue to eat. "What can I do? He's going to be forty this year. He's a grown man now."

I stared at my grandmother. She could've come to my defense! I was disappointed in her lack of support for me.

"Well, one would think," Pearl chimed in, "that you could control the boy in *some* way, dear sister."

*Control the boy*? I looked over at Gran and she just shrugged once again. Celia was still screaming and Dillard was holding her too close, to the point of distress for the child.

"Look how he's made her cry!" he said.

"*Me*? Hey, *I* didn't make her cry! *You're* the one cutting her breath off!"

I looked around the table as Dillard continued to rant and Aunt Pearl continued to lecture my grandmother about my behavior. To my left, Gloria, the child's mother, was shoveling food into her mouth, oblivious to the ruckus going on around her. Randall sat staring at me with a smirk on his face. For two cents I would've reached across the table and grabbed him by the front of his crisp white shirt. Gran continued to eat and shrug. And Helen, dear Helen, sat smiling at the young brat, Randall. Only Derwood rested his chin in his palm, shaking his head at the chaos that surrounded him.

I'd had enough. I rose from my chair, my food barely eaten, and threw my napkin in my plate, where it immediately began soaking up the gravy from my potatoes. I excused myself, grabbed my cigarettes and matches from the top of the radio, and headed out to the front steps. Before I reached the screen door, I heard Helen say, "Look, Ruby, he's acting like a big baby now."

It was going on 3:30 and off to the west, I noticed the sky becoming slightly darkened with soft gray clouds that were heading our way. The wind had picked up and there was a definite chill in the air. There was a good possibility of rain later on. I heard loud voices from inside, but couldn't make out what was being said. I didn't care. It was just good to be away from all of them. The one thing that really bothered me was that a plate full of food was left at the table and I was hungry.

I lit my cigarette and inhaled deeply. It calmed me almost immediately. Looking back, I thought about how Dillard had been a truly odd boy. He'd been the one in the family who tattled on the rest of us children at every opportunity. He'd worn thick glasses back then, and he still did. His light auburn hair was curly and frizzy, and he had a slight overbite.

As much of a social buffoon as Dillard was, he was also smart as a whip—book smart, that is. He worked as an accountant for a furniture manufacturing plant in Plymouth, a city just west of Detroit in which he and his family lived. Pearl and Derwood lived three blocks from him, their only grandson in the midst of eleven granddaughters. Even though I didn't know for sure, I'd heard Dillard earned a good wage. Maybe that's what held the attraction for Gloria, because I sure couldn't think of anything else about him that would. Looking across the street, I saw that he had driven separately from his grandparents. Good! Maybe that meant he would be leaving early. I could only hope.

I'd been sitting there for about twenty minutes, and now my thoughts turned to Myrna Lou. When I'd posted the flyer at White Castle back in Dearborn, I had high hopes that someone, *anyone*, would call with something. It seemed to me that the lure of five dollars would have been enough for one of the kids to call hoping their information, no matter how trivial, would be enough to steer me onto the right track in my search. I'd been wrong. No calls had come in so far. I felt like I had nothing as far as the case was concerned. I was no farther ahead than I'd been on Wednesday when Johnny first told me his story. Last Sunday night Myrna Lou had been upset about something she learned, or saw, at church. Whatever happened, it had the effect of her not wanting to go on the youth outing to Camp Arcadia with the other kids, something she was eagerly looking forward to before that night. What was it? Had someone said something to her that made her angry? Had she witnessed something that triggered her? It could've been any number of things. Finding out what it was would be given top priority on my list of things to investigate. I grabbed another Lucky Strike and lit up.

The opening of the screen door behind me made me turn. Uncle Derwood stepped out onto the porch and eased himself down on the step beside me. I inched over closer to the railing on my right side, making more room for him. He turned toward me and pointed at my cigarette.

"Ya wouldn't happen to have another one of those for an old man, would ya, lad?"

"Help yourself," I said as I handed him my pack of cigarettes along with the matches.

I watched as he put the tobacco stick between his teeth and lit it with a steady hand. Derwood Flanagan was eighty-eight years old and could've passed for a man of at least ten years younger. My grandfather's brother was one of my favorite people.

"Derwood? You're not smoking that, are you?" my aunt asked while looking out of the screen door at us. My uncle handed me the cigarette. Now I had two.

"Nope," he said without turning around to look at her.

We heard movement behind us and knew Pearl had moved away from the door. I handed the cigarette back to Derwood.

"Can ye imagine that, son? I'm almost a hundred and still havin' to answer for what I do. I've lived me whole life doin' what yer aunt has told me to do. Don't get me wrong, I love her more than I've loved anything in me whole life, but I wish she had yer grandmother's temperament." He sighed. "It was Ruby I was with when we first met the O'Malley girls. I liked her...I liked her a lot, but she had eyes for me own brother. I could tell that right away. Ah, and ye know the rest of that story."

We were silent for a few moments, enjoying the sounds of nature and our cigarettes, and then he spoke again. He poked a thumb behind him, toward the house.

"About what happened in there; don't let it get you down. The boy's an idiot...a real dope. I never liked him. I know t'is awful to say, but there it is. He was always a brat and he'll always be a dope."

I turned to Derwood, looking surprised.

"Aren't you being a little hard on him? After all, he's only, what, six or seven years old?"

He turned to face me with his eyebrows knit together.

"T'is not Randall I'm speakin' of; although he, too, is turnin' out to be a handful. T'is his father I'm speakin' of. Me own daughter's boy. I can't stand him."

Derwood took another drag on the Lucky Strike, looking straight ahead. I started to chuckle.

"Of course, if ye repeat even one word of what I've said, I'll deny it." And he smiled.

I could hear the muted ring of the telephone from inside. I almost jumped up to run to it, but I didn't. I could hear my grandmother's loud voice.

"*Huh? Who?* Do you mean *Sam?*"

I rolled my eyes. A minute more and she was at the door.

"A phone call for you, dear," she said through the screen.

I entered the house, leaving Derwood to finish his smoke on his own. The women were in the kitchen, putting the food away and preparing a sink full of hot sudsy water in which to wash the dishes. Through the back window, I could see Dillard in the yard with Randall and Celia.

"Hello?" I said when I reached the telephone and picked up the receiver.

"Happy Easter, buddy," said a male voice. "How's your holiday?"

It took me a moment to recognize the voice of Bill McPherson, my ex-police department partner.

"Hey, Mac! Nice to hear from you. Everything's good. How are you doing?"

"No holiday cheer for me," he said. "I'm planted at the station."

"It never ends, does it?"

"Nope," he said. "Listen, Sam, the reason I phoned was that I got to wondering if your friend's niece ever showed up."

"No, and no one seems to know a thing. We finally went and made out a report yesterday at the Dearborn station."

"Who'd you talk to?" Mac asked.

"A Detective Pete Levasser. You know him?"

"Yeah, yeah, as a matter of fact I do. Good man and a damn good detective, too."

He paused for some moments. In fact, I thought I'd lost the connection, but then he broke the silence. "Uh, we gotta young girl, possibly about the age of that one you're looking for, down here. I wondered if you might get your friend and take a ride down."

"No kiddin'," I said. "What? She's being difficult? Won't tell you her name? Not speaking?"

"Right," he said. "She's not speaking. In fact, she'll never speak again. She's dead, Sam. A fisherman called it in early this morning. She'd been partly in the water off of Belle Isle. We need identification."

# Chapter Fifteen

I felt an uncomfortable electricity shoot through my body. I couldn't speak for a moment or two, trying to process this information. Belle Isle was a 982-acre island sitting between Detroit and Canada. It was connected to Detroit by the Belle Isle Bridge. People would spend weekends picnicking there, enjoying family outings, boating, and fishing. Mac knew what I was thinking and feeling, and he let me have the silence. Finally, I cleared my throat.

"Of course, it might not be her," I said.

"Well, yeah. Hell, I don't even know what your friend's niece *looks* like. But I've had her on my mind today ever since we went out to the scene. I just want to rule out this girl you're looking for. Doc is finishing up his examination and I thought if you could take a ride down...."

"The morgue?"

"Yeah. I'll meet you there, say in about an hour?"

"Make it a half hour," I said.

I wasn't going to call Johnny, not yet. Why upset him and his holiday with this if it didn't turn out to be Myrna Lou? That household was upset enough already. I hung the phone up and stood there, looking down, with my hand still on the receiver.

"Bad news, dear?" Gran asked as she looked at me.

"I don't know. A young woman was found on Belle Isle. I've got to go down and make sure it isn't Grace's niece," I said, still not moving.

"You mean she's dead?" Gran asked.

I nodded.

My Aunt Pearl stopped rinsing the dish she had just washed and turned the water off that was streaming from the tap. She grabbed a towel and dried her hands.

"Ladies," she said. "I think we'd better form a circle and join hands in prayer."

I moved past them as they gathered in the middle of the kitchen and headed toward my bedroom. I picked up my hat, keys, and the money I'd left on my dresser. I returned to the kitchen and waited silently until I heard an "amen" from the women. Placing two one-dollar bills on the table, I told Gran to give that to Albie and Bobby for the work they'd done if they showed up to collect. Then I gave a dollar to Helen for my grandmother's dinner. I knew I was paying out more than I owed, but I didn't want to take the time to count out nickels and dimes at that point.

Once outside, I descended the steps and faced my Uncle Derwood. I told him I had to leave and told him where I was going and why. He grabbed the railing in his effort to stand.

"You wouldn't see fit to takin' an old man with ya, now would ya?" he asked.

"You want to go with me to the morgue?"

"Well, I sure don't want to be left behind with them," he said, pointing his thumb behind him.

"Get your hat then. I'll pull the car out."

\*\*\*\*

I pulled into the lot at the Wayne County Morgue twenty minutes later. It was located on Brush at the corner of Lafayette. Once parked, I killed the engine and sat silent for a moment, staring straight ahead. My chest was tightening and I found it just a bit difficult to breathe. A mild wave of nausea ran over me. There were times when I didn't think this line of work was suited to me, and this was one of those times. Why couldn't I have had a special relationship with numbers, like Dillard? Why couldn't I have followed in my father's footsteps and gotten a position as a machinist in some machine shop in town? At that moment I wanted to view a dead body about as much as I wanted to have my nails ripped from my fingertips. I felt Derwood's hand on my right shoulder.

"It won't get any easier just by sittin' here, lad. Go in and get it over with, and then ye can come out knowin' it isn't her. I'll wait out here for ye."

"Tell me you're sure it isn't her," I said, trying to gather my strength and courage.

"I'll tell ye I'm hopin'," he replied.

Once inside, I found the morgue to be as quiet as a...morgue. I saw no one on the first floor and went directly to the stairs leading to the bowels of the building. Poking my head in Doc Macgregor's office, I found it empty, so I continued on to the lab.

There he was, hunched over the still body of an elderly colored man. He was shining a pen light inside the deceased's wide opened mouth and using a pick of some sort to extract something. I cleared my throat and he looked up.

"Well, long time no see, Sam. How ya been? Mac phoned me you'd be stopping by," he said, smiling widely.

Fergus Macgregor was a native of Scotland who'd arrived in the United States with his parents, three sisters, and seven brothers at the tender age of nine, back in 1889. Now sixty-three, his hair was pure white and worn in a crew cut. He was on the short side and stocky. During the last fifty-four years of American life, he'd all but lost most of his Scottish brogue. He came over to shake my hand, removing his rubber glove first. Fergus wore his white lab coat over dark brown trousers, a light green shirt, and a brown tie.

"Can't complain. How about you and yours?" I asked.

"Ah, doin' well. My youngest just got married last weekend, but the missus and me won't be on our own just yet. She married a military man and while he's stationed in Europe, she'll keep to home with us."

I nodded. Hearing movement behind me, I turned to see Mac enter with a disposable cup containing coffee. He was blowing on the steaming beverage as he walked our way.

"Did I miss anything? Where's your friend?" he asked.

I explained that I'd just arrived and how I didn't want to bother Johnny with this unless I had to. Fergus waved us farther into the room and led us to the gurneys lining the back wall. Four out of the ten gurneys had bodies lying on them with sheets covering their identities. He pulled one out and stood beside it, taking hold of the sheet. He looked at me.

"Ready for this?" he asked.

"Ready as I'll ever be," I said, inhaling deeply.

He lowered the sheet to expose the head, neck, and shoulders. What first hit me was how bruised and swollen the face was. I tore my eyes away and focused on her hair. It was about the same length as Myrna Lou's in the picture I'd been given. It was the same color, but for the life of me, I couldn't tell if it was her. How had I ever thought I would be able to tell if it was Myrna Lou from a photograph I'd seldom looked at?

"I don't know," I said.

"She's fifteen to eighteen years old, I figure," Fergus said. "She's been dead for some days. Maybe even a week."

"What happened to her? What was the cause of death?" I asked.

"Head trauma. She was hit with a blunt instrument on the back of her head and it cracked her skull. In fact, whoever did this hit her twice, but there was no need; she was hit with such force, she was dead after the first blow. Somebody was mighty angry at her. And in case you're wondering, she wasn't violated and she wasn't pregnant. This lassie was pure as the driven snow."

"We found a rock stained with blood at the scene, not too far from the body," Mac added. "We bagged it and it's down at the station. We're going to test for prints, but the weather was sure to affect any that were left behind. I'm not holding my breath; I know it's a long shot at best."

For whatever reason, Doc Macgregor rolled the body to its left, exposing her head wound; a sunken crater. I winced, and then I saw it. This young girl had a purplish birthmark on the back of her right shoulder about the size of my fist. My eyes widened.

"Oh my God!" I said, barely above a whisper. "Can you see if she has a chipped tooth in the front of her mouth? I'm not sure it would still be there, but the picture I had of her showed her having it."

I turned to Mac with a heavy heart.

"You think it's her?" he asked.

I told him of my visit to the Gilbert home, and how ten-year-old Marjorie had told me of Myrna Lou's birthmark. Then the doctor told me that it was affirmative; this girl had a chip on the front top right tooth. My heart sank. I now believed I was looking at the still, lifeless body of Myrna Lou Stevic. I was finally successful in finding Grace's niece.

Judith White

# Chapter Sixteen

Before I took my leave of the Wayne County Morgue, I gave Mac the address of Johnny and Grace Delbeck on Garrison Avenue in Dearborn. Mac volunteered to accompany me to the house, but I declined his offer. I felt this was something I should do alone. He told me to tell the Delbeck's they should expect a visit from him and his partner sometime the following morning.

I was pulling onto Garrison now, with Derwood to my right. I parked at the curb.

"I'll be here when you've finished," Derwood said. "Just leave your smokes this time."

I knocked on the screen door and heard Grace call out, "Come on in, Sam."

I entered and found the four adults sitting in the living room. Johnny and Bart were seated on the sofa and Grace and Vivian were seated in the chairs. The children weren't in sight, but I thought I heard shouts and bantering coming from the backyard.

"I saw you from the window. Who is that in the car?" Grace asked.

"My Uncle Derwood rode out here with me," I answered.

"Well, my goodness, bring him in. I've got a pot of coffee brewing and we're just about to have cake."

Johnny was staring at me, and seemed to sense that this wasn't a routine visit.

"What is it, Sam? What's wrong?" he asked.

"My old partner from the Detroit Police Department is going to come to call on you tomorrow morning," I said, still dreading telling them of the latest development.

"He *is*?" Grace asked, sounding surprised. "Will he be working on the case, too, Sam?"

"Yeah, he's going to pick up the case," I said and then hesitated. "Listen, I don't really know how to say this, so I'm just going to come out with it. The body of a young girl was found on Belle Isle this morning. Some guy had been fishing and called it in. I just got back from downtown. Johnny, Bart," I said, looking from one to the other. "It might be a good idea if you go down tomorrow, too, to have a look. But I believe her to be Myrna Lou."

Vivian jumped up from her chair and I turned to face her. Her breathing became rapid and labored, and her face took on a hard look. She seemed overcome with anger.

"You don't know *anything*!" she said to me. "You've never *met* my baby. How would *you* know if it's her or not? I don't care *what* you believe! My girl isn't dead!"

"I know how you're feeling. Let me just say that this particular girl has a front tooth that is chipped and a birthmark behind her right shoulder," I responded quietly, apologetically.

Vivian's face took on a painful distortion and then she doubled over at the waist. Her mouth was open, but no sound was coming out. Suddenly, it wasn't a cry that emerged, but a deep howl. Grace rose from her seat and tried to hold her sister, but Vivian pushed her away. Johnny's wife buried her face in her hands and began to weep. Bart jumped up and started to pace and rant.

"Oh, well *this* is good! You're hired to find her, and *you* gotta wait until she's *dead* before you bring us any news," he yelled, pointing a forefinger at me. He then looked at his wife. "You see? You see what I told you, Viv? She wasn't nothin' but trouble, and now she's got herself dead!" He turned to Johnny, pointing his finger. "And you! This is all *your* fault, the two of you whiskin' her away down here. If she were still in Harrison, none of this woulda happened. And who in the *hell* is gonna pay for a funeral? *I ain't got that kind of money!*"

Johnny was on his feet instantly and made a move toward Bart with a clenched right fist.

*"Why you rotten bastard!"*

As if by magic, Vivian's tears stopped and she stepped in front of Johnny, placing her hand on his chest. She shook her head.

"No, don't you dare," she said calmly, quietly.

What happened next...well, I never saw it coming. I don't think any of us did. Vivian turned to face her husband, pulled her arm way back, cocked a fist, and let him have it for all she was worth. Her knuckles made contact with his left eye. Bart's head snapped to the right as his hand came up to cover his injury. Vivian squealed with pain and cradled her right fist in her other hand. I could see from my position that her knuckles were a deep red and were beginning to swell already. She began to cry again.

"Don't you *ever* say that again! My sister and her husband aren't to blame!" she screamed. *"You are!* All you've ever done is make Myrna Lou feel like she was an annoyance to you! She was my baby and I loved her. No wonder she acted out all the time. You kept telling her how she was no good in a million different ways!" Vivian straightened. "You're not welcome here, Bart. Go home and pack your things. I want you gone by the time I get back to Harrison."

"You don't mean that, Viv," he said. "What about the boys?"

"I raised my girl by myself for the most part. I can raise them, too. Now leave."

Anger rose in his face as his eye began to swell and bruise. He pushed past Vivian and Grace and went farther into the house.

"You'll be sorry for this, Viv! You mark my words! Within a week you'll be *beggin'* for me to come back, but don't bother!" he shouted.

Grace put her arm around her sister and led her into the bathroom to care for her hand.

Johnny ran his fingers through his hair.

"That's the smartest thing she's ever done," he said, looking at me. "Oh God, Sam, she's dead! I can't *believe* it! What happened? I mean how...?"

I told him about the head wound, and he slumped back down onto the sofa and buried his face in his hands.

When I left the Delbeck home twenty minutes later, Grace and Vivian were sitting at the kitchen table, staring into space with tears streaming down their cheeks, and Johnny was about to call the children in from the yard to explain to them about Myrna Lou. Bart had stormed out moments earlier with a suitcase and screeched down the street in his battered vehicle, leaving his wife alone to deal with the most difficult situation she had ever faced in her life.

"Who was the fella who high tailed it out of the house?" Derwood asked when I climbed in behind the wheel.

"Myrna Lou's stepfather," I replied.

"Seems a helluva time for him to be makin' an exit."

"Believe me, his wife is better off without him," I said.

I pulled away from the curb while glancing back at Johnny's house. There was nothing to see. He'd probably brought the kids into the kitchen where he was now explaining the tragic news.

We drove in silence. There were so many emotions running through me, and anger was at the forefront. As crazy as it sounded, I was mad at Myrna Lou for ending up in that condition on Belle Isle. I was mad at Bart for being such a heel, and I was mad at who'd ever done this to a life that was basically just beginning. And, even though I knew that she was probably dead by the time Johnny entered my office, I was mad at myself for not being successful in bringing her home safe and sound. I knew I wasn't thinking rationally; emotions were leading me. But I somehow *wanted* to feel the anger. It was better than breaking down the way Grace and Vivian were. The last thing Johnny had said to me before I'd left was that he wanted me to find the bastard who'd done this. He had my promise that I would.

# Chapter Seventeen

Uncle Derwood and I pulled up into the drive on St. Aubin at 8:10 p.m. Lights were on in the front, but nowhere else in the house. Dillard's car was gone, thank goodness, as well as Helen's. I parked in the garage and we made our way through a darkened kitchen to the living room where only Gran and Aunt Pearl were sitting, sipping on cups of hot tea. Their conversation ended abruptly and their attention turned to us as we took seats in the room.

"Well?" Gran asked.

Uncle Derwood nodded his head, saying, "T'was her, alright. There's been a bit of foul play in that young one's life. Seems someone was angry enough to take a stone to the back of her head. I took a ride over to her uncle's with the boy here."

The two women lowered their gazes and shook their heads.

Looking up again, Gran asked, "How's Johnny doing, dear?"

I explained everything that had happened from the time I entered the Delbeck home. They listened without interruption while I told of Vivian's initial anger, her belting her husband, and his quick getaway.

"You mean he *left* her? At a time like *this*?" Aunt Pearl was astounded.

"He sure did," I replied.

As I spoke, I noticed out of the corner of my eye that my uncle had been rubbing his left hip with a pained expression on his face.

"What's wrong, Derwood?" my aunt asked him.

"Seems I've got a bum hip this evenin'," he said. "Givin' me a bit of trouble." And then he spoke to my grandmother. "Ruby, you couldn't see your way fit to puttin' us up for the evenin', could ya?"

"You mean you can't drive?" Aunt Pearl asked, sounding disappointed.

"I don't think I should try."

"Well, of course, I can! Come on, Pearl, it'll be fun, like a sleeping over party. How often do we really get to visit?"

"I suppose. But where will we sleep?"

"You can sleep with me," Gran said with excitement. "And Sam can take the couch while Derwood sleeps in Sam's bed."

Uncle Derwood turned to me, silently asking with his expression if that was alright. I shrugged.

"Sure, why not? I don't mind."

Gran jumped off the couch, taking Aunt Pearl's teacup and her own and heading for the kitchen.

"Oh, this will be so much fun! Come on, Pearl, let's go to bed now. We can lay in the dark and talk, just like we used to."

Pearl's eyes followed Gran as she placed the cups on the counter near the sink. She frowned.

"That was more than seventy years ago, ya old fool!" she said.

But she rose from where she was sitting and left the room. Uncle Derwood's gaze followed her as she left. He put a finger up to his lips, cautioning me to be quiet, as he listened for something. We heard the door to Gran's bedroom shut and he turned to me and smiled.

"My hip is as right as rain," he whispered.

"What?" I asked, furrowing my eyebrows.

"My hip is as right as rain; nothin' wrong with it. Let's give them, say, about fifteen minutes, and we'll go raid the macaroni salad and ham. Got anything in the house to drink?"

"I've got some whiskey," I told him.

"Wouldn't happen to be Bushmill's, would it?"

"Nah, sorry."

"Well, no matter," he said. Then as an afterthought, he added, "Got enough smokes?"

I nodded that I did.

"Good," he said. "We're gonna feast on leftovers, have a bit of rye, and ye are gonna tell me all about this case right from the beginnin'."

He rose from his chair and told me nothing was wrong with his hip, but his bladder was about to burst. Saying he would meet me in the kitchen in about ten minutes, he left me alone with the grin I was wearing.

You wouldn't have thought I could eat after knowing of Myrna Lou's circumstances, but I could. My plate was piled high with ham and macaroni salad and I ate like there was no tomorrow. After my plate was clean, I sliced off a small wedge of my aunt's apple pie and consumed that. Uncle Derwood had been done with his snack for some time, and was now watching me continue to shovel food into my mouth while he puffed on a Lucky Strike at the kitchen table.

I finally pushed my plate away and leaned back into the chair, holding my stomach with both hands. I'd eaten too much and I'd eaten too fast. Derwood got up from the table and placed both of our plates into the sink. He reached in the cupboard above the counter and took down two clear glasses, setting one in front of me and one on the table in front of his chair. I moved to the pantry, brought out my fifth of whiskey, and poured us each about three fingers.

"Do ye still record all yer investigatin' on paper?" he asked me.

"I do," I answered him. "But I haven't so far in this case. It's time I do that."

I moved my chair back once again and went to my bedroom, where I kept a notebook in my top dresser drawer. I brought it back to the table along with a sharpened pencil. Opening it to a clean page, I wrote "Myrna Lou" at the top. Before I could add anything else, I looked up at my uncle and saw him looking past me. I turned and saw Aunt Pearl standing in the doorway, wearing one of my grandmother's nightgowns. It was way too large on her and way too short.

"You're not drinking that, are you, Derwood?"

My uncle picked up the glass of whiskey, leaned across the table, and emptied it into my glass.

"Nope," he said.

Pearl continued on to the bathroom. When she'd finished and emerged once again, heading back to bed, Derwood leaned over and poured half of the whiskey back into his own glass.

"Now, as ye write what ye have learned so far, tell me all about it," he said, taking a swig.

I did just that, starting from the beginning where I had run into Johnny at Baker's Keyboard Lounge on Tuesday evening. I told him the story behind Myrna Lou staying at her aunt and uncle's in Dearborn; how I'd taken a ride into the city on Wednesday, stopping at the park to talk to Rick Neller and his two friends; and how it was Joe, at White Castle, who began to paint a picture of the girl's personality for me. Each time I mentioned a new name, I would write that name into my book and make notes beside it, recording what I had learned. I finally ended with our visit to Detective Pete Levasser yesterday at the Dearborn Police Department.

"Hmm," Derwood said. "I don't care for the sound of that teacher...what's his name?"

"Schramm?"

"Yep, him. I don't like the sound of him bein' so close to the girl."

"He claims that it was all her," I explained. "He was stunned at her behavior. Showed me a picture of his wife of a few years, and told me he was happily married."

"I still don't like it. He can say anythin', especially if he already knows the lass is dead."

I put a question mark next to Tony Schramm's name. It might be worth it to look into him further.

"And ye know what I keep thinkin'? I keep thinkin' 'minic a rinne bromach gioblach capall cumasach.'" He saw the confused look on my face. "It's Gaelic for 'an awkward colt often becomes a beautiful horse.' No one liked her now, but who knows what plans the good Lord had for the lass? Who knows what kind of beauty she woulda turned out to be?"

He paused and looked up at the ceiling.

"Of course, there's the girl," Derwood said, rubbing his chin.

I brought my eyebrows together and watched him as he drained his glass of the liquor. I held the bottle out to him and he shook his head, declining my offer. He got up from the table and walked over to the sink, empty glass in hand, and set it with the used plates. He rubbed his hips and stretched.

"I think I've put a curse on meself," he said. "Tellin' that whopper about my hip pain. They're startin' to really ache now from sittin' in the chair so long. I think I'll mosey on to bed now."

I turned in my seat and said, "Wait a minute. What girl? What girl are you talking about?"

"The little one. Your friend's daughter."

"Bonnie?" I asked. "What about her?"

"Well, ye said she doesn't speak, even though the doctors say nothin' is wrong. But she was the one sittin' on the steps with her cousin that day. Either a phone call came in to make her walk away—and I doubt that 'cause the older girl doin' her class work woulda heard it—or someone picked her up that day, and Bonnie saw it." He paused and yawned. "We'll have to figure out a way of findin' out what she saw or what she knows. But we can talk about that in the mornin'."

I watched as my uncle turned away from me and walked towards my bedroom. My mouth was hanging open. He was right! Bonnie may not speak, but there sure was nothing wrong with her eyesight!

Judith White

# Chapter Eighteen

The gray clouds that had rolled in on Easter afternoon finally made good on their threat. A bolt of lightning illuminated the living room and a crack of thunder soon followed. It was 1:19 a.m. and I was sitting on the couch, smoking a cigarette. Before the big splats of rain started hitting the rooftop, the only sound throughout the house was that of soft snoring coming from Uncle Derwood, who was sleeping soundly in my bedroom. I couldn't sleep. What my uncle had said about Bonnie Delbeck kept replaying in my head. Had I dismissed her as being a viable witness because she was only five years of age? Had I thought she'd have nothing to reveal because throughout her short life she'd barely uttered any words? I certainly couldn't dismiss her involvement now. Uncle Derwood brought her position in this case to the forefront of my mind, and it would stay there until I could find out what she knew, if she knew anything. What would she tell me if she could? If she would? What did she know?

I puffed on my cigarette, seeing the sweet young girl in my mind. She was so adorable, so pure and innocent—and she might just be a witness. *A witness*! My blood ran cold and a sharp stab of fear ran through me. If someone had come walking along the sidewalk in front of the Delbeck home, if someone had pulled up in a car and called out to Myrna Lou, Bonnie would've seen them. *They* would've seen *Bonnie*! Had they done what I did, underestimated her because she was only five? Or did they know her well enough to know about her speech problem and feel a certain safety in that fact? Either way, I now felt the urge to warn Johnny and Grace of the danger that may surround their youngest child.

I stamped out my cigarette in the ashtray and reclined on the couch, covering myself with the blanket up to my neck, trying to ward off the chill of fear I felt. I wanted to speak to someone about this, but there was no one at this hour. The Dearborn boutique owner, Patti Ann, surfaced in my mind. How I wished she were there to listen to me. I didn't even know her last name or where she lived, but I was drawn to her...attracted to her. To come home and share all of my thoughts with someone just like her would be wonderful. Sharing my days with someone was what I wanted. Gran wasn't that someone, even though I loved her with all my heart. I needed someone of my own.

I don't know what time I finally fell asleep, but I woke at a few minutes before 8:30 on Monday morning. I could hear soft humming coming from the kitchen and could smell coffee and the wonderful scent of frying ham. I sat up and looked out the window. It was wet outside, but the rain had stopped. Low hanging gray clouds threatened a further downpour. Derwood moved through the dining room and stood just inside the living room entryway.

"Oh good, yer up. I was goin' to wake ye. Breakfast is almost done."

He turned to walk away and I called after him, asking if I had time for a shower.

"If ye take more than five minutes, I'll be eatin' without ye and ye'll find a cold breakfast waiting for ye."

I sat at the table with a damp head of hair, feeling wide-awake and refreshed. The breakfast looked good. On a plate waiting for me were scrambled eggs, fried slices of ham, a potato cake of some sort and reheated biscuits with butter and honey. I asked about the potato cake.

"I took some of the leftover mashed potatoes," Derwood said, "and made a patty, dipped it in egg and flour, and fried it in the hot grease."

I cut into it with my fork and took a bite. The potato cake was browned and crispy on the outside, and creamy smooth and hot on the inside. It was delicious.

I asked the whereabouts of Gran and Aunt Pearl. It seemed they were out and about with Helen already.

"So what's on the schedule for today? Pearl wanted to go home, but I told her not until we find out what Bonnie knows. Ye don't mind a foolish old man helpin' to investigate, do ye?"

I shook my head while stuffing my mouth with egg. "Not at all. You're the least foolish man I know."

After breakfast, we jointly cleaned the kitchen and then decided we'd ride into Dearborn and talk to some of the people that I hadn't seen yet. Audrey Sweeney was the first on my list. Tony Schramm, the general science teacher, had told me that Myrna Lou sat next to the girl in his class. We pulled up to the address I had in my little notebook and looked at the house. Large paint chips were missing from its exterior. The drapery at the picture window was shabby and hanging unattached from the rod in the middle. The lawn was mostly weeds and dirt. Derwood and I approached the door and knocked. It was opened by a young lady, and the odor that wafted out of the house reminded me of wet animal fur.

"Are you Audrey Sweeney?" I asked.

She nodded her head silently. Audrey was a very petite girl who had delicate facial features. Her long black hair was worn in a ponytail with bangs across her forehead. Her face was filled with apprehension, almost as if she'd done something wrong and we'd come to call her on it.

"You know a Myrna Lou Stevic?" I asked.

She nodded again, but said nothing.

"Audrey," Derwood took over. "Myrna Lou had been missin' since last Monday, and yesterday she was found dead on Belle Isle. Can ye give us any information about who may have done this? Was she involved with any young lad that ye know of?"

Her eyes widened and she gasped. "*Dead?*" she asked in a whisper.

"That's right, Audrey. Someone did this to her, and that's why we need any help ye can give us," my uncle said.

Before she could respond, we heard an angry, gravelly male voice call out from farther back in the house.

"*Audrey, who the hell is it?*"

"Just a couple of guys, Daddy!" she called out over her left shoulder. She rolled her eyes and her face reddened.

"What did I *tell* you about talking to boys?" her father yelled.

"Oh, Daddy! They aren't boys, it's two policemen!" she yelled back.

Within seconds, the door was pulled open wider and Audrey's father was facing us through the screen door. His pants were shabby and ill fitting, and he wore only a graying sleeveless undershirt covering his chest. He looked like he'd just woken up, with his black hair going in all directions. He needed a shave.

"What's this all about? What do you want?" he asked, gruffly.

Derwood continued to speak. "Your daughter attended school with a girl who was found murdered yesterday, and we're two private investigators who are lookin' into the case. We'd like to hear all she has to say about this lass; see if she knows anythin' that could shed light on this."

Audrey's father kept his eyes on Uncle Derwood. His mouth formed a smirk.

"*You're* an investigator?" he asked.

Derwood nodded, telling the man he was the *senior* investigator in the case. I wanted to laugh. Uncle Derwood was playing this for all he was worth. Mr. Sweeney snickered, and then he looked at his daughter.

"You know anything about this?" he demanded.

She shook her head, indicating no.

"She don't know nothin'," he said.

What happened next shocked and angered me. Mr. Sweeney slammed the door in our faces, and we heard a dead bolt catch from the inside. Derwood and I looked at one another, and I shook my head.

"Ah, the world t'is filled with idiots, boy. *That's* the lass we should be prayin' for. Her father's nothin' but a dope."

We made our way slowly back to the car. I was still reeling at the insensitivity Mr. Sweeney had displayed. He had showed no concern that a classmate of his daughter had her life taken from her at such an early age. He showed no compassion or sympathy. I was about to get into the auto when I looked up and saw my uncle standing near his door and staring past me over the top of the Chevy.

"Better go see what the young lass wants, boy," he said.

I turned and saw Audrey standing outside near the side entrance to her house. Her arms were wrapped around her, fighting off the damp chill in the air as she stared at us. I hurried over to her.

"I have to make this quick," she whispered to me. "Myrna Lou *was* involved with someone. She told me in class a couple of weeks ago about a guy she was thinking of marrying. I don't know who it is, but she said he was the best thing that'd ever happened to her. She said they would probably marry and move far, far away. She seemed real happy about it." She paused and looked down. When she looked up again, her eyes had formed tears. "Hey, she's really dead?"

"Yeah, Audrey, she's really dead. I've got to find out who this boy is she was talking about. You don't know anything further?"

She shook her head. "No, but you'd better find him. I'm wondering if he even knows what's happened to her." She turned suddenly, opening her side door. "I gotta go." And then she was gone.

Derwood and I next found where Rose Peterson, a student Myrna Lou had been seen having lunch with, lived. There was no response to our knock, so we continued on to the home of Louise Elliot, which was right around the block from the Peterson residence. She, too, had been seen having lunch with Grace's niece by Mr. Schramm. She could shed no light whatsoever on anything further going on in Myrna Lou's life. In fact, she was unaware of the girl's matrimonial plans.

"It's funny you say that, though," Louise said. "That could be true because Myrna Lou's changed recently."

"How so?" I asked.

"Well, lately, she hasn't been acting all khaki wacky," she said.

She noticed the confusion on Derwood's face and started to laugh.

"That means *boy crazy*," she explained. "She hasn't been coming on to the boys at school like she used to. Not that I really *cared*, anyway…I don't have much time to socialize with the girls or boys at school, usually. My parents are pretty strict about my school work. My

dad says it's *mandatory* I get into college!" She paused. "Did you say Myrna Lou is missing?" she asked.

"She was," Derwood replied. "But we found her."

"Oh," Louise smiled. "That's good."

"No, t'is not so good. She was found dead, lass."

When we left Louise Elliot, she was wearing a blank look on her face. I suspected she was trying to let sink in what she had just been told. We sat in the Chevy at the curb, and before pulling away, Audrey Sweeney's words surfaced in my mind. "But you'd better find him. I'm wondering if he even knows what's happened to her." I started the engine, wondering something completely different. I wondered if the boy that Myrna Lou was planning on marrying was the one who had taken her life in a fit of rage.

# Chapter Nineteen

I wasn't quite sure where to go next. The church was a definite possibility, but I didn't know if anyone would be there or not at this hour on a Monday. I felt like I needed to talk some things out first. Maybe discussing what was on my mind with my uncle would help me to focus better.

"Could you use a cup of coffee?" I asked him.

He looked at his watch, noting it was twenty minutes past eleven in the morning.

"Well, I guess I wouldn't mind."

We drove in silence until I reached White Castle on Michigan Avenue. I pulled into the parking lot, having my choice of parking spaces…Joe had no business at this hour on the day after Easter. I pulled into the space closest to the door. My uncle exited the car and stretched, looking at the sign on top of the building.

"I've never had one of these," he said.

"What? A White Castle burger?"

"Yep."

"Come on, I'll buy you one," I told him.

By the time Joe emerged from the back of the restaurant, Derwood and I had hopped up on the red leather stools and had each lit a Lucky Strike. The coffee maker was sputtering and emptying itself into a glass pot which sat on its burner, and the intoxicating smell of fresh brewed coffee filled the air. The grill sat cold and shiny clean. I swiveled to look out the front window as we waited and noticed Paul's Barber Shop was still lifeless, and a

"Closed" sign was hanging on the glass door that led to the interior of the business. Few people were out walking the streets of Dearborn on this cool, gray day. I swiveled back at the sound of the swinging double doors opening.

"Hey! I didn't know anyone was out here," Joe said, smiling. "Been here long?"

"A few minutes," I said, shrugging my shoulders.

Joe's gaze focused on my uncle and he extended his hand.

"Who ya got here with ya today, Sam?"

"This is my Uncle Derwood. Derwood, this is Joe. He owns the place."

"Nice to meet ya, old timer. Well, how did Easter go for the two of you?"

"Not too well, Joe," I said. "That gal I was looking for was found yesterday."

Joe leaned on his side of the counter with his forearms and looked at me blankly.

"Well, that oughta be a good thing. I don't get the problem," he said.

"The thing is, this young one was found dead, Joe," Uncle Derwood said.

Joe straightened and shook his head. He turned to the coffee pot and poured three cups of coffee, setting two of them in front of Derwood and me. He placed cream and sugar by Derwood. My uncle added cream but ignored the sugar. Joe leaned on the counter in front of us once again.

"Okay, so tell me; what was it? A car accident?" he asked.

Derwood shook his head as he stirred his coffee. "Nope; someone disliked her enough to end her life for her."

I watched Joe as he took that in. His face became reddened and his breathing quickened slightly. He straightened once again and folded his arms across his huge chest.

"You mean to tell me that someone *killed* that young girl?"

"That's what we're tellin' ye."

"Excuse me a minute," Joe said, and he disappeared behind the swinging doors.

I looked at Derwood and he shrugged. While the owner of White Castle was gone, we sipped at our coffee and sat silently. I hadn't figured the news would affect Joe in the way that it did. That three hundred pound man had a sensitive side, a real soft spot in his heart for people.

When he returned, he was placing a white handkerchief in the back pocket of his pants. His eyes looked as though he had shed a tear or two in the privacy of his kitchen. He stopped at the grill and turned the knob to the on position, heating it up for the day.

"You two want something to eat?" Joe asked.

"Yeah," I said. "Why don't you give us each a couple of burgers?"

He threw four meatballs on the grill. No hissing sound came from the surface; it wasn't hot enough yet. He smashed them with his utensil and then turned to us, waving the spatula.

"What I don't get is why someone would want to do that to her. This is a nice town, Sam, with nice people living here. I haven't heard a thing of this throughout the city. What part of town did they find her in?"

"She was found on Belle Isle yesterday morning by a fisherman," I said.

"Well, then anybody coulda done this to her; doesn't mean it was somebody from here," Joe said. "Doesn't mean it was someone she knew, right?"

"I suppose that could be the case, but I'm still following some leads. Derwood and I are working on it, as well as the Detroit Police Department; maybe the Dearborn department, too."

Joe walked the length of the counter and came around to the front, where Derwood and I were sitting. He continued on to the cash register and tore down the flyer I had made just days ago. He crumpled it into a ball and then threw it in the trash container sitting by the door.

"This world ain't right!" he said, heading back to his grill. "The whole damn world is going to hell in a hand basket!"

After our burgers were set before us, Joe said he had to attend to a leak in his sink in the back. Ernie didn't come into work until

1:00 p.m., but Joe wanted to have it fixed by the time he arrived. He told us to give a holler if someone else came in as he disappeared in the back of the store. I actually welcomed the opportunity to be with Derwood alone to air my concerns.

"You know what you said about Bonnie last night? That she may have seen something?"

He nodded and I continued.

"Well, what bothers me more is that that someone may have seen her."

"Aye," he said. "T'is a possibility."

"Yeah, and that scares the heck out of me. I don't want to put more stress on Johnny, but I've got to tell him about this."

Derwood nodded and continued to eat his sandwich.

"And another thing; I didn't believe this story about Myrna Lou considering marriage at first. I thought it might be her way of getting attention or trying to make the other girls jealous. But with Audrey telling us the same thing; well, I just don't know. I'm thinking it just might be possible now."

"I agree," said Derwood. "But the likes of a young lad who's a classmate of hers doesn't seem right to yer old uncle. Seems like these lasses would know who she was talkin' about, but they haven't seen her with anyone. Nah, my money is still on that teacher of hers. If not him, maybe another teacher she had. I think t'is a man involved and not a boy."

I mulled this over in my mind while we finished eating. At eighty-eight, maybe Derwood saw seventeen year olds as being very young boys still. Maybe he didn't see them as capable of committing such an act, but I saw it differently. Boys that age were nearly men and capable of violence just as anyone else would be.

When we'd finished eating, I walked around to the coffee pot and refilled mine and Derwood's cups—I didn't think Joe would mind. We smoked a cigarette while we finished up. I called out to Joe when we were leaving and laid a dollar and a quarter on the counter. I knew the bill wasn't that much, but he could have the rest as a tip. Right then I wanted to ride by Christ the Divine Lutheran Church to see if anyone was there.

I pulled into the lot when I noticed three cars parked at the church. Two were brown and the other was a dark blue Ford coupe. We heard organ music being played when we entered. The same elderly woman that I'd seen on Good Friday was now sitting at the instrument. I knew that Grace played the organ there, but maybe this woman alternated Sunday's with her. She was playing "The Old Rugged Cross." Two people, a man and a woman in their thirties, were waxing the pews in the chapel and listening to her play.

Derwood followed me as I retraced the same direction I'd gone three days ago. Pastor Mayhew's door was shut and I got no response when I knocked on it, so we moved to the next office. That door was shut, too. When I knocked softly I heard a "Yes?" from within. I didn't know how to answer that, so I didn't...I just knocked again. This time I heard movement, and within seconds the door was opened to us. The young man who opened it was about twenty-three or twenty-four years of age, I assumed, with light brown hair cut very short. He was of medium height and average build, and he wore black trousers and a white shirt opened at the collar. His dark brown eyes looked at us questioningly behind tortoise shell glasses. He wasn't a handsome man, but he wasn't what I would call unattractive, either.

"Are you Matthew Coady?" I asked.

"Why, yes, I am," he said, looking surprised.

"I'm Sam Flanagan and this is Derwood Flanagan," I said, gesturing to my uncle. "We'd like to talk to you about Myrna Lou Stevic. May we come in?"

He removed his spectacles and his face took on a look of sadness. He opened the door wider and waved us in, gesturing to two chairs facing his desk.

"Please do," he said. "Mrs. Delbeck called this morning with the sad news. She also wanted to let us know that Jake and Susan wouldn't be going to youth camp this morning with the others."

We took our seats at his desk and he sat down, facing us on the other side of it. Behind him, on the wall, he had several pictures of what I assumed were his college days. One was of the young man and a few of his buddies, in caps and gowns, arms around one another, smiling broadly. Two were of the football team. It looked as though he played during his years at the university. Others were of him and friends in social situations.

"What can I tell you that would help? I assume you're investigating Myrna Lou's death; is that right? Are you policemen?"

"We aren't policemen," Derwood said. "But we *are* investigatin' her death. We're private investigators."

"I'll tell you anything I can that will help," the young man said.

"First of all, I'd like to have something cleared up," I said. "We were told by the girl's aunt that she seemed a bit upset a week ago yesterday after the evening church service...or at least she appeared to be upset when she got home that evening. Grace Delbeck said that her niece told her she didn't want to go with the youth group to Camp Arcadia, when before that time, she'd seemed eager to go. Do you know what that was all about?"

He frowned, shaking his head.

"No, I sure don't. I wasn't aware that she'd made that decision, and I can't think what would have upset her. Myrna Lou wasn't all that close to any one person in the young people's class, but she wasn't in a feud with any of them, either."

"You said you know of no one who was particularly close to Myrna Lou. I've heard the name Lonnie Orwick mentioned by the pastor as maybe having a crush on her at one point. Did you notice this also?"

The youth pastor snickered and then said, "That could very well be, but nothing ever came of it...at least, I don't think so. Lonnie is a big, shy, teddy bear. He's tall and muscular, but he's not real confident. I doubt he ever acted on his feelings. He's one of the kids Duane and I pick up on Sundays. He lives on the east side of the city—not a real good home environment. That's why we want him to keep coming to Christ the Divine. He's a good kid, Mr. Flanagan. I'd hate to see him thrown by the wayside because of the lack of encouragement he gets at home. I was really wishing he could've accompanied the group on their trip. He said he couldn't make it, though." He sighed and shook his head.

"Why aren't ye there?" Derwood asked. "Don't youth pastors normally go with the group?"

"Yes, of course, but something came up. I got a call from my wife in the afternoon a week ago Sunday. She'll be home tomorrow and I wanted to be here to see her. You see, my wife has been gone on a mission trip to Arizona for the past six weeks. She's staying with a few others on a Navajo reservation. She was supposed to be gone until the first week in May, but she got homesick." He smiled widely. "I'm very excited to see her. We've only been married a year and a half."

I nodded in understanding.

"You realize that this is now a murder investigation, Mr. Coady, so don't take personally what I have to ask you. Where were you around 4:30 on Monday, April 19th?"

His eyes widened. "Is that the day she went missing? Pastor Mayhew told me they couldn't find the girl, but I wasn't quite sure what day that was." He stared at the ceiling in thought. "To tell you the truth, I'm not sure."

He moved his chair out from his desk, opened his top drawer, brought out a black leather bound book, and started leafing through the pages. We waited for him to answer the question.

"Oh," he said, looking up suddenly. "Yes, I remember now. That was the day that we had a basketball game in the afternoon after school. Most of the boys showed. I try to schedule activities for them so they stay off the streets and stay out of trouble."

"Was Lonnie Orwick at this game?" Derwood asked.

"I believe he was. Duane took the bus and picked up some of the boys."

"Can we have his address, Mr. Coady?" I asked.

"Sure," he said, opening another drawer and pulling out a small plastic container which held index cards.

I watched as he leafed through them until he finally removed one which had information for Lonnie Orwick written on it, and then I jotted down where the young man lived in my own notebook and replaced it in my suit jacket pocket. Derwood and I stood to take our leave.

"I may have to come back with further questions," I said.

"No problem," he said. He hesitated a moment and then added, "Myrna Lou wasn't really a bad person. She was a bit complex, but she was troubled and most of the kids her age didn't understand that she acted out because of it. Please tell the Delbeck's again how sorry we are to hear of their tragedy. I hope you find whoever did this, Mr. Flanagan."

I assured him I would and we walked out, heading for the Chevy.

# Chapter Twenty

Derwood was getting tired. I could see it in his eyes when we climbed into the car. I actually welcomed him on this case—I welcomed his insight—and I knew he was having the time of his life playing detective, but I had to be aware of his moments of winding down. At his age, he didn't have the same stamina I did. I didn't want to over work him.

"Getting tired?" I asked.

"Aye, that I am," he said. "But since we're in town, I think we should head on over to the boy's, that Lonnie Orwick."

"I was thinking the same thing," I said.

\*\*\*\*

The houses on Horger Street were nice two and three bedroom bungalows, but the farther north we drove away from Michigan Avenue, the seedier the area became. I pulled up to 879 and shut the engine off.

Lonnie Orwick lived in a yellow wood frame whose yard was ankle deep in mostly weeds. In the middle of the front lawn sat an old and battered dark green Ford, missing three of its wheels, hoisted up on cinder blocks. Directly across the street from this row of houses sat an abandoned warehouse of some kind. During its heyday, I was sure it had employed many of the area residents, but now its yard was littered with papers and broken bottles. The windows in the old building were shattered, and I could see a few half-starved cats rummaging through the debris.

Derwood and I carefully climbed the two steps leading up to the porch on Lonnie's house. They were crumbling and badly in need of repair. A yellowed bed sheet was hanging at the front picture window in place of draperies, and the inside door was opened. I looked through the screen before knocking. Lying on an old tattered brown couch was a gentleman with more than a few days' worth of whiskers. His mouth was hanging open and he had his left hand half way down the inside of the front of his trousers, in which the zipper was down. An empty liquor bottle was on the floor near the couch. I raised my hand to give a knock when a young man emerging from a hallway caught sight of my uncle and me. He hurried over to us and half whispered through the screen.

"Hi," he said.

Then he opened the door gently and joined us on the porch as we backed up to make room for him.

"Lonnie?" I asked.

He nodded. The boy was tall, standing at probably six feet. He wasn't overweight, but he was huge with bulk and muscle. If he wasn't on the high school football team, he should've been. His dark brown hair was way too long and fell in oily strands covering his dark eyes. His hand swiped at it, moving it to the side. Gesturing for us to follow him, we descended the steps and stood in the drive.

"Did you want to see my pa?" he asked. "'Cause I really don't wanna wake him."

I wondered if his father was sleeping or if he was passed out cold from too much drink.

"T'is actually ye we want to see," Derwood said.

"Lonnie, we know you go to Christ the Divine Lutheran Church," I added. "You know a Myrna Lou Stevic who attended also."

He nodded, smiling. "That's right. But I already told 'em that I couldn't make that trip. Money's a bit tight right now, sir. Gee, I thought they'd already be on their way. They didn't send you to come fetch me, did they?"

"No, nothing like that. Myrna Lou hadn't been seen for almost a week, and then she was found yesterday morning over on Belle Isle. She's been murdered, Lonnie," I told him.

I watched as his smile turned into a slow frown. The boy tucked his hands into his denim pants and looked down at the cement under his bare feet. His brown sweater was fraying and hung loosely around his hips. He looked up again.

"Are you *sure*?" he asked, squinting with his eyes.

Derwood and I nodded.

"We're investigating this matter. Can you tell us anything that might give us a clue as to who might have done this to her? Was there anything that she was into that could've resulted in her death?" I asked.

"Gee, like what?"

"I don't know. Was there anyone that she might have been arguing with? Do you know of anyone that hated her enough to want to do this to her? Her aunt said she came home from the evening service a week ago yesterday and she was a bit upset over something. Do you know what that was all about?"

"No, sir, I don't."

"Someone at the church said ye may have had special feelin's for her at one time. Is that so, lad?"

The young man's face reddened and he looked down again, moving a small pebble around with his toe.

"Well," he said. "I guess I did a little when she first came here. I don't get to meet too many girls my age, and she seemed real nice. I mean, she paid attention to me at first. It was kinda nice is all. But shoot, I could see right away that she wasn't *really* interested. And I still like her, but not in that way anymore."

"Why can't ye meet lasses yer own age?" Derwood asked him. "What about school?"

"Eh, I quit. Things haven't been so good around here, and I needed to help Ma out by gettin' a job. She does odd jobs in the neighborhood for people, but she can't carry the whole load. I work as a bag boy down at the market on Michigan Avenue. As soon as I fix this up," he said, gesturing to the green automobile sitting in the yard, "I figure Pa will have a better chance of lookin' for work, too."

"How do ye get to the job, lad?" Derwood asked.

"Walk," he responded.

"Mighty long walk, t'isn't it?"

"Eh, it isn't so bad. Cold weather is the worst, though."

"Were you at a basketball game at the church a week ago?" I asked him.

"Yeah, I was off of work that day, so I went."

"Mr. Coady and Mr. Whelan ran the game?"

"Pastor Whelan did. I think Pastor Coady was doing some kind of paper work in his office. He stuck his head out when we first got there, and then he was there for the last fifteen minutes or so of the game."

My uncle and I exchanged glances. I asked Lonnie when he got there and what time he'd left. The boy had been picked up from his house by Duane Whelan at 3:45 in the afternoon and they headed out on the bus again about 6:00, he said. *Hmm, that was interesting,* I thought. Would that have been enough time for the youth pastor to pick Myrna Lou up at Johnny's house, take her to Belle Isle, kill her, and return? I sure didn't see why not. But why would he was the question. Was *he* the man Myrna Lou had spoken of marrying to the girls at school? The man seemed happily married. Why would he speak of marriage to a young girl in his youth group?

We talked another ten minutes or so to Lonnie, but learned nothing else. We thanked him for his time and started to head back to the car when he called out to us and we turned.

"Sir, could you please let me know about a funeral or a showin'? I'd sure like to be there to pay my respects if I can make it. I thought she was a real nice girl."

Pulling away from the house, I noticed that Lonnie had opened the hood on the clunker, and had his head buried underneath it.

Had I been alone, I would've headed over to Johnny's. I was curious about Mac's visit this morning, but by the time I'd reached Michigan Avenue, Derwood was already snoring softly in the front seat next to me, with his head leaning back. I thought about Audrey Sweeney. She was telling the truth when she said she believed Myrna Lou had her sights on marrying some young man. She believed the story, so why shouldn't I? I thought about Lonnie, and knew for a fact that if he had a mean streak in him, he could've wielded a rock into the back of someone's head and wiped the life right out of them. He was big enough and strong enough to do it. The thing was, though, I didn't think he had that sort of temperament. He seemed nice, gentle, and respectful, and I honestly believed he liked Myrna Lou at face value. None of the classmates and none of the kids who attended church with Grace's niece were capable of this kind of monstrosity...at least, I didn't think so.

When we arrived home, Derwood wiped the drool from the side of his mouth and announced he was going to go lie down and take a nap. I decided I wasn't going to think about this case at all for the next forty-five minutes to an hour. I was going to pull the lawn mower out of the garage and pray the grass wasn't too wet to cut before we got another dose of rain. Gran and Aunt Pearl still weren't home and it was 1:30 in the afternoon. I wondered where they had gone and what they were up to.

Judith White

# Chapter Twenty-One

The grass cut, I entered the house through the back door and stepped into the kitchen. Gran had her head stuck in the icebox, removing dishes of leftovers from the Easter Sunday dinner. She turned to look at me.

"There you are, dear," she said.

"I cut the grass. Where've you been?"

"Helen took us to Pearl's in Plymouth. We brought back some clothes for her and Derwood."

In the dining room, right outside of Gran's bedroom door, sat an old brown suitcase. The bathroom door opened and out stepped my Aunt Pearl, and she gave me a stern look. I wondered what I had done to disappoint her, but I didn't have to wait long to find out.

"I hope you realize your uncle isn't as young as he used to be!" she said. "It's fine to ask his advice, but to ask him to help you work on this case is going too far. I see he's sleeping. I don't want you running him down."

I frowned, but said nothing. This had to have been Uncle Derwood's idea—telling his wife I'd asked him to help me on this case. I wasn't going to blow his cover by correcting her. I'd take the fall for this one—for him. Pearl turned to my grandmother.

"I'm going to unpack," she said. And then turning back to me, she added, "I wish you would've taught your grandson some common sense, Ruby."

I almost called her on that remark, but I let it go. First of all, I had two parents that raised me, not my grandmother; and second of all, I *did* have common sense. She entered the bedroom with the suitcase and shut the door. My grandmother was slicing ham off the bone at the kitchen table.

"Why don't you ever defend me to her?" I asked.

She looked up at me. "To *Pearl*? What good would that do? She knows everything— always has. There's no point in arguing with her. Besides, we both know better, don't we? But dear, if you needed help with your work, why did you have to ask your uncle? I'm sure you have lots of policeman friends who would've been happy to do that."

I rolled my eyes and went to the telephone on the kitchen wall next to the back door. After dialing the Detroit Police Department, I asked for Bill McPherson. I waited only seconds before he picked up, and then I asked him about his visit to the Delbeck's.

"We wanted your friend to accompany us down here to the morgue. The mother of the victim…well, she insisted on coming, too. We needed to be sure of the identification, and they confirmed what you told us, although there really wasn't any doubt from what you'd said. It wasn't a pretty sight, Sam…a lot of screaming and crying down here. And your friend looked as though he was going to lose his breakfast. It's a bad thing when the vic is so young. I'm going to need to see the people you've talked to on this one. Tell me where you're at in this case. And no need for you to contact Levasser over this. I'm sure the Dearborn station will want to know the particulars, but I'll share it all with him. And by the way, that rock produced no other evidence than confirming it was her blood. That was indeed the murder weapon."

I told Mac everything I'd done in working the case, starting from the beginning. I gave him the names and addresses of everyone I had talked to and told him all I'd learned from them. Before hanging up, I asked him to let me know if he learned anything different than I had. Next, I put in a call to Johnny.

"Geez, Sam, it's a nightmare around here. I couldn't settle Vivian down after returning from Detroit. I finally gave her a couple shots of straight whiskey and made her drink it. She slept for three hours. I went down to the funeral home in Allen Park and made some arrangements. I suppose the body's already been taken there. They say they can have her ready by tomorrow late afternoon. I've got to take Vivian there in the morning so she can pick out a casket." He lowered his voice. "Between you and me, I don't know how I'm going to pay for this, and now I have to miss work tomorrow, too. Grace is staring into space. I think she's blaming herself for this, Sam. Susan and Jake are holed up in their rooms. I think they're more disappointed in not being able to go to camp than anything else. Ah, kids! Bonnie is the only one acting half way normal, and even she knows something is wrong. She's confused. I feel as though I have to hold everything together here, and I'm reeling from this just as much as they are."

"Uh, Johnny, speaking of Bonnie…well, I realized something. If Myrna Lou was picked up in a car by someone, or if someone was just walking along the street, I'm figuring Bonnie may have seen that someone. What really worries me is that Bonnie may have been noticed by them, as well."

There was dead silence on Johnny's end. I could almost feel the fear he was experiencing.

"*Oh God, Sam,*" he whispered.

"Don't get so worked up about this yet," I said. "Bonnie hasn't said anything and they may be banking on that. They might know of her condition and feel she isn't a threat. But, Johnny, I wouldn't leave your girl alone at any time, either."

**\*\*\*\***

The four of us sat down to dinner around the kitchen table at 5:15. I told my Uncle Derwood about the two phone conversations I'd had while he slept. Each time I glanced at my aunt, she was staring at me with narrowed eyes and tight lips. I ignored her and tried not to look her way.

"When we're finished here, why don't ye give Johnny another call? Tell him to go to his job in the mornin' and ye can take his sister-in-law to do her business. I have an idea. I want to spend time with his young lass."

I wasn't completely at ease about him spending time with Bonnie. He wouldn't tell me his idea just yet and I was worried it wouldn't be a good idea, but I did what he asked me to do. Johnny was relieved he wouldn't be missing another day's wages, and he agreed to my taking Vivian to pick out Myrna Lou's casket tomorrow. After the kitchen was cleaned, Gran, my aunt, and my uncle retired to the dining room to listen to the radio. I got my notebook and sat on my bed with the door closed. I needed to go over my notes again. Maybe something I hadn't seen before would pop out at me.

# Chapter Twenty-Two

I woke early enough on Tuesday morning to see the sunrise. It was April 27<sup>th</sup>, and I would be going to a funeral viewing that night. Making my way to the kitchen, I started the coffee brewing. While it perked on the burner, I treated myself to a long, hot shower. As the water covered my body in warmth, I thought of the Delbeck household. I wondered if Grace and her sister were able to sleep throughout the night. I didn't know what it was like to lose a child to tragedy. Hell, I didn't even know what it was like to *have* a child, but I knew it must be devastating to give someone life and see that life snuffed out all too soon. Vivian would never be the same.

Stepping from the tub, I dried off and put my pajamas on again. The clothes I would wear today were in my bedroom and I didn't want to disturb my uncle's sleep. It was way too early to rouse him yet. I poured coffee and took it into the living room. When I heard the newspaper hit the porch, I went to retrieve it. The air outside was cool and damp, making the paper a bit moist. Low gray clouds hung in the sky.

I sat in a living room chair and scanned the front page. A young Detroit man had been arrested the day before. He had failed to answer a Selective Service questionnaire that had been sent to him by the Detroit, Michigan Draft Board, and he did not show for his scheduled physical examination. Roger Wheaton, age nineteen, was being questioned by the Detroit Division of the FBI. Another headline read, 'WHO SAYS THE JAPS DON'T GIVE UP?' There was a photograph showing several Japanese men standing in a line and the caption read, "Wounded Jap prisoners at an American prison camp in the South Pacific area contradict the suicidal enthusiasm to which they are driven to the code of Bushido. These Nipponese soldiers seem pleased to be out of it all as they line up for medical attention."

I turned to page two. At the top, an article caught my attention. It was about finding Myrna Lou on Belle Isle on Easter morning. I read it with interest.

"The body of a young girl has been found on Belle Isle, the apparent victim of foul play. Myrna Lou Stevic, 17, had been staying with her aunt and uncle in the city of Dearborn. Detroit Homicide Detective William McPherson encourages anyone to come forward with any information on this case. He and his partner, Lawrence Brown, will be heading the investigation. An early morning fisherman, who discovered the body on Sunday and who wishes to remain anonymous, is quoted as saying, 'I never seen nothing like it. I didn't know what I was looking at at first. It was awful.'"

I placed the paper on the end table, picked up my coffee, taking a sip, and lit a cigarette. I thought about what Joe had said. He said that it didn't necessarily have to be someone from Dearborn who had committed this dastardly crime. He said it didn't necessarily have to be someone who knew Myrna Lou personally. While that was certainly a possibility, I thought it was a very remote one. In my gut I felt that it was someone close to the girl who had murdered her, and I kept coming back to the last Sunday night she'd attended church. Something had set her off. Something bothered her enough to make her want to cancel her plans for going away while she was out of school for the week. I kept thinking that was the key here. What could it have been? Who knew what made the girl angry? Was someone holding back information?

I stamped out my Lucky Strike in the ashtray, leaned my head against the back of the chair, and closed my eyes, picturing all those I'd questioned. I went over their statements again in my mind. Who wasn't telling me the whole story? Derwood thought Mr. Schramm, the general science teacher, warranted another look. Maybe, just maybe, Myrna Lou was upset about something that had nothing to do with the church, but rather with school. Then Matthew Coady came to mind. Was he really in his office attending to some paper work during the basketball game on that Monday afternoon? Or had he left the church for awhile, possibly to make a quick trip to Belle Isle?

I'm not sure at what point I dozed off, but I did. I woke when I heard a door opening. My uncle was emerging from my room, but when I opened my eyes, I saw Aunt Pearl sitting on the couch across from me. She was sewing a button onto a black suit jacket of my uncle's while still in her nightgown and robe, and she was staring at me. I straightened in the chair.

"What time is it?" I asked, clearing my throat.

"It's twenty minutes past eight," she said, coolly.

I jumped up from my seat and grabbed my cup from the end table. I took it out to the kitchen, where I found my grandmother making toast and pouring coffee for herself, her sister, and her brother-in-law. Derwood had just entered the bathroom. I poured myself another cup of the hot black beverage and grabbed a blueberry muffin out of the basket that was sitting in the middle of the table.

"Good morning, dear," Gran said. "I just got off the phone from Helen and I told her we would pick her up about 4:00 this afternoon."

I stopped chewing. "Pick her up for *what*?" I asked.

"The viewing tonight, of course."

"The *viewing*? Why are we picking Helen up? In fact, what's this *we* stuff? It isn't a party, Gran."

"Well, I know *that*, dear. A party would be lots more fun. This is a sad event, and Helen wants to go. She has nothing else to do tonight and she gets bored and lonely. I told her to eat a late lunch or an early supper, because who knows how long we'll be there."

I couldn't believe my ears—my friend's niece was lying cold in a mortuary, and these old people were looking at it as an opportunity to go out for the evening. I stared at her as she buttered the slices of toasted bread. I was at a loss for words for some moments. Finally, I spoke.

"You mean to tell me that the five of us are going to waltz into that funeral parlor because you don't have anything *better to do tonight*? None of you even *knew* her!"

She placed the toast on a plate and set it on a tray along with three cups of coffee, all lightened with cream. She picked it up and headed for the living room. As she walked through the dining room, she called back over her shoulder.

"Well, neither did you, dear."

****

Johnny told me he had made arrangements at the Paar-Chandler Mortuary on Park Street in the neighboring city of Allen Park. I knew how to get to Allen Park, but I had no idea where Park Street was. I was confident I'd find it, though. My gas gauge was low, so before we left the Detroit city limits, I decided to stop in at Hep Martin's filling station. I pulled next to the pump just as another car was pulling out, then I got out of the auto and stretched.

Hep emerged from the front door of his business, smiling and waving when he recognized who I was. As Derwood sat in the passenger seat of the Chevy, I stood near my friend as he filled my tank and cleaned my windows. I told him what I'd been working on for the last week, and he gave a low whistle.

"No kiddin', Sam. I just read about that young gal this morning."

I changed the subject, telling Hep I had been at Baker's Keyboard Lounge one week ago, listening to him jam with Bill Harris and his band. He beamed with pride and his face colored slightly. He put his hands in the front pockets of his pants and he rocked back and forth on his heels.

"No kiddin'!" he said. "I didn't know you were there. I got my picture taken with them in their dressing room in the back during break time. Next time you come in, I should have it. They're going to send me a copy."

I paid Hep what I owed him in rationing stamps and got back into the car. It was 9:30, and I wanted to be at Johnny's no later than 10:00.

****

Grace and Vivian were waiting for us when we arrived. They'd been sitting in the living room watching out the picture window for me to pull up. Derwood entered the house with me. I didn't need to explain about his desire to speak to Bonnie because Grace told me that her sister wanted her to go along with us.

"I've told Susan and Jake to keep an eye on the young ones for us while we're gone," she said.

"If ye like, I can stay here to watch over all of 'em," Derwood offered.

Grace's face looked relieved.

"Oh, would you?" she asked.

My uncle nodded his head and told her it was no bother. I still didn't know what my uncle was up to and I prayed it didn't backfire on us. I didn't know the reason Bonnie refused to speak, but I knew that we had to be gentle with the girl. Derwood was a very tall man with wisps of white hair that barely covered his balding and freckled head. I just didn't want Bonnie to fear him.

Before Grace could get her sweater on, Vivian had gone out to the car and climbed into the back seat. She seemed to be robot-like in her movements. Her face was expressionless, with puffy dark circles under her eyes. Grace told me it would be best if she sat in the back with her sister. I'd feel like their chauffeur, but I agreed with her.

Once inside the city limits of Allen Park, I stopped at the first service station I spied and asked for directions to the Paar-Chandler Mortuary on Park Street. I had no trouble finding it after that. The building was a three-story structure that had once been a

Victorian home. It was painted a dark maroon on the outside and was trimmed in white.

When we entered, we stepped into a large seating area. Three solid black sofas formed a semi-circle with a large square coffee table sitting in the middle of them. In the center of the table sat an arrangement of fresh cut flowers that were pink and red and white. A few ashtrays were placed near the edge, close to the seating area. Maroon and white striped wallpaper hung on the walls.

A short, stout man was making his way down the stairway that was located to the left of the entrance. He had thick, wavy black hair and wore large glasses on a nose that was barely big enough to keep them on his face. He walked up to us, extending his hand. For some reason that wasn't hard to figure out, he picked out Vivian as being Myrna Lou's mother. She was the one who wore the most suffering on her face.

"Ah, Mrs. Stevic," he said. "We've been expecting you. I am so sorry for your loss."

Her name wasn't Stevic, but neither she nor Grace corrected him. That small error didn't seem to matter at a time like this. He took her hands in his and then reached around her shoulder, guiding her into the middle of the room. We followed and sat on one of the sofas, Vivian and this man sitting on the one opposite us. He turned to face her once we were all seated.

"I'm Edgar Paar. We will do everything we can to make sure that your daughter has the best in the way of her final farewell."

As he talked to her, I looked around the room, taking in more of the detail of the décor. At the far end of the room, directly opposite the entryway, there was a huge gray stone fireplace. It sat empty and cold for this time of year. Above the mantel was a portrait of an elderly man wearing a black suit with a gold pocket watch inserted in his coat pocket, only the expensive fine chain being exposed. Everywhere I looked, the area radiated comfort and warmth. Johnny had done well in coming here, but this had to be quite pricey. I was brought back to Vivian and Mr. Paar when they rose from the sofa and he told her to follow him.

"Now, we have four viewing rooms," he said, guiding us to the left, the side of the parlor where the stairway was located. "This room is called 'Serenity.' We've given each of our rooms a different name. This will be the room your daughter will be in."

Vivian looked up to a piece of rough, unfinished wood that was nailed above the doorway. Etched in the wood was the word 'Serenity.' Without saying anything, she went to the next room and looked up. She read the word 'Jubilation.' The third room was across the seating area and was called 'Glorify,' and the fourth, right next to it, was called 'Homeward Bound.' She stopped in front of the last room.

"I want this one," she said while continuing to look up. "I like that. She's homeward bound."

Edgar Paar smiled and told her they could accommodate her, and then he led the women into a back room in which, I assumed, the caskets were kept. I stayed in the large lounging area and waited for them, smoking two cigarettes, and tried to give my mind a rest, thinking of nothing in particular. An hour and ten minutes later, the ladies reappeared, but without Mr. Paar. Grace had her arm around her sister and Vivian's eyes were moist. They headed for the door and I followed.

When we arrived back on Garrison Avenue, I pulled up to the curb directly across the street from Johnny's house. As I turned the key to shut the engine off, my head turned to the left. Through the large picture window, I saw the back of my uncle's head. He was sitting on the couch and Bonnie was on his lap, facing him. She had her arms locked around his neck, and from this vantage point it looked as if she was speaking to him.

I craned my neck to focus. Were my eyes deceiving me? I then saw her break out into laughter and she threw her head back, pulling him a bit forward, toward her. Grace and Vivian seemed not to notice and climbed out of the car, and I followed them. We entered the living room and Derwood stood, Bonnie in his arms. The young child saw it was her mother and stuck a thumb in her mouth and laid her head against my uncle's shoulder. He kissed the top of her head.

Laying her purse on the table, Grace said, "I see you two have gotten along."

"She's a sweetheart, that she is," Derwood said. "The others are in one of the bedrooms playin' some sorta game. They been good as gold."

Vivian headed straight for Grace's room, sighing with exhaustion. Before she was completely out of sight, she turned and said, "Grace, I can't thank you and Johnny enough. Thank you, too, Mr. Flanagan." And then she disappeared around the corner.

Grace held out her hands for Bonnie and the child went to her willingly and yawned.

"Thanks, Sam. It was very nice of you to take us down there this morning. I don't know how Vivian is going to get through tonight and tomorrow. The service will be tomorrow afternoon at 1:00, and then she's being buried at Woodmere Cemetery. My folks are there. She'll rest near them."

"What time tonight, Grace?" I asked.

"We'll be there by 4:30, and others can show up at 5:00 or after," she said.

We headed out to the car. I was about to question Derwood about his little experiment and ask him if I had witnessed what I thought I had, when a voice shouted to us from the right. It was a deep and gravelly voice.

"Hey! Hey, you two, hold up there!"

We turned to see a man of about seventy-five to eighty years old hobbling toward us as best he could. His sprinting days had long been over. Derwood and I turned and started walking his way to meet him.

"Hold on up," he said again. "You the men looking into the murder of that little girl?" he asked, out of breath.

My uncle and I looked at each other and then nodded to him.

"Well, follow me. I gots ta get off this bum knee of mine. Come on inta the house. I think I might have some information for ya."

# Chapter Twenty-Three

We stepped into a house that was across the street and in the next block from Johnny's. The place smelled of cooked onions and tomatoes. A fine layer of dust covered the tables in the living room, and the carpeting needed a good cleaning. Animal fur was visible in some areas on the floor and furniture.

"Go ahead and take a seat on the divan. I'll be right back. I needs to take my pills," the man said.

I looked at Derwood and shrugged. We sat down on the faded green and gold floral sofa. It was only then, when we looked up, that we noticed an elderly woman sitting in a brown and gold striped chair directly across the room from us. She was wearing a yellow cotton housecoat that snapped up the length of the front, and she was wearing fuzzy bedroom slippers—one yellow and one a dark blue—over a pair of white stocking feet. Her short, steel gray hair was sticking out from the sides of her head. A walker was right in front of her to assist her should she need to rise. I nodded and she did nothing—she said nothing. Her eyes never left us.

"That's better," the old man said, returning to the living room.

He eased himself down into a solid light blue chair. None of the furniture in this house matched. It was a hodgepodge of colors, patterns, and styles.

"The name is Onus Higby, gentlemen," he said. "I gotsa knee that's been failin' me for a few years now and the doctor says I needs to keep usin' it or else I'll lose all movement in it."

"*Who's that?*" the old woman blared. Her voice was high pitched and shaky.

"These fellas are the ones investigatin' that there young girl's death," Onus shouted at her. He turned back to us. "Anyway, I gotsa exercise reglar."

"Uh, Mr. Higby, you said something about some information you might have for us?" I interrupted him.

"Don't be so impatient, young fella. I'm gettin' to it," he sighed loudly.

"*Who's that, Onus?*" the woman asked again, speaking louder than the first time.

*Uh oh*, I thought. *We've stumbled onto a couple of nuts.*

He turned to her, frustrated. "Them's the two men who are tryin' to find out who killed that young girl what was stayin' with Johnny Delbeck!" he yelled. "Now, damn it, Almeada, don't innerrup me again!" He pounded his fist on the arm of his chair. Then he turned back to us, pointing his thumb in her direction. "Been married to her for fifty-four years, and five months ago, she woke from a nap and didn't know who I was. She comes and she goes now. Don't pay no attention to her. Anyway, like I was sayin' I gotsa exercise, so I takes walks. Have you two talked to that boy what lives down the street?"

"What?" I asked him, bewildered.

I was all for getting up and leaving. This man and his wife were both nuts, as far as I could tell. I made a move to rise from the sofa when I felt my uncle's hand on my arm, stopping me.

"Now what lad might ye be talkin' about, Mr. Higby?" Derwood asked.

"That one what lives right next to the park at the end of the street. I don't know his name, but he lives in that corner house down there," he said, pointing.

My uncle looked at me. Rick Neller came to mind.

"I've talked to a boy named Rick Neller who lives in that house. I've only spoken to him briefly, and he told me he had a class with Myrna Lou, but that was about it."

"Huh! Well, talk to him again. He knew her better than he's tellin' ya. When I takes my walks, I goes down the block to the park, sits on the bench and rests a spell, and then I heads back. I cain't be gone too long because a her," he said, gesturing to his wife. "I sees him out there all the time. A few weeks ago, I sees him at the park one mornin' with this girl, the one that got killed. They's havin' words, but I cain't hear what's bein' said."

"*Onus, I see'd somethin'. Tell 'em what I see'd!*" his wife belted out suddenly.

I jumped at the sound of her voice and Onus Higby's face got red.

"Meadie, go inta the bed! How many times I gotta tell ya, ya didn't see what ya think ya see'd! You was takin' a nap when that girl went missin'. Ya didn't see a thing!"

"*Did, too!*" she yelled. "*I had to use the commode. I was gonna mess myself. I see'd her through the winda.*"

Right then, I wanted to be anywhere else but there. All I wanted to do was walk out that front door and light up a cigarette. Given the choice of getting a tooth pulled or listening to much more of this, I wouldn't think twice about laying in a dentist's chair. I ran my fingers through my hair and sighed loudly. I was getting antsy.

"Let me get her ta bed," Mr. Higby said. "Then I can go on with my story."

He hobbled over to where she was sitting and pulled her into a standing position, placing her hands around the top bar of the walker. She stood but wouldn't budge, just staring at us, moving her false teeth part way out of the front of her mouth with her tongue and then sucking them back in.

I felt as though I was going to go crazy. I looked at my uncle and rolled my eyes. He frowned and shook his head slightly at me. I felt as though I was a child he was telling to behave. Taking in a deep breath, I tried to relax.

"Come on, Meadie, quit bein' so stubborn!" he pleaded with her. "After yer nap, I'll take ya outside ta sit a spell."

She was finally on the move, but moving painstakingly slow. At last, they reached the hallway leading to their bedroom, but she suddenly stopped and turned her head toward us.

"*Tell 'em what I see'd!*" she yelled in her shrill voice before continuing.

This time her husband ignored her. We waited while he got her settled in the room. When he returned, he fell back into his chair, out of breath.

"We raised six girls, and none of 'em can give us the time a day now. Not one of 'em comes ta help out. Our youngest lives twenty minutes away, but we never sees her. Them's kids for ya! I cain't even lie down an' die 'cause I gotta takes care a her!" he said, waving his hand in the direction of their bedroom.

I coughed into my fist and he looked at me.

"Yeah, yeah, I'm gettin' back ta the story," he said. "Anyway, the two of them was havin' harsh words. Then all of a sudden, she turns around and hightails it back toward her aunt and uncle's. But not before she musta said somethin' purdy bad ta him, 'cause...well, let me shows ya. *Lucky! Lucky!* Come 'ere, girl!" he yelled out.

To my right, I heard clicking sounds on the linoleum floor in the kitchen. I turned to see a brown and white dog limp toward Mr. Onus Higby. The dog's left rear leg was bent at an awkward angle. The animal sat at the old man's feet and Mr. Higby bent to scratch behind the dog's ears.

"This here dog was that boy's. But she's mine now! I calls her Lucky, 'cause that's what she is," he said defiantly. "She was with 'em in the park that mornin'. When that there girl left, he took a stick he found on the ground and beat this pup ta within an inch a her life. I got up off that there bench as fast as I could and willed my legs ta move. I took this dog and brought her home. Lookin' back, I don't know hows I made it. Now we both have bum legs. It took a lotta nursin' ta get her inta this gooda shape. Now, if I was you, I'd talk ta that boy again. Somethin' ain't right with him. Anyone that could get mad enough ta beat a poor little dog like that might not be able ta holds his temper in other sitiations."

168

I looked at my uncle and he looked at me. I was stunned. Never did I figure Rick Neller to be capable of that type of violence. My first impression of him was that he was a respectful boy. If what Onus Higby was telling us was true, and I didn't doubt him for a moment, Rick Neller was someone to speak to again.

We stood and thanked the old man for the information, and he asked us to stay for lunch—it seemed he'd just made a big pot of chili. He was old and he was lonely, and wanted the company. Had it been any other day, I might have considered it. I was starting to feel sorry for the elderly man and his situation, but we had a lot to do. Onus Higby walked us to the front door. When we reached it, I turned to him with my hand on the knob.

"What was it that your wife seems to think she saw, Mr. Higby?"

He waved his hand in the air. "Aw, don't go payin' no attention to her," he said. "She don't know what she's talkin' 'bout. I tell ya, she was sleepin' at the time. I'd just checked on her 'fore I went out in the backyard that day."

"If ya could just see your way fit to humorin' us then," my uncle said. "What was it she told ya?"

"She says she see'd that girl talkin' ta someone in a car. She didn't know who, but she said the car was brown was all she said." He shook his head. "But she musta been dreamin', 'cause when I went out back, she was sawin' logs."

We stepped out onto the porch and heard the door shut behind us. I fished in my pocket for a smoke, put it between my lips and lit it. When I looked up, I tapped Derwood's arm with the back of my hand. I pointed down the street.

"Look," I said.

He looked where I was pointing and then turned his head back to me.

"That him?" he asked.

I nodded. Rick Neller was in his front yard with his back toward us, tossing a baseball in the air and hitting it into the park with a bat as it fell back toward the ground. He'd then run to retrieve the ball and do it all over again.

"Let's take a wee walk," my uncle suggested.

We strolled leisurely toward the Neller residence. We were two houses away when the boy noticed us. He paid no attention, though, and hit the ball into the park again. When he came running back to his yard, he saw we were standing in his driveway, waiting for him.

"Hey," he said when he recognized me. "You're that guy from last week. I just heard about Myrna Lou today. That's awful." He shook his head in sadness.

"Seems you were closer to her than you let on," I said. "You didn't tell me the two of you had a relationship."

He shrugged. "It wasn't important. We've *had* no relationship for about a month now. Besides, I don't kiss and tell. And whatever *relationship* we had wasn't common knowledge. You came around here when I was with my buddies."

"Oh, I get it. You were embarrassed of her. Afraid your pals might not approve?"

"Nah, I didn't say *that!*" He shrugged, looking a bit ashamed.

"What'd she do, break it off with you?" I asked.

"Hey, that's none of your business. I don't have to explain things to you!"

He was getting angry now. I could see his fists clench by his sides.

"I look at it this way, Rick. I figure somebody with a very mean temper hit Myrna Lou with that rock. I figure it was someone like you. She said something to get you mad enough to do just that. After all, you're man enough to beat up on dogs, aren't you?"

His face reddened and he was clenching and unclenching his fists now. Suddenly, a girl of about fourteen rode up the drive on her bicycle, letting it fall on the front lawn when she hopped off of it. She ran to the side door of the house and entered, ignoring us.

"Who told you that?" he finally yelled out. "That old, fat bastard down the street?"

"Rick! Watch your language!"

We looked up to see Rick's mother step out onto the porch.

"Go into the house, Ma!" he yelled, turning his head to her. "Get in the house!"

There was something very scary about this boy. His voice had taken on a frightening growl, and she did exactly what he told her to do. She went through the door without another word, shutting it, and I could hear a lock turn. I dropped my cigarette butt on the drive and stamped it out. My gaze returned to him, matching his stare.

"I didn't kill Myrna Lou and I don't have to say another word."

"I'm afraid ye do, lad."

"And just who the hell are *you*?" he asked, turning to Derwood.

"I've heard enough," Derwood said, tapping my arm with the back of his hand. "Get me back to the courthouse. I'll send some men from the station over to pick him up. They can do their questionin' down there. I've got to be on the bench by 2:00."

Rick's eyes widened. I thought I saw a flicker of fear cross his face. I wanted to laugh, but I didn't dare even crack a smile. My uncle was brilliant!

"Wait," Rick said. "You a judge or something?"

My uncle said nothing and neither did I. Rick looked from my uncle to me and then back to Derwood.

"Okay, okay," he said, running his fingers through his hair. "We were hanging out. I liked her, okay? Then all of a sudden, she's acting real distant. She told me right in the park here that she was seeing someone else. She told me that "the Skipper" was more man than I'd *ever* be. That's what made me mad! And I want my dog back from that old geezer, too!"

"Mad enough to take her to Belle Isle and kill her, Rick?" I questioned him.

"*NO! I DIDN'T KILL HER!*"

"Ye own a brown car, lad?" Derwood asked.

"No, I don't own a brown car!" he said sarcastically. "I don't *own* a car!"

171

"Does ye father?"

"No, it's green; why?"

Derwood didn't answer him. Now it was my turn to ask a question.

"'The Skipper'? Who did she mean by that?"

"I don't know. She didn't say and I didn't ask," he answered with impudence.

I was growing tired of this young punk's attitude. He was a little too sassy for my liking. My uncle pointed his finger at Rick.

"Yer not gettin' that pup back. She's stayin' right where she's at. And if I get wind of anythin' happenin' to that fine gentleman down the block, I'll have ye in custody and in me courtroom faster than ye can figure out what shoe fits on yer right foot."

We slowly turned and walked toward the Chevy with Rick staring after us. We were in the middle of the street, a few houses down, when we heard loud banging coming from behind us. We stopped and turned and watched as Rick Neller repeatedly wielded his bat into his sister's bike. My uncle shook his head at the sight.

"You still think only a grown man could've committed this murder?" I asked him.

He didn't answer, but started walking toward the car again. I walked along with him.

"Why ask him about a brown car? You think Mrs. Higby really might have seen something?"

"I know she did, boy."

"How can you be so sure?" I asked.

"'Cause that darlin' lass, Bonnie, told me her cousin got into a car the color of me trousers."

I stopped and watched as my uncle continued his stroll. I looked down at the pants he was wearing. They were brown.

# Chapter Twenty-Four

Before heading back into Detroit, I wanted to make one more stop. I pulled into a parking space right outside of Patti Ann's Boutique, and told my uncle I would only be a moment. I saw her through the window, dressing a mannequin in a red negligee. Her blond hair was worn down today, just grazing the tops of her shoulders. It was smooth, parted on the right side and only bent slightly under at the ends. Her bangs were feathery and straight, softening her beautiful face. She wore a navy blue pantsuit with shoulder padding and a white turtleneck underneath her form-fitting jacket. She turned her head toward me when I entered and smiled.

"Well, hello again," she said.

"Hi there! Listen, I don't have much time, but I was wondering something."

"And what is it you were wondering?" she asked me.

"I'm working on a case right now, but—"

"Yes, I remember," she interrupted me. "The case of the missing girl."

"Well, she *was* missing. We found her, but there's a bad ending to the story."

"Oh?"

"She's been murdered," I said.

She gasped and her hand came up to her throat. Her smile disappeared.

"Oh my goodness! Was it the girl who came in here with Mrs. Dade?"

"No, that was Mrs. Dade's own granddaughter," I replied. "But what I was wondering was if you'd like to have dinner some evening once I'm free of this case?"

Her smile returned. "I think I'd like that very much."

I started to back up toward the door with the biggest smile I'd ever worn on my face. When I reached it, I told her I would see her soon.

"I hope so," she said, and then waved her hand at me as I left her shop.

****

It was now 3:30 and the four of us were seated around the kitchen table eating bowls of ham and bean soup. The conversation I had had with my uncle on the way home was about Bonnie; how he'd gotten her to speak, what she had said. It seemed Derwood played the game with her; pushing on his nose to make his tongue pop out...the same game I had played at the dinner table on Easter Sunday with Celia. He'd been much more successful at it than I had been. After a while, he started to question her. *Did ye see Myrna Lou leave the day ye were sittin' on the porch?* She nodded yes. *Did ye see her get into a car?* She nodded again. *What color was the car?* She pointed to Derwood's pants. *Do ye know who she got in the car with?* She shrugged. *Ye didn't recognize who was drivin' the car?* She shook her head and said, "He was wearing a hat." *Do ye know ye are a very good lass?* Nodding her head, she said, "Yep, and I'm five," holding up her right hand with fingers and thumb spread out.

All this time, Bonnie had held onto this information, and I could only blame myself. No one, including me, thought to just ask her. We had all just assumed she had no information to offer since she was only five years old. I watched my uncle now as he brought Pearl and Gran up to speed on the case as he ate his soup. He told them about babysitting Bonnie and about our visit with the Higby's. He told them about Rick Neller, and how he had placed the fear of God into the boy. After his tale was told, my grandmother sighed.

"Do you think she was really going to run away to marry the skipper of a ship? Maybe that's why he took her to Belle Isle...to board the boat. It sounds sort of dreamy, doesn't it?"

Aunt Pearl frowned and stared at her sister.

"You say the craziest things, Ruby! Yes, it's dreamy alright; all except the part about him smashing her head in with a big rock! You can be such a fool!"

Gran ignored that comment and went right on talking.

"Remember when we were young like that, Pearl? I remember being head over heels in love with what's his name. I can't recall it now, but I can see his face. That was long before you and Paddy came over, Derwood. I must've been fourteen at the time. If Papa had ever found out, he would've thrown a holy fit. A lot of us used to go and talk to that young pastor...not our senior pastor, but his assistant. I can't remember his name, either, but he was young and good looking, and we just thought he was the cat's meow and we could trust him with our feelings and problems. The senior pastor frightened us."

"Well, *I* never went to him with any problems! You and your friends acted foolish back then!"

My grandmother sighed. "Ah, I wish I were young and pretty again."

****

We pulled up into Helen Foster's drive at twenty minutes to five—I'd had Gran call her to tell her we wouldn't be picking her up at four. She came out of her house carrying a large black purse at her side, dressed in a black dress with beige lace around the collar and belted around her tiny waist. Over her forearm was a black lightweight sweater. She opened the back door and climbed into the seat next to Pearl and Gran. Derwood sat in front with me.

"Where's this place at?" she asked, as I cruised down her street.

"Over in Allen Park somewhere," Gran answered.

"Well, if you ask me," Pearl complained, "this is just wrong! Family should be laid out in the home, like they used to be. Laying them out in a public building is disgraceful. It's cold and it's disrespectful. I don't know *what* kind of friends your grandson has, Ruby."

I had had my limit with my aunt. Pulling over to the curb, I stopped the car. I fully turned around in my seat, looking directly behind me, and stared Pearl straight in the eye.

"Listen, you've had a problem with me ever since you arrived at the house. I don't know what that's all about, but I'll tell you one thing. You are *not* going to go into that funeral parlor and insulting my friends! Is that understood? If you think you're going to voice your opinion during the viewing, you can just sit in the car when we get there."

Her face reddened and her lips tightened.

"Are you going to let your grandson speak to me in that manner, Ruby?"

My grandmother looked to her left and stared calmly at her older sister. She seemed to consider the question and then she finally spoke.

"Yes, Pearl, I think I am. You've had it comin' to you."

I turned my gaze to Helen. "Now, do *you* have anything to say?"

Helen made a gesture with her fingers of zipping her lips. She then turned to her right, gazing out the window.

"Good!" I said and started to pull away from the curb.

"*Well, I never!*" Pearl said.

From where he sat, Derwood started to chuckle. "No, Pearl, and ye never will," he said.

If I could have, I would've hugged my uncle and kissed Gran right then and there. The rest of the trip was made in silence. I could just imagine how my aunt was fuming inside. Me, on the other hand; well, I was pretty proud of myself for standing up to her.

The parking lot at the Paar-Chandler Mortuary was almost bare when we pulled in. I spotted Johnny's car along with three others, none of which were brown. We were met with soft music when we entered...somber music. I led the others to the "Homeward Bound" room. Grace and Vivian were seated on a sofa a few feet directly in front of the casket. Johnny was sitting in the back of the room with Bonnie on his lap. Pastor Coady was seated in a chair next to Johnny. Jake and Susan were behind their mother on folding chairs, with Vivian's two young boys sitting on either side of them. Up near the casket was Pastor Bertram Mayhew. He was kneeling on a low, short, red padded bench, his head bent and his hands folded in prayer.

Lonnie Orwick was respectfully waiting for Bertram Mayhew to conclude his prayer before advancing. I suddenly felt guilty for not calling Lonnie to tell him of the funeral arrangements; it had totally slipped my mind. But someone must've called the boy to let him know. He was dressed in dark brown trousers that appeared as though they had seen better days. The suit jacket he wore was black and looked a bit too small for his wide shoulders. He'd probably borrowed it from his father. His white shirt was buttoned tightly around his neck, but he wore no tie. On his feet were badly scuffed black shoes. His hair was still way too long and he kept pushing the front of it out of his eyes. He turned to us as we entered the room and gave a smile and a wave in our direction. Derwood waved back and I nodded. Johnny spotted us and came over, carrying Bonnie in his arms.

"Hey, Sam," he said.

I introduced him to the group. He said hello to everyone and bent to hug my grandmother with his free hand.

"Mrs. Flanagan, it's been so long. I'm so glad to see you; you're looking well."

Gran offered her condolences and asked about his mother while I made my way to the front to talk to Grace and Vivian.

"Hi," I said in a half whisper. "How you holding up, Vivian?"

She tilted her head to meet my gaze and I could see her eyes beginning to water. The woman looked terrible. Her face was blotchy and her eyes were red and puffy. She sniffed and shrugged. Grace turned toward her sister and leaned in, kissing her cheek.

Rising from the sofa, Johnny's wife took my hand, leading me away and to the front corner of the room.

"I'm so worried about her," she said of Vivian. "None of us are doing too well, but she just sits and stares into space. She cries occasionally, but she doesn't speak. I'm afraid Viv is holding too much in."

I gazed around the room again.

"I take it her husband hasn't shown up or called?" I asked.

"No, can you believe that? Not one word from him."

"To tell you the truth, Grace, I don't know if that's good or bad."

"True," she said.

She looked toward the rear of the room as a man entered, removing his brown fedora. He looked familiar to me, but I couldn't figure out where I'd seen him before.

"Oh, excuse me a moment, Sam. There's Jim Wieboldt, our neighbor. You remember meeting him at the church, don't you? Karen had the baby yesterday morning."

I nodded and she walked away from me and toward him. She left me standing up near the casket, but off to the side. I didn't want to look at the prone, lifeless body of Myrna Lou Stevic, so I didn't. I made my way to the back of the room where my uncle was now sitting with Bonnie on his lap. She was giggling softly as she stuck her fingers in his mouth and he pretended to nibble on them. I smiled and sat down in the chair next to them. My grandfather and his brother always had a way with children, and it was evident that Derwood hadn't lost his touch over the years.

By 6:30 the room was filled with visitors, some I recognized and some I didn't. Most of the adults could've been teachers, neighbors, or people associated with the church. I didn't know which. Vernon Wagner, the principal at Dearborn High School, had come in with a tall woman on his arm...Mrs. Wagner, no doubt. I saw his young secretary come in briefly to pay her respects, leaving soon afterward. Agnes Dade waltzed in with her granddaughter shortly before 7:00. She spotted me and gave me a dirty look, went up to view her former student, and then turned around and left without speaking to anyone. *What a personality!* I thought. Several students ambled in and then went out to sit in the gathering area outside of "Homeward Bound." They took seats on the sofas and a couple of them pulled out cigarettes to smoke. I recognized Art Gellert among them. Mrs. Gilbert arrived with her husband and their youngest daughter, Marjorie. Carlene would be at camp. Mr. Gilbert's appearance surprised me. He was shorter than his wife by probably an inch or maybe an inch and a half, and she was heavier than he was by about fifty pounds or so. Yet, his face was very handsome. While Marjorie's parents went straight to Grace and Johnny, who was now up front with his wife, the young girl made a beeline for me.

"Hey, Mr. Flanagan, remember me?" she asked.

"Well, of course I do, Marjorie."

"Gee, you even remember my name," she said. "Guess what?"

"What?"

"I think I'm gonna be sick. I don't wanna go look at her."

"Then don't. Why don't you just remember her the way she was the last time you saw her? It's probably better that way."

"Yeah, I think you're right. I guess the last time I saw her wasn't last Wednesday, either, huh? I could've sworn it was her going into that dress shop."

"We all make those kinds of mistakes. It was someone who looked a lot like her."

"Yeah, I guess. So the last time I saw her was at church over a week ago. Myrna Lou and Carlene walked out of their class that night and I went up to them. She messed my hair up and then said she had to go and talk to Pastor Coady. That's the last time I saw her, when she was walking into his office."

My ears perked up.

"Marjorie, did she seem upset to you at the time? Did she say what she wanted to talk to the youth pastor about?"

The girl shrugged. "She didn't say what was on her mind, and I really didn't notice if she was upset. She didn't seem like it to me, though."

179

I nodded and rubbed my chin. Hmm...the youth pastor hadn't mentioned talking to her privately afterward at the church. Maybe it had slipped his mind, but then again...I'd have to pay him another visit soon. Here and now wasn't the place or time to question anyone, so I made a mental note of it. Marjorie took the chair next to mine and we sat in silence for quite a while.

My eyes scanned the room. Pastor Mayhew was sitting by himself in a corner, wiping his brow with a handkerchief. He looked pale to me. He appeared as though he might be coming down with something. Pastor Coady was standing in another corner with Lonnie, talking. I saw the science teacher from Dearborn High, Mr. Tony Schramm, enter and hesitantly make his way to where his one time student lay quiet and cold. He didn't notice me. After he paid his respects at the side of Myrna Lou, he turned and introduced himself to Vivian, shaking her hand and then squatting in front of her to speak.

I was getting antsy. I felt as though I needed some fresh air and I wanted a cigarette. I didn't feel like joining the six or eight teens on the sofas just outside the room, so I rose and made my way toward the front exit of the building. I stood just outside the door and breathed deep. I was lighting a Lucky Strike when the door opened behind me and out stepped Jim Wieboldt. Our eyes met and he tilted his head.

"I know you, don't I?"

"We met in the church parking lot. I'm Sam Flanagan, Johnny's friend," I explained.

"Ah, yes! I saw you inside, and it's been bothering me where I recognized you from."

"I hear congratulations are in order," I said. "How are mother and baby doing?"

His smile grew wide. He put his hands in his pants pockets and looked down at the ground.

"Doing fine," he said, looking back up at me. "We've got ourselves a son, James, Jr. I feel sort of guilty being so happy. I mean, that girl's mother is in there devastated to have to say goodbye to her child, and I'm welcoming one into our lives."

"Nah, you go ahead and feel all the joy that's due you," I said.

"Well, it's nice seeing you again. I need to get going. You know, I haven't told Karen about this yet." He nodded his head toward the doorway of the funeral parlor. "I just found out about what happened late yesterday afternoon. I didn't want her upset. She'll find out about it soon enough, and there's nothing she can do right now, anyway."

"I understand. That was probably wise."

"Anyway, nice seeing you," he said once again as he started for his car. He stopped in the middle of the parking lot and retraced his steps back to me. Reaching into the top pocket on his suit jacket, he pulled out a cigar and handed it to me. "That's for you," he said. And he was off again.

"Who was that?"

I turned to see Derwood coming out of the door. I told him about Jim Wieboldt and how he had just become a new father, then held up the cigar and asked him if he wanted it...I didn't smoke them. He took it and ran it under his nose, savoring the aroma. We watched as Johnny's young neighbor made his way to the back of the lot, got in his car, and started it. He backed up slowly, and it was only when he passed under a lamppost heading out onto Park Avenue that I noticed his car was a 1939 Packard 120...and it was brown. My eyes turned quickly to my uncle, and he nodded his head.

"Aye, I see. If me wife were about to be havin' a wee one, I wouldn't want another lass thinkin' I was goin' to run away to wed her."

I had to agree that that would be a pretty powerful motive for wanting to get rid of a gal I was fooling around with on the side. I also had to stop myself from jumping to conclusions. There had to be thousands of brown cars in the area, and any number of acquaintances of Myrna Lou's could be driving one of them. But I found it rather curious that a young man who lived across the street from Johnny and Grace drove a car that was the color of the one Myrna Lou had been seen getting into. Had his euphoria been solely because of the arrival of his son? That in and of itself would be enough to cause any man to be on cloud nine. But, was his happiness also the result of relief felt at knowing now his wife would never find out about an affair he'd been having with the young girl who lived near them and attended the same church they did? I took one last drag on my cigarette and stamped it out with the heel of my shoe. One thing I was sure of; Myrna Lou was murdered by someone known to her. He was probably in attendance here tonight, or would be tomorrow at the service. I was going to find whoever did this to her. It was the least I could do for the young woman and my dear friends, Grace and Johnny Delbeck.

# Chapter Twenty-Five

I looked at my watch; twenty minutes until eight. Gran was up front with the Delbeck's and Myrna Lou's mother. She had Vivian's hands resting in her own and was speaking to the woman. Whatever Gran was saying, it seemed to have a comforting effect on Grace's sister. Ruby Flanagan could be very compassionate when the need arose. I'd seen this over and over again when she'd come to the aid of people who were hurting.

Aunt Pearl was seated in the back of the room. She was in between the arm of the sofa and Helen, and Helen had her head tilted, half resting on the back of the couch and half resting on Pearl's right shoulder, her mouth hanging open...she was asleep. Pearl didn't look too pleased with the situation. *Thank the Lord for small favors*, I thought, because Helen wasn't snoring. I pointed her out to my uncle.

"We'd better get these women home," I said.

**\*\*\*\***

"I was havin' a dream in there," Helen said as she climbed into the car.

"About what?" Gran asked.

"I was dreamin' that I was ridin' a huge white horse and I was naked, just like Lady Guinevere. Only I didn't have any fig leaves coverin' me up."

"It's Lady *Godiva,* and her *hair* covered her, not *fig leaves*," Aunt Pearl corrected her with disgust in her voice.

"You don't know that she didn't have fig leaves on under the hair, Pearl," Gran chimed in.

Pearl sighed.

"I wonder if that means anything," Gran continued.

"If what means anything?" I asked from behind the wheel.

"Dreaming about being naked on the back of a white horse while you're at a funeral viewing," she said. "I hear your dreams can mean something. Like it might mean there's money on the horizon or a bunch of good luck coming."

"For who?" I asked.

"Maybe the dreamer, or maybe the deceased; or maybe the person you're dreaming about."

Derwood chuckled and I looked in the rearview mirror. *Was she kidding?*

"Well, I can guarantee you, no money is coming to Myrna Lou, and I'd say her luck has run out. And as for Lady Godiva," I added, "nothing's coming her way, either."

"I'm hungry!" Helen belted out from the back seat.

"I'll have you home in just a bit," I said.

Out of the corner of my eye I saw Derwood reach into his pocket and bring out his wallet. He opened it and began to count the bills he had in it.

"Why don't ya swing by that friend of yers and I'll buy the ladies one of his sandwiches?" he suggested.

We walked into White Castle at ten minutes after eight. From the hours posted on the door, I knew Joe was closing up in twenty minutes. I felt a bit guilty for arriving so late with four others. I was relieved to see his grill wasn't cleaned for the night, nor was the coffee pot empty. He actually seemed pleased to see us.

"Well, howdy! And who are these lovely ladies with you tonight, Sam?" he asked, and then turned to nod at my uncle. "Hey, old timer, good to see you again."

I made the introductions. Helen and Gran smiled at him and Aunt Pearl knit her eyebrows together in a frown. Geez, she'd grown into a miserable old cuss. Helen hopped on the stool next to the cash register with surprising ease and Gran gingerly mounted the one to her right. Pearl stood behind the seat next to my grandmother and asked if there was a restroom.

"Right there," Joe pointed. "The red door at the end of the counter."

As Pearl headed that way, Helen asked Joe, "Do you have orange juice?"

"That sounds good. Order me one also," my aunt called out over her shoulder.

"Make that three," Gran said.

"And put some ice in them," Helen told him.

I narrowed my eyes, watching Helen. *She wouldn't, would she?* And then she did. She pulled out a fifth of vodka from her oversized handbag. It was three quarters full.

"*Whoa ho!*" Joe said, and then laughed.

We watched as Helen poured a good amount into her juice, and then she handed the bottle to Gran, who did the same. I was surprised because my grandmother liked beer, but didn't really care for hard liquor. I rolled my eyes and shrugged my shoulders at Joe, but I jumped up when Gran started to add some to Pearl's juice. Before I could move to stop her, or say anything in protest, I felt Derwood's hand on my arm. He shook his head.

"Are you crazy?" I asked him. "There's going to be hell to pay for this one."

"Ye just let me worry about that."

The ever stingy Helen watched as Gran added the alcohol to Pearl's glass.

"Well, don't give it *all* to her," she said.

"Oh hush! I just want her to relax and loosen up for a change. I don't want to *kill* her!"

"Well, that bottle has to last me for a few days!"

"Oh phooey! That's not going to last you for a few days and you know it!"

Joe leaned his elbows on the counter in front of Gran and Helen.

"How about getting up and turning that lock on the door, beautiful?"

185

Helen slid off her stool faster than I thought she ever could and did what he told her to do.

"Hey," my grandmother protested. "How do you know he was talking to *you*?"

"Oh, really Ruby, who else would he be talking to?" she said as she climbed back onto her seat.

Gran gave up the fight and took a sip of the fruity concoction.

"I don't mind having one, myself," Joe said. "But of course, if you don't think you have enough...."

"Oh, Ruby's right. This'll never last me anyway. You just get yourself a glass."

Helen was smiling wide at the restaurant owner and batting her lashes. Joe winked at her and reached for the juice. I couldn't believe it. Helen was flirting with Joe, a man thirty or more years younger than she was, and he was actually going along with it. I felt like I was watching a cheesy comedy at the moving picture theater. Joe poured a good amount into the glass and handed the bottle back to Helen. She replaced the cap and returned it to the inside of her bag. She zipped the top of her purse just as my aunt emerged from the bathroom. I got off my seat and moved five stools farther into the eatery.

"If you're smart," I said to my uncle, "you'll do the same."

He did, and then Joe took the orders. When he got to me, all I wanted was a cup of black coffee in front of me and an ashtray.

As Joe cooked, I heard my aunt say, "This tastes funny. Has this orange juice gone bad, young man?"

"Oh just shut up and drink it," Gran told her. "It's good for you."

"*Well, I never!*"

"No, you haven't, Pearl, but you are now. Quit being my cranky older sister for a change."

I saw Joe's girth jiggle with his laughter as his back was to us, wielding his spatula on the sputtering meat. After that, I refused to listen to them any longer or look their way. If I could've, I would've walked out, leaving them all there. I didn't want to witness the fallout from all of this. But I couldn't do that, so I sat right where I was, sipping the strong coffee and smoking my cigarette. I alternated between watching Joe do his thing with the hamburgers and swiveling my stool to glance out onto the main street of Dearborn. I watched the trees bend with the strong gusts of wind that had kicked up outside. It was like a ghost town tonight. No one was out walking or driving on Michigan Avenue.

Joe placed the plates in front of the others and I noted how the women ate as though they were ravenous. Derwood bit into his burger and looked straight ahead, keeping his thoughts to himself.

Gazing out the window again, I saw a car moving slowly up the street. It pulled to the curb directly in front of Paul's Barber Shop and turned its lights and engine off, but no one got out. Sipping my coffee, I continued to watch. A good five minutes passed and I began to get a bit nervous. Was someone watching us? I couldn't tell. I couldn't even make out who was in the car, or if it was a man or a woman. Another set of headlights approached from the way the first had come. The second car pulled up in front of the one that was already parked. The lights went out and the engine was shut off. This was curious.

I tapped on my uncle's arm as he was wiping his mouth with a paper napkin. I discreetly gestured out the window, telling him about the separate arrivals in a low tone. He swiveled in his seat. We watched as a man got out of the second car to arrive and went back to the first, opening the driver's side door and helping a woman to exit her vehicle. They then hurried to his car on the passenger side, which sat under the street lamp. I breathed a sigh of relief. I had hated to think that whoever had murdered Myrna Lou was now tailing me and wanting to cause trouble, especially with Derwood and the ladies here. The man opened the door to his car for her, and then all of a sudden pulled her to him and embraced her, leaning in to kiss her deeply. As he did this, his hat blew into the wind. He hurriedly chased after it, catching it, and carried it back with him. As he approached the car and the woman, his face became illuminated in the light. I sucked in my breath and then let out a soft whistle.

"Well, I'll be...."

Derwood turned to me.

"What; haven't ye ever seen a man kiss a woman before?"

I nodded my head and said, "Yes, I have. But that man shouldn't be kissing that woman. She's not his wife."

"How do ye know? Who is she?"

"Because I've seen a picture of his wife and that's not her." This woman's name suddenly came to mind. "That's the secretary, Becky Timmons, from Dearborn High School, and that's the one and only Tony Schramm, Myrna Lou's science teacher."

We both watched as the two got into Tony Schramm's car. They pulled away slowly and drove out of sight.

# Chapter Twenty-Six

We left Joe's White Castle a little after 9:00. Pearl didn't appear too steady on her feet when she slid off her stool, so I took her by the elbow and gently guided her out to the Chevy Coupe. Before sliding in the middle of the back seat, she turned to me and roughly patted my cheek.

"You're sush a good boy! And sho hanshome, too. I wish Dillard wash more like you."

There was no doubt about it, she was feeling tipsy. For her to place me in a better light than her own grandson was very irregular. I'd probably never hear words to that effect coming out of her mouth again. She let go of a loud and long belch in my face. I could smell the fruity vodka mixture on her breath. She rubbed at her stomach.

"I think I might get shick before we get home," she moaned.

I voiced a suggestion that maybe it would be best if my aunt sat near a door on the ride home. If need be, she could open a window and hang her head out. But my grandmother shot down the idea, saying that Pearl would be just fine. I sighed, prayed, and climbed in behind the wheel. We hadn't travelled more than five minutes when I heard soft whimpering coming from behind me, so looked in the rearview mirror. Well, it wasn't Gran. She was looking to her right with a confused look on her face.

"What's the matter with *you*?" I heard Helen ask.

My aunt uttered something indistinguishable.

"You feeling sick, Aunt Pearl?" I asked her over my shoulder.

189

Again, I couldn't make out what she said. Derwood turned in his seat to look at his wife.

"What's the matter, girl?" he asked.

"I've carried sush a burden for yearsh naw."

"About what? Why don't you let it out? You might feel better," Helen suggested.

"Oh, Derwood, can you ever forgive me?" Pearl asked, and then she let go of another loud belch.

*Uh oh*, I thought. My aunt was feeling weepy from the drink she had had. I half turned in my seat, feeling a bit of panic, and suggested that Pearl may want to stop talking. All she needed was some rest. When we arrived home, she could crawl into bed. Ignoring my advice, she kept right on speaking and spilled her guts over something that had happened years ago. I couldn't help but laugh out loud when I'd heard the story. From directly behind me, my grandmother slapped the back of my head. I then glanced over at my uncle, who was looking straight ahead and out the windshield with a smirk on his face.

****

We pulled up to Helen's house and she hopped out, only to stick her head back inside the car.

"I wouldn't worry about it, Pearl. Once when my Frank was alive, we had a terrible argument and I told him to his face that I wished I had married Rudolph Valentino. He told me he wished I had, too. So you see? It's really no big deal. Shoot, I'd say it's normal."

*That'd be something to see*, I thought. *A fifty something Helen married to a twenty something Valentino!*

She shut the back door and climbed the steps to her porch. I waited while she unlocked her door and disappeared inside. I tried to hold back, but couldn't. I broke into laughter again.

Once at home, I stood in the kitchen and ate the last blueberry muffin. Derwood went into the pantry and retrieved my bottle of whiskey, pouring himself a bit of it over a few ice cubes he'd placed in a glass. He reached into his top pocket and pulled out the cigar that Jim Wieboldt had given me. As he was holding a match to it, his wife emerged from Gran's bedroom dressed in her nightgown and robe. She gasped.

"You're not going to shmoke that—"

"Yes, I am, Pearl," he said determinedly. "I've had me a bit of a shock and I need this to calm down."

She then spied his glass of amber liquid, but said nothing. Her eyes began to tear up slightly and she returned to Gran's room without another word and shut the door quietly.

"Hey, you're not really upset by all that stuff, are you?" I asked him.

He waved at me dismissively and puffed on the stogie.

"What, do I look daft to ya, lad? 'Course I'm not upset by it. Just feedin' her a bit o' the blarney and it worked. I got her to shut up 'bout me smoke and drink now, didn't I?"

It seemed that some years ago, 1932 to be exact, Pearl had gone to the moving picture show with her eldest daughter to see a film that had just come out. *Red Dust* starred a young Jean Harlow and an upcoming celebrity named Clark Gable. Seeing him on the big screen, Pearl thought he was possibly the most handsome man she'd ever seen. He affected her so much that she thought of nothing but him for the next two days and periodically afterward. And *this* was what she felt guilty for. At the time, Gable was probably thirty years old to my aunt's seventy-three.

Later, when everyone was tucked in for the night, I took my notebook into the living room and worked on a list of people I thought to be suspects. The way I saw it, I had four of them. I started writing on a clean sheet of paper, listing them one by one and giving my reasons for suspecting them. First I wrote down Jim Wieboldt. Under his name, I wrote the obvious reason for including him on the list. He had a brown car. I also listed a possible motive; he was having an affair with Myrna Lou. Of course, that wasn't fact. I was just putting out a theory. But if he *had* been involved with her, he had a pretty good motive for murder. He surely wouldn't want his pregnant wife finding out about his relationship with the girl across the street. He couldn't risk losing what he had if Myrna Lou was the type to cause trouble.

And how involved was he in the church? He probably wouldn't want to risk his pastor and the congregation finding out he was unfaithful. How would that look? Could the seemingly polite and decent young man be 'the Skipper'?

What bothered me about it being Jim Wieboldt was that Bonnie hadn't recognized him. Wouldn't even a five year old see that it was a man who had been living right across the street from her, although his hat was pulled down over his eyes? And wouldn't she see that it was her neighbor's car? Wouldn't she have seen that the vehicle had come from right across the street while she was sitting outdoors on her porch steps? My mind suddenly traveled back to the day I'd gone over to the Delbeck's to obtain a list of Myrna Lou's friends; the day I'd first laid eyes on Bonnie. I thought of how she had pointed out the front window. She'd been desperately trying to tell us something. She didn't want to go and play with her neighbor's dog…I was certain of that now. What was it she had been pointing at? I closed my eyes and tried to visualize what was visible out that window. The elderly man had been cutting his lawn. The dog was running in circles, and then disappeared behind a car and then reappeared.

I quickly opened my eyes. *The car! It was a brown car!* Was it Jim Wieboldt's car? I tried to think if it was the same make and model I'd seen him drive away from the funeral parlor in. I couldn't be certain, but I didn't think so. Yet, I didn't cross him off my list because the motive seemed to be a good one and the circumstances seemed to fit.

Bonnie had acted that way another time. I remembered her pulling on my suit jacket sleeve and pointing. Now where was that? I closed my eyes again, trying to picture where I'd been that day. It was in the church parking lot. She and Grace had just exited the building on Good Friday. I had turned and watched as a man had been pulling his child along and yelling at him. At the time, I thought she was upset by the man's harsh words, but now I wasn't so sure. What had she been pointing at? *It was the cars, again!* The father and son had been walking in between two brown cars! She'd been trying to tell us all along that Myrna Lou had been picked up in a brown car.

Next, I listed Tony Schramm. Seeing what I had seen that night convinced me he couldn't be trusted. He was Myrna Lou's teacher. He'd have access to her at least five days a week. How close had they grown? Had they had a relationship that wasn't just that of teacher and student? Agnes Dade had caught them standing close; too close. Was it really as Mr. Schramm had said, with her being too forward and acting flirtatious? Becky Timmons had to be about twenty years of age. If a thirty-year-old man could have an affair with a twenty-year-old, what would stop him from getting involved with a seventeen-year-old? And I had noticed something else. His automobile was a deep burgundy, just like my Chevy. Could Bonnie and Mrs. Higby have mistaken the color for brown? Again, his motive would be his wife *and* his career. His life as a teacher would be over if anyone caught wind of him fooling around with one of his students. Maybe he was the type to play, but not for keeps. Myrna Lou obviously had another idea in mind, according to a few of the girls she went to Dearborn High School with, and I doubted that she was the type to be discreet if he tried to break it off with her.

I then thought about the youth pastor, Matthew Coady. I'd heard nothing to indicate that anyone had suspicions about him and Myrna Lou. He seemed like a decent young man whom the young people at Christ the Divine Lutheran Church seemed to like and admire, but I couldn't discount the fact that he was missing, according to Lonnie Orwick, for most of the basketball game at the church that Monday afternoon, and he hadn't told me about his own absence. He also hadn't told me that he had a visit in his office from Johnny's niece that last Sunday night she'd attended services there. I found that to be strange. My guess was that she went in to discuss something that was bothering her, so he knew what that was. And he'd lied to us. Again, he was married, and that was a pretty good motive for not wanting Myra Lou around. Matthew's position at the church was another good motive. Certainly he would be scared to death to have it be known that he was fooling around with a young lady in his youth group. But I didn't want to believe that he could be involved—not him, not a youth pastor. Something inside of me didn't want to think that a man who had made God the focal point of his career could do such an evil thing. And yet, I knew better; I knew that even a man of God could falter and then try to cover up his sin.

I rubbed at my temples and laid my notebook down on the coffee table. Standing, I stretched and yawned. It was getting late and I was getting tired. I went into the bathroom and changed into my pajamas, getting a drink of water on my way back to the living room. Picking up the notebook once again, I sat in the chair where the light from the lamp was brighter. There was one more person I wanted to add to the list—Rick Neller. Could he have killed Myrna Lou? Out of all of them, he certainly had the temperament. I had no doubt that he could inflict a lot of damage if he got angry enough at someone, and it didn't seem it took much to get him to that state. The problem was he didn't have a car. Not only that, but if he picked Myrna Lou up in a car at all, I'd assumed it would be his father's, and he told us his father's car was green. If he lied, it was easy enough to follow up on and find out for sure. I sat back and pictured Rick cruising down the street and stopping in front of Johnny's house, summoning to Myrna Lou, who had been sitting on the steps of the porch. I pictured him wearing a fedora down over his eyes. I chuckled. I just couldn't see it.

What I *did* see though, out of the corner of my eye, was a car pass by the house on St. Aubin outside the picture window. I watched, through the opened draperies, as it seemed to be traveling very slowly. I turned off the lamp that was on the table next to me and continued to watch outside. I moved to the window once the car was no longer in sight, and glanced at my watch to try to make out the time by the light of the moon filtering in. It was 12:46 a.m.

Suddenly, thunder struck outside with a huge reverberation, and I jumped and retreated farther into the room, sitting in the padded chair once more. If the car passed by again, I'd catch full sight of it. I hadn't caught the color of the car, although I knew it was dark, and I wasn't sure of the make.

Feeling for the ashtray on the end table, I set it on the arm of the chair. I needed a smoke. Sitting in dark silence, I puffed away and listened as the heavens opened up and spit massive drops of rain down to earth with a vengeance. In a matter of minutes, the huge living room window was drenched on the outside and my visibility for looking out onto the street was severely limited. I stayed where I was and continued to smoke, relatively sure the car hadn't passed again since I'd seen no headlights. I was growing very sleepy, but I decided to give my watch a few more moments.

Wracking my brain, trying to mentally go over again the list of four people I'd made, I wondered if the passing car could've contained one of my suspects. If one of them had driven by, watching the house, which one of them could it have been? Or could it have been *anyone* connected with this case? Could it have been just an innocent passing of a car late at night?

Then I heard it. I jumped so suddenly that I dropped my cigarette to my lap. I felt the heat immediately and reached out to retrieve it, then stubbed it out in the ashtray. What had caused that noise? I couldn't think what had caused it, but I knew it had come from the back of the house.

My thoughts turned to the German Luger I'd purchased early in the year. It was in the bedroom and Derwood was sleeping. No, it *wasn't* in the bedroom. I suddenly remembered that it was in the glove compartment of my Chevy! *Damn*, I thought. The sound repeated itself. It sounded like the rattling of the screen door at the back of the house. Was someone trying to get in? Had that car gone around the block and then parked on the street behind us, its occupant making his way up through the yard and to the door off the kitchen? Or could it be that I had nothing to worry about and that the wind was causing the sound?

I quietly and slowly rose from the chair, stood for a moment right where I was, and strained to listen. Okay, I admit it; I was spooked. I willed myself to move toward the origin of the sound, watching my step. The house was as dark as it could get, the moonlight being obscured by the heavy downpour outside. I'd just entered the kitchen when I heard the noise again. *Someone was rattling the back door*! Pulling a drawer out soundlessly, I reached in, feeling around. I recognized the shape of my grandmother's wooden mallet and grabbed it. I didn't know how much protection it would give, but at least it was *something*! Moving closer to the inner door, I slightly parted the curtains that hung covering the upper glass portion, but saw no one. I searched the yard as best I could and saw no movement. Only rain could be seen pelting the lawn.

My heartbeat was starting to return to normal when the sound came again. This time I could hear that it was coming from the bottom of the screen door. I had to make a move and find out what or who this was. As quietly as I could, I unlatched the lock, leaving my hand on the knob. Taking in a huge breath of air, I yanked it open. Slowly and cautiously, I opened the screen door, raising the mallet above my head. Looking down, I found two frightened, light blue eyes staring back at me.

# Chapter Twenty-Seven

I could hear their soft voices. They were trying to be quiet so as not to wake me, but it wasn't working. I didn't want to pry my eyes open just yet, though, so I tried to retreat back into sleep.

"I think we should call him Blackie," I heard my grandmother half whisper.

"And just why would ya be callin' him that when he isn't black?" my uncle asked.

"Well, he's gray and that's close enough to black," she replied.

My uncle grunted and I heard paper rustle. What in the world were they talking about? I willed my left eye to open and looked over at them. Uncle Derwood was hidden behind this morning's newspaper while sitting in the chair I'd occupied the night before. Gran was in the other chair, cradling a soft ball of fur in her lap. She caught my head movement out of the corner of her eye.

"Well, good morning, dear. I hope we didn't wake you, but we have a visitor."

She held the kitten up so I could see him.

"Somehow," she continued, "this little fellow got into the house while we were sleeping. I think it's a gift from God. He's telling us we need a pet."

She brought the animal's face close to her own and rubbed her nose against the top of his head, cooing to him in baby talk. I ran my open hand over my face and rose to a sitting position, placing my feet on the floor. I yawned and asked the time.

"T'is ten minutes to seven o'clock," came my uncle's voice from behind the newspaper.

I groaned. I so much wanted to go back to sleep for another hour, but I knew I wouldn't be able to. I watched my grandmother as she held the small animal close to her chest and hugged it gently. She rocked back and forth in her seat and started to sing a lullaby softly, as if this kitten were her own newborn child. I didn't need this. I didn't need to listen to her voice trying to keep a tune when it couldn't. She hit a high note and I cringed. My uncle didn't seem to mind or notice, or maybe he was just afraid to come out from behind the paper. Then I saw the Detroit News shake in his hands and I knew he was silently laughing while hidden. She suddenly stopped and looked at me.

"Isn't it strange, dear?"

"What?" I asked with a thick morning tongue.

"Well, I can't figure out how he got into the house."

"I let him in," I said.

"You *did*? Well, I'm glad you did, but what made you think to do that? How did you know he was outside?"

"He knocked," I said, while rising to head for the bathroom. I stretched. "He was half drowned in the storm. I dried him off and gave him some tuna. Last thing I remember, he was lying across my chest."

"That's where I found him this morning, dear. It's a sign from God, Sam. I just know it is. What other kitten do you know would come here and knock on the door? It's a miracle!"

I rolled my eyes and called over my shoulder as I entered the kitchen, "Yeah, well don't get too attached to him. We've got to find out who he belongs to."

****

I emerged from the bathroom, showered and shaved and feeling fully awake. I removed a cup from the cupboard in which to pour coffee. Gran was now at the sink, filling it with sudsy water while the tiny gray ball of fur rubbed against her ankles. She placed a couple of bowls in the hot soapy water. It appeared that she and Derwood had each had oatmeal for breakfast.

"Aunt Pearl still sleeping?"

"She's not feeling too well this morning. I hope she isn't coming down with something. Influenza can be bad at her age."

I stared at my grandmother, stunned but not really surprised. She was kidding, right? *Influenza*? My aunt wasn't coming down with anything and Gran knew it! She had to know the cause of Pearl's discomfort.

"She isn't coming down with anything," I said. "You know exactly why she isn't feeling well. It was the liquor in her juice that got her sick."

"Well, between you and me, you might be right," Gran said, and then added with anger in her voice while shaking her head, "*That dern Helen!*"

"What do you mean, *Helen*? *You're* the one who poured it in her juice last night."

"I think your memory isn't very good, dear. It was *Helen's* vodka, and it was *Helen* who brought it along with her last night. I really had nothing to do with it."

I stared at her in disbelief and replaced the coffee cup on the shelf in the cupboard. I loved my grandmother and Uncle Derwood. I even had to admit to loving my Aunt Pearl to some extent, mainly because she was Gran's sister. But I knew what I had to do. I had to get away, even if it was only for a couple of hours. I needed a break! I could always pick up some coffee at a diner.

****

I took the stairs to my second story office two at a time. It felt good to get away from the house and the battiness that Gran sometimes displayed. Turning the corner, I saw that Oliver Treadwell's door was wide open. Ollie occupied the office next to mine. He was a photographer who had his own business here in the building, and he also freelanced for the Detroit News. He was a short, bald gent with short and stubby hands, who wore black rimmed glasses and talked in a soft, singsong voice. I stuck my head in his door.

"Well, good morning, Ollie. How's life been treating you?"

He jerked in his chair behind the desk and looked up from the monthly photo rag that he subscribed to.

"Oh, Mr. Flanagan, you nearly gave me a heart attack!" He put his hand across his chest and smiled with relief. "Where *have* you been? I haven't seen you around here in days, and your phone has been ringing off the hook," he said. "I was beginning to think you'd met with an ill fate! I'm very happy to see I was wrong!"

"Nah, me Ollie? Never!"

I was glad the little man was speaking to me once again. A few month's back, I'd discovered, quite by accident, that Oliver Treadwell was paying rent of thirty dollars a month. Yours truly was being charged thirty-two dollars and fifty cents for my downtown Detroit office space. That put me up in arms, and I went to the building supervisor to correct this mistake. I told him I wasn't going to put up with the discrepancy, and why should I? Our offices were the same size. I didn't see why one should be paying any different than the other. After my tirade, the man calmly told me I was right. It had probably just been an oversight; one that he would see was corrected. I'd left his first floor digs feeling good about my assertiveness in the matter, and I felt elated to know that I could now count on an extra two dollars and fifty cents each month. The world was good! But when the rent came due, I'd gotten the same bill I'd always gotten, and I also got an irate Ollie Treadwell beating down my door. His rent had been raised by two dollars and fifty cents. He hadn't spoken to me for a couple of weeks after that.

I left him to his magazine and went next door. As I entered my office, I stooped to retrieve the handful of envelopes that had been shoved inside. The very top one was my office rent reminder. Ollie Treadwell was right; I hadn't been here in a week, and it was time to catch up with things, mainly these bills. Tossing them on the top of my desk, I went to the window and looked down on Woodward Avenue. The day was as gray as it could get and there were few people strolling along the walk. Fortunately, the rain from the night before had stopped, but it left behind a dull sky and a bone-chilling breeze. Continuing to gaze down upon the streets of Detroit, I took the lid off the steaming black beverage and gently blew across its surface. Before I got the chance to take a sip of it, the telephone rang.

"Flanagan Investigations," I said into the mouthpiece.

"I wanna talk to the detective. Put him on."

The voice was loud and demanding. I didn't recognize it.

"You're speaking to him."

"You're Flanagan?"

"Yes sir, what can I help you with?"

"What kind of place are you running there? I've been trying to reach you for days," he said.

"Well, you've reached me now, so why not tell me what you want?"

"I want Daisy back and I want you to get her back for me. I've lived with that girl for the past six years and I want her home again. I don't care what you have to do to get her back, either. Just do it!"

I laughed into the mouthpiece. I had the feeling I was dealing with a real goofball here.

"Well, isn't that up to *you* to coax her back home? I mean, hey, if you can't hold her, what can *I* do about it?"

"Don't be a smart aleck, Flanagan. I don't like smart alecks. I want her back home and the sooner the better. Now what's your fee?"

"Now wait a minute. Obviously, you've had a spat with the little woman, but that's going to take *your* doing to convince her to come back to you. I'm going to have to pass on this one."

"What little woman?" he asked. "The *woman* in this instance is the problem! I don't want the *woman* back. Married to her for a couple of years and she cleans me out in the divorce, including taking my *dog* along with her! And the dog wasn't part of the divorce settlement. Now, I want my Daisy back and I'm willing to pay for your service."

I sighed. "I charge ten dollars a day. What kind of dog is it, and where'd your ex-wife go? Give me a description of Daisy."

His voice softened. "Daisy is the sweetest thing you've ever seen. She's all black except for the lower jaw. It's tan. She's a Rottweiler, and Miranda has gone to Cleveland with her."

I frowned. "Uh, I think you'll have to find another P.I. I don't do Rottweiler's. Besides, I'm currently working on a case and couldn't get away at this time."

"Well, when can you get away?" he persisted.

"I don't think you're hearing me. Even if I could go to Cleveland, I wouldn't. Rottweiler's scare the hell out of me, okay?"

"Now what's the *matter* with you? She's a big, gentle teddy bear! Has never had a mean streak in her," he said, and paused. "Well, *hardly* ever. You say you get ten dollars a day? I'll make it thirteen."

I rolled my eyes and said nothing. He continued his begging.

"Okay, I'll give you fifteen dollars a day. How's that?"

I straightened in the chair and grabbed a pencil from my top drawer. I took down his name, address and phone number, just in case. I mean, after all, how vicious could a Rottweiler *really* get?

# Chapter Twenty-Eight

The light mood I felt while walking into my downtown office had dissipated. Now I was brought back to the reality of Myrna Lou Stevic's funeral this afternoon. I stood outside on the front walk, smoking a Lucky Strike while I waited for my uncle to finish getting ready for the sad event. I turned at the sound of a screen door opening and saw Albie, the kid from next door, come outside and head toward me.

"Hey, Mr. Flanagan! You look mighty sharp today. Goin' somewhere?"

"Yeah, I'm going somewhere. So, how was your Easter Sunday?" I asked him.

"Purdy good. We went to my aunt's house, and it was crazy with people over there. I was sorta glad to get home again." He brushed his hair out of his eyes and looked up at me. "I need to ask ya somethin'."

"Okay, ask away."

"I need some money. Ma's birthday is comin' up, and I wanna get her a hair brush I seen at the five and dime. It's got what looks like a pearl handle."

"So, you want to borrow some money? How much is the brush?"

"No, no, I don't wanna borrow any; I thought maybe you could hire me to do somethin'…you know, like ya usually do. The brush costs fifteen cents, and I only got a nickel."

"What happened to the money I paid you for washing the windows?"

"Aw, heck, Mr. Flanagan, me and Bobby went to the show yesterday, and I sorta squandered the rest on candy and different things. I love those blackjacks," he explained.

I watched as the boy kicked a pebble from the sidewalk out into the street. There had to be something I could have him do to earn the dime. And then an idea came to me. I told him about the kitten who appeared at the door last night during the storm. He'd save me some legwork if he could ask around the neighborhood to see if anyone was missing a pet.

"Sure, I can do that for ya, Mr. Flanagan, but I gotta tell ya, that job sounds like more of a twenty center to me."

"Okay, it's a deal. Here, just in case I don't see you for a while."

I reached in my pocket, brought out my change and handed him two dimes. He looked up at me in surprise, wearing a sweet smile.

"Gee, that was too easy. I shoulda asked for a whole quarter," he said.

"Yeah? Well, don't push your luck. Just find out who the cat belongs to."

I watched as he ran back to his house and disappeared around the side of it, heading into his back yard. I thought about Gran, who was in the living room right now, fawning over the little animal. When Albie found out who the kitten belonged to, it was going to break her heart. I turned again at the sound of my own front screen door opening and saw Uncle Derwood emerge from the house. He was wearing his black suit, a white shirt, black tie, and black shoes, and his face had the shine of cleanliness on it. His overcoat was draped across his forearm. The wisps of white hair on top of his head had been neatly combed to the side. I took a good long look at him as he descended the steps. At eighty-eight years old, he still was a handsome man.

"Aunt Pearl feeling any better?" I asked him when he'd reached me out on the walk.

"Eh, she's sleeping, so who knows? Would ye like to take me car? I can drive."

"Nah, let's just take the Chevy," I said and headed for the garage.

The drive to the Paar-Chandler Mortuary was a silent one. I had the impression that even Uncle Derwood was feeling the sadness. When we parked in the lot and got out of the car, I saw Mac pulling up in a parking spot not too far from mine. His current partner, Lawrence Brown, was with him. I had never cared for Lawrence Brown. As far as I was concerned, he had a personality that stunk. He rubbed people the wrong way...he was a know it all, and when I was part of the department, most officers avoided him. Lawrence Brown was only about five feet seven inches and his build was slight. He had dark brown eyes and a massive head full of dark brown curls. When he smiled, a wide space showed between his top two front teeth. Personally, I thought he was goofy looking. For some reason that escaped all of us in the department, the chief liked him enough to bump him up to a detective in the homicide division. He was forty-six years old, married to his high school sweetheart, and had one daughter who was married and pumped out babies like it was her career.

Derwood and I waited until the two of them caught up with us in the parking lot. Right before reaching us, Mac discarded his cigarette on the cement and stepped on it with his shoe.

"Hey, Sam," Mac said. "I've been meaning to give you a call. Anything new on your end?"

"There are a couple of things my uncle and I have found out."

I looked over at Brown before continuing. He was wearing a smirk. Mac knew I didn't like him. He could sense my hesitance.

"Why don't you leave it to the big boys now, Flanagan? You've done your part, and it looks like you're not getting any further with it. Leave it to us now."

I said nothing, but Mac turned to him.

"Why don't you go on in and find the girl's mother? Let her know we'll be here observing, just in case."

Brown smirked again, but moved toward the funeral home with his hands tucked inside his trouser pockets. I waited until he was far enough away before I spoke.

"How do you stand him? He's an idiot," I said, but Mac just laughed.

I told him what we'd learned from the Higby's and Bonnie herself. I told him about the four people I thought could be suspects and why. He didn't respond until after I was done speaking.

"Well, we contacted most of the people you'd already spoken to. That kid...what's his name, Neller? He said something about you and a judge coming to see him. Said he knew the *judge* sent us to question him, but he swore he didn't know anything about his friend's death. He seemed a bit shook up at our visit. Know anything about that?"

Mac looked straight at my uncle and smiled. Derwood returned his gaze, scratching his head.

"I think I'll just mosey on inside, lad."

Derwood followed the way Lawrence Brown had gone. When he had disappeared inside the building, I turned to Mac.

"That kid has serious problems...I mean his temper. I don't doubt he could've killed her had he been with her that day. I just don't see how he could've been with her."

"Well, whoever killed her won't get away with it. That I am sure of," Mac said. "And just some friendly advice, Sam; maybe your uncle shouldn't impersonate any city official again. You know, just in case there's a law against it."

# Chapter Twenty-Nine

It was warm and stuffy inside the "Homeward Bound" viewing room, even though the air was damp and chilly outside. My uncle and I were sitting four rows behind the sofa where Vivian, Grace, and Johnny now sat. Their children were sitting in folding chairs directly behind them. In between the sofa and the casket where Myrna Lou was lying prone was a small podium. Pastor Bertram Mayhew stood behind it, scanning some notes and wiping his brow with a white handkerchief. Soft hymnal music was piped into the room and people sat silent for the most part, waiting for comforting words to come from the man. I turned to my right as Lonnie Orwick took the seat next to mine. He put his hand on my forearm as he lowered himself into the chair. He leaned over to me.

"Do you mind if I sit next to you, Mr. Flanagan?" he asked.

"Not at all, Lonnie."

The young man wore the exact same clothes he'd had on the previous night. I gazed at him as he shoved his hair out of his eyes.

"Gee, I didn't know if I was gonna make it in time for the service," he whispered. "I left the house about ten minutes after eleven, but seems like I should've left a bit earlier."

I looked at him in surprise. "You mean to tell me you walked here from home?"

He nodded while looking straight ahead as Pastor Mayhew shuffled his papers. I glanced at the man again, and then turned back to Lonnie.

"He seems to be coming down with something," I said. "Last night he looked pale, too."

"I don't know," the boy said quietly. "I rarely see him. I'm always in the teen room during his sermons. We hear a sermon from Pastor Coady on Sunday mornings." And then he laughed softly. "Gee, I guess I don't really even know Pastor Mayhew all that well."

The music stopped abruptly and so did any whispered conversations throughout the room. The pastor cleared his throat, and then he began to speak.

"The family of Myrna Lou Stevic would like to thank you all for taking the time to come and pay your respects. They want to convey their gratitude for all the sympathy and kind and comforting words spoken. They are grieving, as we all are, for a life that has left its earthly home all too soon. For those of us who knew this dear child, even in the slightest way, she was one who touched our lives. For the Lord tells us in Romans, 'For none of us liveth to himself and no man dieth to himself.' We know not why the Lord chose to call her home. We know not what His plan is. But what we do know is that we shall see this child again in a Heavenly setting if we just trust in Jesus Christ our Lord...."

I stopped listening as I looked around the room. I could hear the soft sniffling of Vivian and Grace up ahead. Someone behind me erupted into a coughing fit, and I could hear them rise from their seat and make their way out of the room. Vernon Wagner sat in the row ahead of me, alone...his wife had not accompanied him today. Mr. and Mrs. Gilbert were sitting behind Jake and Susan and Vivian's two boys. Their young daughter, Marjorie, sat next to them, resting her head on her mother's arm. I knew that a couple of rows back was Mr. Tony Schramm, with a blond woman next to him that looked very much like the woman he'd told me was his wife in the picture he had shown me. I did not see Agnes Dade.

Many of the students who had come to the viewing the night before were not there for the funeral. Art Gellert was not in attendance, but I did notice Audrey Sweeney, who sat in a chair in the back of the room. When I'd entered the mortuary, I'd seen her father sitting on one of the sofas in the waiting room, smoking a cigarette, looking bored and impatient. He hadn't joined her to listen to the eulogy. I specifically looked for the Neller boy. He hadn't come to say his goodbyes the previous night, and he wasn't there now. Johnny's neighbor, Jim Weiboldt, wasn't there, either. I felt that Matthew Coady must surely be there somewhere, but I hadn't noticed him.

The pastor spoke for about ten minutes and then ended with a prayer. I was relieved when it was finished. I didn't like funerals. I didn't like to be reminded of certain and impending death; not Gran's, not Uncle Derwood's, and hell, not even my own. It was something I didn't want to think about, and this was forcing me to do just that. It also caused me to ponder the outcome of this case. Whenever I was on a case, the fear of not being able to solve it was always in the back of my mind. I was distinctly aware of my possible lack of success on this one. It scared me.

When it was all over, people rose from their seats and formed a line to say a final farewell to Myrna Lou up near the casket. I didn't see any need in doing that, since I didn't know her. Lonnie got in line, but not before I asked him if he'd like to continue on to the cemetery. I offered him a lift if he wanted to go, and he took me up on it. Derwood and I meandered out to the parking lot to have a cigarette while we waited for him. The air, although chilly, felt good on my face. It was only moments, though, before I put my overcoat on.

****

The Chevy Coupe was the fourth in line in a small procession of cars that followed the hearse to Woodmere Cemetery. Woodmere was designed and created by some prominent men living in Detroit back in 1867 who wanted a rural cemetery to grace the city. Many of the graves contained the remains of the early movers and shakers of Detroit and of Civil War veterans. It was located on West Fort Street in southwest Detroit. The grounds were perfectly manicured. The grass had been freshly cut and was a healthy green. Flowers sporadically rested at the base of headstones.

We walked up the hill to the newly dug grave, which sat there waiting for the arrival of its occupant. Johnny and Jake Delbeck were pallbearers, as well as Lonnie Orwick. I didn't know the other three men who carried Myrna Lou to her resting place.

When we were all assembled around the grave, Pastor Mayhew began to talk of the greeting Myrna Lou was receiving in Heaven, and began to describe her new eternal home. Vivian went from silent tears to heart wrenching sobs. She turned to Johnny, burying her face in his chest, and he held her tightly.

Directly across from me were Tony Schramm and his wife. I studied her as she stared at the inconsolable Vivian, her own eyes growing moist. She was short and a bit pudgy, but her face was as cute as a button, with big and full lips. The woman's hair was a light blond and fell in wisps around her cheeks. She looked up at her husband and he took her hand and held it tight. She gave him a slight smile. The look he returned to her was a look of pure love. What in the world was he doing with Becky Timmons? He was gambling with his life...with his entire future. So intent was I at studying this couple that I'd hardly heard anything the pastor said. The graveside eulogy was over before I knew it.

Derwood and I started to descend the hill. We stopped halfway down and turned back to look at the others. Many were waiting in line to express their sympathy and condolences to Johnny's sister-in-law. Now would come the hard part for Myrna Lou's mother and siblings. They would wake up tomorrow and the day after that, and realize she was really gone and wouldn't be coming back. They would realize that they would never know her beyond the age of seventeen.

The first one to leave the graveside and start walking toward us was Matthew Coady, Lonnie Orwick walking by his side. They were coming to talk to us, and when they were ten feet away, I decided to try something.

"Hey, Skipper," I said.

Coady furrowed his eyebrows and cocked his head to one side. He was confused by my greeting, but didn't question me about it. Instead, when he'd reached us, he offered us an invitation.

"The ladies from the church have prepared a little luncheon. I hope you two will join us back at Christ the Divine."

"Uh, well, thanks for the offer, but I have to get my uncle home," I lied.

The truth was I just didn't want to go. I looked at Derwood and silently begged with my gaze for him to go along with me on this.

"Me wife isn't feelin' too well and I need to look in on her," he said to the youth pastor.

The young man nodded and said, "I'm so sorry to hear that. My own wife came back feeling a bit under the weather. That's why she isn't here today. Please give Mrs. Flanagan our regards. And, in that case, Pastor Mayhew and I can give Lonnie a lift back to Dearborn then." He turned to Lonnie. "You're welcome to come back to the church and have something to eat before returning home."

Lonnie shrugged and said, "Sure, I can do that."

They shook our hands, said their goodbyes, and then continued down the hill and toward their car. I watched as they climbed into a black vehicle.

Others were now descending the grassy hill. I suddenly noticed that I didn't see Mac or Lawrence Brown. They must not have been in the procession to Woodmere. Audrey Sweeny wasn't there either. Her father had probably told her he wouldn't make the drive into Detroit. He probably told her enough was enough and that she was lucky he allowed her to pay her last respects at the funeral home.

I waited for Schramm and his wife to approach. When he did, I repeated my phrase to him.

"Hey there, Skipper," I said.

He didn't seem to know I was talking to him and he continued past me with his arm circling his wife's waist. As he walked by, I called out to him.

"Mr. Schramm! Mind if I have a word?"

He stopped and turned toward me. Derwood and I walked up to him. His wife looked at us questioningly, wondering who we were.

"We'd like to have a word with you, if you don't mind," I said again.

I said nothing after that and glanced at the lady standing next to him. He understood my silent message. Tony Schramm turned to his wife and told her he wouldn't be long, and he suggested she continue on to the car. She did as he asked. When she was out of earshot, he asked how he could help us.

"Nice lookin' lass there," Uncle Derwood commented. "I'm assumin' that's yer wife. Or am I mistaken? Maybe yer wife was the little lass ye were seen with last night?"

Tony Schramm's eyes grew wide while the rest of his face turned to stone. He suddenly looked all around him, making sure no one was within earshot.

"Are you crazy?" he asked, just above a whisper. "Keep your voice down! I don't know what you're talking about!"

Derwood started to laugh. I watched as a fine sweat began to dot the teacher's forehead. He eyed the last of the approaching mourners with nervousness.

"No sense in lying about it, Schramm," I said. "We saw you last night in Dearborn with the Timmons dame. For shame, for shame! I thought you didn't play with the young ones?"

"It wasn't me!" he said in a last ditch effort to clear himself.

"T'was ye, alright. Now how 'bout ye quit with the nonsense? We want ye to tell us if ye ever had the same type of relationship with Myrna Lou, and don't lie 'bout it."

He buried his face in his hands and groaned. When he looked up, he wore a look of surrender.

"No; I may be a cad, but I've never come on to any of the students. I swear that's the truth. I'll break it off with Becky. Just please don't tell my wife!"

"I'm not going to tell your *wife*! What kind of Joe do you think I am? That's *your* business. If you want to throw away the love that your wife obviously has for you, you'd be a fool, but it's still up to you. What *is* my business is finding out who killed the girl. And if I find it was you, I won't rest until you're locked up and the key is thrown away."

"Oh God, how could you think I killed her? *Why* would I want to do that? There was nothing between us, I swear!"

"You'd better hope and pray I don't find out differently," I said.

"I believe yer wife is gettin' a bit antsy," Derwood said.

We followed his gaze and saw Mrs. Schramm step out of the car and look over the top of it toward us. The three of us strolled down the hill, Derwood and I walking the general science teacher to where she waited.

"What is it, honey?" she asked when we reached her.

"Nothing. These gentlemen are investigating Myrna Lou's death," he said. "They just had a couple of questions, but I really can't help them."

"Oh," she said softly.

My uncle smiled at the woman and then suddenly asked, "Do ye own a boat, Mrs. Schramm?"

She was taken by surprise and said, "No, we don't. Is that important to the case?"

"No, not really," he said.

We said our goodbyes, but not before my uncle spied an empty box on the back seat of the Schramm's car. He asked what they were going to do with it and when they answered nothing, that it was from a new radio that had been recently purchased for Mrs. Schramm's mother, Derwood asked if he could have it. We then headed for the Chevy, leaving Johnny, Grace, Vivian, and the kids still at the gravesite.

We were half way home when I questioned my uncle concerning the box he'd tossed in the back seat.

"I'm goin' to cut it down and fill it with dirt from out back in the alley," he said. "That kitten needs a place to do his business." He suddenly leaned forward, opening the glove compartment. "Got any mints or chewin' gum?"

He didn't find either, but he pulled out my German Luger. He held it up and asked me how I'd gotten it, and I told him how some months ago I'd purchased it at the hardware store across from my office on Woodward Avenue. I told him about how the storeowner was selling it for his wife's nephew who had returned from the war with it. He started to replace it, but I stopped him. I thought of last night when I was afraid someone was trying to break into the house—I didn't want to be in that position again. The Luger always needed to be close by, just in case. I took it from him and slipped it into my overcoat pocket.

"Well," he said. "What's on the schedule for the rest of the day?"

"How about nothing? Let's go home and see what's on the radio. Let's just take the rest of the day off."

"Sounds good to me, lad."

# Chapter Thirty

Thursday was a repeat of Wednesday as far as the weather was concerned…overcast, chilly, and gloomy. I awoke at twenty minutes after nine o'clock and didn't get fully dressed until twelve thirty. I only did so then because Gran asked me to run to the store for a couple of items. She wanted to make a beef stew for dinner and needed onions and carrots. When I pulled up in the driveway, returning from the market, Albie was crossing his lawn and heading my way.

"I know who the cat belongs to," he said.

My heart did a little dive inside of my chest. I was secretly hoping he wouldn't find its owner, so Gran could keep it. Actually, I was growing fond of the little creature myself.

"Okay, who then?"

"Bucky Steers. He's in my class. He lives around the block and a few houses down."

"Is he the tall kid with the red hair and freckles?" I asked.

"Yep," Albie nodded.

"Well, hang on then and you can take the cat back to him," I said, and started to move toward the house.

"Nuh uh. Not me!" Albie replied.

I turned back to him and rolled my eyes. "Oh, I suppose I have to pay you to do that, right?" I sighed loudly.

"Mr. Flanagan, you don't have enough money to pay me for that one. I'm not havin' that on *my* head," he said. He could see the confusion on my face and began to explain. "Bucky's cat had a litter some weeks back. She gave birth to six of 'em. A couple of nights ago, Bucky's pa tossed 'em out of the house…not their cat, but the kittens. He said he couldn't afford to feed more than one animal, and if they came back, he was gonna have to drown 'em. And Mr. Steers is the kinda guy who only says somethin' once and he means what he says. So, if I was you, I'd keep the kitten and I wouldn't let it wander around outside. You know, just in case it wants to go see its ma."

Albie then asked if he could come in the house to see the animal and I gave him my consent. He cupped his mouth with the palms of his hands and yelled toward his own home.

"Bobby! Bobby! Get on out here! We can go visit the cat!"

****

The boys had left about ten minutes earlier. We all got a kick out of seeing Bobby roll around on the living room floor in a fit of laughter while the kitten playfully nipped at his ears. Gran told the boys she wanted to call the pet "Blackie," but Albie objected to that. He scrunched up his face and rubbed his chin as if deep in thought. He then turned to my uncle, and being fascinated with his brogue, asked him what a detective was called in 'Irish.' When my uncle told him, he clapped his hands together and cried out.

"That's it! Mr. Flanagan investigated the noise that night and found this little guy, so I think you should name him *Shamus*!"

As Gran stood at the kitchen sink and peeled the potatoes for the stew with a curious Shamus circling her ankles, I went to the phone and dialed the Detroit Police Department, asking for Mac. Before a full minute had passed, I heard his voice speak into the other end.

"Hey, Mac, I didn't notice you at Woodmere yesterday," I said.

"Nah, we didn't go. Instead we paid a visit to the neighbor, Wieboldt. He's the only one we hadn't been able to get hold of. We finally caught up with him at his place of work, which is First National Bank down on Michigan Avenue there in Dearborn. He's one of two assistant managers. We wanted to know his whereabouts on that Monday around four o'clock. He says he was at work until about four fifteen, and then he left early to stop by a confectioners to get his wife some chocolate. Seems she called him around noon telling him she had a craving. He usually gets off work at five, but the manager told him he could leave a bit early. The manager confirmed this, but just to be sure, we went to where he bought the candy. It's a small shop over in Lincoln Park on Fort Street. The woman who owns it and Wieboldt's mother are longtime friends, so he travels the distance to give her the business. She says he was there, alright. He stayed awhile and they caught each other up on what's been happening. She says he left about twenty minutes after five with a whole pound of chocolate. She knows this because she closes down for the day at 5:30."

I told him of my little experiment of first calling Pastor Coady 'Skipper,' and then repeating the greeting to Tony Schramm.

"Neither of them seemed to even flinch, though. I honestly don't think they recognized the name, Mac."

"And Wieboldt can't be the Skipper, either, because of his alibi."

"My gut tells me that when we find out who the Skipper is, we'll have our murderer," I said.

"And I think what your gut is telling you is right."

"Yeah, but the Skipper could be anyone. It's like finding a needle in a haystack."

After disconnecting with Mac, I dialed the operator. I needed the number to Christ the Divine Lutheran Church. Even though I now highly doubted Matthew Coady was the Skipper, he still might know what had upset Myrna Lou that last night she'd attended the service. Either he had overlooked her visit to him, or he was keeping the information to himself for some reason. While I had her on the phone, I had the operator give me the number to Patti Ann's Boutique, also.

I dialed the church first. After letting it ring ten times without being answered on the other end, I hung up. I had more success with my next call. Lucy, her assistant and seamstress, answered and handed the phone to the owner when I asked for Patti Ann. She seemed surprised and pleased to find it was me on the line. We talked of little incidentals for the first five minutes, which included a lot of laughter. I finally asked her when she could get away. We could do lunch, we could have dinner, we could go dancing; I didn't care, I just wanted to see this woman. She told me she always took inventory on the first Sunday of each month, and this coming Sunday would be the second day of May. She arrived early and was usually done by two in the afternoon. Patti Ann asked how I felt about a late lunch, and I told her that would suit me just fine. We disconnected after agreeing I would pick her up at the boutique at two the following Sunday. Even though I felt the case was far from being solved, I needed a break. I'd been working steadily on it, but I needed some 'me' time, and I wanted to spend that time with Patti Ann.

I replaced the receiver but kept my hand on it, my smile stretching far and wide. When I looked up, Gran was staring at me in an odd way.

"What?" I asked.

"Oh, nothing," she said. "You just look kind of funny is all, dear."

We sat down to dinner at 5:30. Aunt Pearl was feeling much better today. No one spoke of the cause of her "mysterious" illness, not even her. I told my uncle about my conversation with Mac, and how it didn't appear that Jim Wieboldt should be on our suspect list any longer due to a cast iron alibi. I also voiced my doubt that either Matthew Coady or Tony Schramm was involved. I was almost sure it was the Skipper who had lured Myrna Lou away from the Delbeck's front steps, and neither of them were that man.

"But something was bothering the girl and I think the youth pastor knows what that is," I said. "Maybe Myrna Lou told him of her feelings for this guy at some point. Maybe she confided in him or asked for his advice. Maybe Matt Coady knows the identity of Myrna Lou's killer without even realizing it."

"Well, sure," Gran interjected. "It's like I said before; when I was a young girl we always went to the assistant pastor with troubles. He was young and we felt we could trust him. Our senior pastor was too scary!" She shuddered and then placed a spoonful of beef and gravy in her mouth.

Derwood nodded at Gran. "I agree with Ruby there. Me thinks Myrna Lou went to him that evenin', and maybe the lad doesn't see the connection. He should be next on our list to visit."

We all looked at Pearl as she tossed her spoon on the kitchen table, causing it to bounce and fall to the tiled floor.

"Derwood, I've been patient," she whined, "but enough is enough! I want to go home! I want to sleep in my own bed and go to my own church on Sunday!"

Before my uncle could respond, Gran butted in.

"I think you're being unfair, Pearl. There's a murderer out there and that little girl deserves justice." She shrugged. "If Sam can't get the job done, then Derwood has to step in and help him."

I wasn't sure I liked her assumption that I didn't have the ability to be successful in solving this case. I frowned, but didn't say a word. Derwood, on the other hand, chuckled softly. He turned to his wife, who was sitting beside him, and put his arm around her, drawing her to him. He kissed her cheek.

"Yer right. If the case is to be solved at all, me thinks I need to be solvin' it quickly." And then he chuckled again while he gave me a sly little wink.

# Chapter Thirty-One

Friday morning the sun was streaming brightly into the living room. I nearly bounced off the couch with a limitless amount of energy and enthusiasm. When I reached the kitchen, I saw that the clock read ten minutes to seven. It was the last day of April and in two days' time, I would be sitting with a beautiful woman having a bite to eat. I couldn't wait to see Patti Ann!

Using the last of the coffee, I put a pot on the stove to perk while I took a shower. Thank goodness tomorrow was May the first and we would get our renewal of rationing stamps. Exiting the bathroom, I made my way toward the front of the house to get the morning paper off the porch. Even though it was a sunny day, the breeze that blew outside was on the verge of being downright cold. I snagged the Detroit News and quickly stepped back inside. I thought I could hear my uncle stirring inside my bedroom, so I made my way back to the kitchen, threw the paper on the table, and began to make breakfast. Whistling softly, I broke several eggs into a large bowl. For the ladies, my uncle, and myself, I was going to make ham and cheese omelets, a rare thing to have in the Flanagan household. There was no special occasion—I was just feeling exceptionally good. As I cut the last of the ham off the bone and chopped it into bite sized pieces, Derwood entered the kitchen, grabbed a cup, and poured himself some coffee.

"Whatcha makin' there, lad? Is there anythin' I can do to help ya?"

"Omelets," I answered. "How about peeling some potatoes? Want some fried potatoes with it?"

My uncle scratched at his nearly bald head and sighed. "No," he said. "I wasn't serious 'bout helpin' ya out, so let's skip the taters."

I laughed as he disappeared behind the bathroom door, leaving his full cup on the counter. I heard him turn the lock and then I heard water running in the tub. I continued to whistle my upbeat tune. When the omelets were just about ready to put on the plates, I went to Gran's room and softly knocked on the door.

"Breakfast is ready," I called, and then reentered the kitchen to toast some bread.

My Aunt Pearl was the first to arrive in the kitchen. She entered and then crossed the room to look out the window, pulling the curtains to the side.

"What a beautiful day!" she said, and then turned to me. "How nice of you, Sam, to fix us breakfast."

What was this? I didn't dare show the frown of confusion I was feeling inside, not wanting to jinx the moment. This was the nicest, the most cordial, my aunt had treated me since arriving on Easter afternoon. Swallowing the smart aleck remark I tasted on the tip of my tongue, I smiled at her instead.

\*\*\*\*

By 10:00, I had filled the kitchen sink full of hot, soapy water and dropped the dirty dishes in. Derwood was going to take the ladies to Ben Franklin, the five and dime. Before they left, Gran kissed me on the cheek and, once again, thanked me for the omelet.

As soon as they left, I resumed my whistling. I felt a little guilty for loving life so much on this Friday in April. I still hadn't solved the case of Myrna Lou's murder, and the only place I had left to go was to the youth pastor at the church she'd been attending for the past four months. If I didn't get any answers there, where was I going to go? Where would I get the next tip leading me in the right direction? I didn't know, but I didn't let it bother me. There were times when working a case when I felt like

I was getting nowhere and it was good to just stop thinking, to back away from it to get a larger, clearer view. At the moment, my mind and sight was on the boutique owner. I'd try to arrange a meeting with Matthew Coady for either today or tomorrow, spend Sunday with the woman I was attracted to and wanted desperately to get to know, and then return full force to the case on Monday. Taking a small break had worked in the past, and I was hoping and praying it would work again.

I was rinsing the last plate when the phone on the wall by the back door rang. Drying my hands, I went to it.

"Hello?"

"Where's your grandmother? Put her on."

"Well, good morning, Helen. And how are you today?" I said sweetly, exaggerating my smile. Nothing was going to ruin this mood I was in, not even Helen's abruptness.

She grunted and then asked for Gran again.

"She isn't here. They went to the five and dime."

"For what?" she asked in a demanding tone.

"Oh, I don't know," I said casually. "Maybe just to browse. She didn't tell me."

"Well, have her call me when she gets in. St. Peter's is having bingo tonight and I don't feel like staying ta home." She hesitated and then said, "Pearl can come, too, if she wants."

With the promise that I would have my grandmother return her call, we hung up. Since I was by the phone anyway, I thought this would be a good time to ring the church. I dialed the number that was written on a paper that now sat on the countertop. After eight rings, I hung up. It was only 10:20. I would call back in an hour or so.

Since I had the house to myself and nothing to do with my time, I decided to clean up. I took some bleach and a pail and headed for the bathroom. Opening the door, I saw Shamus the cat standing on the toilet rim with his head bent forward, lapping up the cold water. I gently lifted him off the seat and set him outside the room. Not wanting him to get curious about the bleach or to be overcome by its fumes, I shut the door behind me and got to work.

It took me no time at all to scour the tub, toilet, and sink. I then got to work scrubbing the beige linoleum floor. After that, I removed the soiled towels and put up a fresh set. Since the flooring was beige and the tub, toilet, and sink were white, Gran had just about every color of towel there was. I put up the dark green set today. Derwood had placed the kitten's box in the corner of the room, so I cleaned that out, too.

The living room was my next target. The tables gleamed after I'd rubbed them with lemon oil, and the floor was spotless after I ran the sweeper over the throw rugs. The dining room needed little attention, so I quickly straightened it. I left my own bedroom alone for now. After all, Uncle Derwood had personal items lying in there and I didn't want to disturb them.

It was now 12:45 and I went to the wall phone again. I redialed the number I'd tried over two hours ago. This time, Pastor Bertram Mayhew picked up on the third ring.

"Christ the Divine Lutheran Church; this is Pastor Mayhew speaking," he said in his deep and melodious voice.

"Hello, Pastor, this is Sam Flanagan."

He was silent on his end of the phone. I could picture him frowning, trying to figure out who I was. I continued.

"Johnny Delbeck's friend? The man looking into the Stevic case," I further explained.

As if a light had been turned on, he said, "Oh, oh yes, Mr. Flanagan. You wouldn't happen to be calling in response to the pamphlet I gave you, would you? Can I help you with any questions you might have?"

"Uh, actually, no sir."

"Ahhh," he said, sounding disappointed. "Let me just remind you, son, there will come a day when the Lord's patience will run out. Don't take too long making your decision."

I rolled my eyes and said, "Pastor, I appreciate your concern about the state of my soul, but believe me, the Lord and I have an agreement. There's nothing for you to worry about."

"It's not an agreement He wants with you, Mr. Flanagan; it's a relationship."

"Well," I said, "we have that, too."

There was no immediate response from him, so I forged ahead with my reason for calling.

"I'm wondering if Pastor Coady is there. I'd like to drive into Dearborn to talk to him if he is."

"No, no he isn't here at the moment. Is there something I can help you with?"

"I don't think so. The last Sunday night that Myrna Lou attended church, I was told she went into Pastor Coady's office after the service. Then, when she arrived home with her aunt and uncle, she announced she wouldn't be going on the youth outing. Something upset her, and I think she may have discussed whatever it was with Matthew. I'd like to find out what their conversation in the office was about. Do you have any idea when he'll be at the church? Or maybe you could give me his home address."

He hesitated before saying, "I can't think of anything that would've upset the poor girl."

"Well, I believe Pastor Coady might know what it was. When would be a good time to come and speak to him?"

"I can assure you, he said nothing to me about counseling the girl. He didn't mention a visit from her at all."

"I'd feel a lot better if I covered this base with him. He may not even realize that what she told him might lead us to her killer. Surely, you can understand that. Pastor, is there a good time to catch him at the church?" I asked yet again.

Was this man deliberately trying to keep me away from his youth pastor? I wasn't sure what was going on. He didn't answer right away, and I was wondering if he was looking at an appointment book or a schedule of some kind. I gave him a few more seconds to respond. When he didn't, I asked the question yet again.

"He should be here this evening. Usually, Matthew spends Friday evenings preparing for his Sunday teachings. He should be here sometime after six, and I've known him to work until nine or ten o'clock. Should I have him call you, Mr. Flanagan?"

"I can just swing by the church later. No need for him to call."

We rang off after saying our goodbyes and I scooped up the kitten, which had been rubbing against my ankles, and went into the living room. I sat in the chair, looking out the window as the trees across the street bent with the force of the wind. I petted the animal and tried to think of nothing. I laid my head against the back cushion and closed my eyes. Shamus curled into a ball on my lap, and we both fell asleep.

****

"But that's gambling, Ruby! You know that!" my aunt whined.

"It benefits the church, Pearl. We'll be doin' work for the Lord," Gran said, trying to justify going to bingo on Friday evening.

"Yes, but it's the *Catholic* church," Pearl protested, with distaste on her lips.

"Now, now; what's wrong with the Catholic church, girl? Remember, me own mother and father, God rest their souls, raised me to be a Catholic before ye converted me all those years ago," Uncle Derwood chimed in.

"That's true," Gran said. "Besides, what difference does it make what church it is? There's still only one Lord and He's the head of all of 'em."

My aunt wrung her hands together and her face wore the anxiety of indecision.

"Oh, I don't know. What should I do, Derwood?"

"Go if ye want. If ye win any money, just donate it back to the church. That way, ye won't be gamblin' at all."

"Yes, Pearl; do that!" Gran said with enthusiasm in hopes of her sister agreeing to the prospect of a night out.

****

Gran and Aunt Pearl climbed into Helen's car at half past four, taking with them a large sack filled with sandwiches, crackers, and apples. I watched out the picture window until the vehicle disappeared out of sight down St. Aubin, and then I turned to my uncle. "What should we fix for dinner?"

"Nothin'," he responded. "Let's head out now and stop and get us a sandwich from Joe's place. We can then make our way to talk to the lad at the church."

It sounded good to me. I didn't feel like messing up the kitchen, anyway. We grabbed our overcoats and hats and headed out the back way, locking up behind us.

\*\*\*\*

It wasn't very busy for a Friday evening at the Dearborn White Castle, and that surprised me. When we pulled into the lot, there were three other cars parked there. One, undoubtedly, was Joe's. We entered and found the owner ringing up a man at the cash register who had come in to buy a sack full of burgers and fries and carry them home with him. Down the counter, halfway into the restaurant, sat a young man, his wife, and their son, who looked to be about seven years of age.

As we took our own seats, Ernie emerged from the restroom carrying a pail and mop. He'd evidently just finished cleaning the facility. He caught sight of me and waved, wearing a huge smile. I nodded, smiling also. We put in our order for cheeseburgers and fries. Uncle Derwood wanted a root beer with his and I chose an orange soda. Joe wanted an update on the case, but there was nothing of importance to tell him. I told him about the funeral and that I was still working to find who the murderer was.

When we began to eat, the owner busied himself with cleaning the shelves under the counter on his side. We ate in silence, watching him remove coloring books, crayons, comic books, and a game of checkers. He set the items on the countertop behind him right next to his grill, and got to work cleaning with a hot, soapy rag.

By the time we pushed our plates away it was only 5:33. I pulled out my Lucky Strikes and offered my uncle one. We smoked as Joe finished up, taking his pail into the back room, then watched as he returned and started to replace the things that would keep a child's interest. He held the game of checkers in his hand, ready to put it back underneath the counter, when he looked up at Derwood.

"Hey, old timer," he said. "Care for a game of checkers?"

My uncle moved his root beer off to the side, making room for the board and said, "Sure, but me bets I beat ya."

I watched as they played three games, my uncle winning the first two, and Joe taking the third. Tapping Derwood on the arm, I suggested it was time for us to head on out. It was almost twenty minutes after six.

"Aww, and I was just going to up the stakes by suggesting we put a quarter on the next game," Joe complained.

My uncle eyed the board and then turned to me, saying nothing. I sighed and told him to go ahead. Joe became twenty-five cents richer when the game was over.

"Double or nothin'," Joe said.

I watched as they each laid two quarters on the counter. The sun was starting to fade into the west and I was anxious to get to the church. It was a few minutes after seven o'clock. The young family who'd been eating there earlier was long gone. No one else had entered the eating establishment. Derwood and Joe were thoroughly enjoying themselves and I hated to break up their fun, but I had a job to do, so I rose from my seat and made a suggestion.

"Why don't you two go ahead and play while I go talk to Pastor Coady? I shouldn't be long. I'll tell you what was said when I swing back here to pick you up."

"Sounds good to me, lad," Derwood said as he studied the board, trying to figure out his next move.

I left Joe's White Castle in Dearborn without either one of them really noticing, and headed out to the Chevy.

Five minutes later, I pulled into the parking lot at Christ the Divine Lutheran Church. Only one other auto was sitting in the lot, a dark blue 1940 Ford coupe. I was relieved to see that Pastor Coady obviously was there.

The church was quiet inside. Lights were on in the chapel, but I didn't see anyone as I passed and headed down the hall to the youth pastor's office. The door was open a few inches and even before I knocked, I could see Matthew sitting at his desk, head bent over a book. He looked up when I tapped softly.

"Yes?" he called out while he stood and looked my way.

I shoved the door open wider and removed my hat. "Pastor Coady?"

He smiled and then came around to greet me. "Ah, Mr. Flanagan."

I told him I needed to talk to him and he showed me to one of the chairs facing his desk, and then moved around to sit in his own.

He was dressed in denim pants tonight and a dark blue v-neck sweater, with a tan shirt which was open at the neck underneath. His hair on top was a bit messy and looked as though he'd been running his fingers through it as he read from his Bible. Removing his glasses and laying them on the desk in front of him, he sat back in his seat, intertwining his fingers together, waiting for me to explain the reason for my visit. I got right to the point.

"Pastor, I've told you before that we believe Myrna Lou was upset about something after the last service she'd attended. She went home with her aunt and uncle that night, but told them she didn't want to go to Camp Arcadia the following week with the other youths. I've learned since then that immediately following the service that night, the girl came in here to talk to you. Someone saw her enter this office. I'd like to know what that conversation was all about. No matter how trivial it may have seemed to you, she may have said something that could point me in the right direction on this case. Can you tell me what she was upset about that night? Did she say anything to indicate that she *was* upset?"

He shook his head slowly and shrugged his shoulders. "I have no idea what it would've been. Whoever told you she came to see me was mistaken. I don't recall her being here in the office that night, Mr. Flanagan."

I looked down at the fedora I was holding in my hands and mindlessly twirled it. Marjorie had been mistaken when she said she saw Myrna Lou going into the boutique with who she thought was the girls' grandmother—could she be wrong again? Frustration was building inside of me. The young girl told me she'd seen Myrna Lou enter the youth pastor's office. I believed her. She didn't seem to say it with doubt in her voice. Could Myrna Lou have walked in, but caught others in the room wanting to see Matthew Coady? Could there have been a long line to speak to the young man, and in seeing this, she decided not to wait? I voiced that possibility.

"No, I don't recall that *anyone* had come back to talk to me. It's strange, isn't it? Maybe she changed her mind and turned around before reaching the office," he suggested.

I had to admit, that could be a possibility. Now what? Where was I to go in this investigation from here? I'd just hit a huge brick wall in this case.

We both looked up at the door to his office when a soft knock sounded on it. There stood the elderly woman whom I'd heard playing the organ when I'd paid a couple of other visits to the church. I hadn't known she was there; I hadn't seen her when passing the chapel. She looked embarrassed at her interruption.

"Oh, excuse me, Pastor. I just wanted to let you know I'll be leaving now."

The young man rose from his seat. "Done playing for the night? Let me walk you out, Mrs. Rousch." Over his shoulder, he said to me, "I'll be right back."

I nodded, even though he didn't see me. My eyebrows were furrowed and my mind was in a whirl. What was I missing? What couldn't I see? Maybe I would never find the answers to all my questions. Maybe this was going to be one case I couldn't solve.

I sighed with anger and frustration and stood to stretch, tossing my hat back onto the chair. Removing my overcoat, I tossed that over the empty chair that faced Duane Whelan's desk. Noticing the university pictures of Matthew Coady which hung on the wall, I moved forward to get a better look. He really didn't look that much different in the photos than he did now. Of course, these had to be taken within the last five years, I figured. Matthew looked happy, standing with his buddies from school. I eyed the one of him in his football uniform, wondering what position he played. He was standing with two other young fellows and the caption underneath told their names. When I read Matthew Coady's name, my blood ran cold. I was badly shaken. Suddenly, things fell into place. Rick Neller had been mistaken. Myrna Lou hadn't said "the Skipper" was more of a man than he'd ever be…she'd said "the Biffer" was more of a man! There it was in black and white: Matthew 'the Biffer' Coady. I felt my blood pressure rise as I anxiously waited for him to return to his office.

Judith White

# Chapter Thirty-Two

Now, you see, this was the type of stuff which got my dander up—it was the kind of thing that made me grumpy. I'd been working for days trying to find answers, trying to put the pieces of this puzzle together. Coming to this young punk for help, I thought I could trust him—I thought he'd be a straight shooter. I was wrong! He'd been holding out, hiding things, and I didn't like that one bit.

Suddenly, everything about Matthew Coady left a bad taste in my mouth. Being a man of God, he was no better than anyone else. What was he doing here anyway? Why wasn't he in military uniform, serving God *and* country? Matthew Coady had to have been somewhere in his early to mid-twenties—the right age for being shipped overseas to enter the fighting. Instead, he was leading a secure life of teaching the community's youth about God, while preying on the young females in his class. If he'd been spending his time as he should've been, maybe Myrna Lou would still be breathing at this very moment. I wanted to knock him around and loosen a few of his teeth—and in the house of the Lord, no less.

He reentered the room, eyes down, head shaking from side to side, a smile formed at the corners of his mouth.

"Mrs. Rousch; what a beautiful soul," he said. "She lost her husband a few months ago and likes to spend time playing the organ here. It helps to lift her spirit."

He looked up and stopped, the corners of his mouth starting to drop when he saw me standing behind his chair. Maybe he noticed something in my eyes that put him on guard, or took in the scowl on my face; or maybe, just maybe, he could feel the fury running through my veins. Whatever he saw, he was now unsure of how to proceed with me.

"So, you're the Biffer, huh?" I said, calmly.

His smile returned and grew wider as his gaze drifted to the photos hanging on the wall just beyond and above my right shoulder. He started to laugh and nod his head.

"That's right," he said with enthusiasm. "But no one's called me that for a few years now, Mr. Flanagan."

"Oh, I don't think that's the case, now is it?"

His eyes drew together in a look of confusion. He didn't know where I was going with this.

"Pardon me?"

"Well, you know, I figure Myrna Lou called you that as a term of endearment. You were in love with her, weren't you? Or, at least, you led her to believe you were."

His face reddened and he looked shocked as his eyes grew wide. "Where on earth did you get an idea like that? That just isn't true!"

I moved to the chair I'd been sitting in, bent down and picked up my hat, and sat down once again.

"Sit down, Matthew. We need to discuss some things."

He headed toward his chair, and by the time he'd reached it, I noticed the fine layer of sweat dotting his forehead and the space between his nose and upper lip. This boy was getting nervous, and that was a good sign. I figured I'd have his confession within minutes.

"Now, you tell me what Myrna Lou was upset about the last night she set foot in this church. I want some answers!" I demanded.

"I don't know what you're talking about! I didn't see her after our service!" he yelled.

He was lying, of course. His face gave him away. I could see it in his eyes and hear it in his voice.

Okay, that was it! I was through with this pull and tug game. I stared at him, never moving my eyes from his face, and rather enjoyed watching him squirm. Then I reached for the black telephone that sat on top of his desk. Lifting the receiver, I began dialing.

"What are you doing? Who are you calling?" he asked in a panic.

"Someone who can get the truth out of you," I answered him. "I'm sure Detective McPherson from the homicide division will have a more successful conversation with you."

As I heard a second ring start to sound in my ear, Matthew Coady jumped up and reached across the desk, yanking the receiver from my hand. He slammed it down on the base of the instrument, severing my connection.

"No, wait!" he yelled. He looked up at me, and fatigue and resignation seemed to run through his whole body. He sighed loudly and slumped back down in his chair. "Okay, okay," he said, weakly. "I *did* see her after the service."

The young man paused, but I didn't say a word. I just waited until he was ready to continue. His bottom lip quivered, and I feared he might break down into tears.

"She came in here because she was upset that I wasn't going to go on the youth outing. I had announced to the class that night that I would not be accompanying them because Sheila was coming back from Arizona and I wanted to be here when she arrived home." Matthew's voice was faint, and I had to strain to make out every word he was saying. "She told me if I wasn't going, she didn't want to go, either."

"You'd told her you were falling in love with her, didn't you?"

I felt heat from anger run through my body. The desire to knock his teeth out returned, but instead, I waited for his response.

"No!" he shouted. "It wasn't like that at all!" The youth pastor ran the palm of his hand over his face. He glanced at me and then turned his face away, saying nothing. Finally, he gained the strength to continue. "It wasn't that way," he said in a much calmer voice, while staring down at his desk. "When Myrna Lou first came here, I could tell she was a troubled girl. I tried to draw her out. I introduced her to the other kids and hoped she'd feel like she belonged. Well, I could see right away that the others were willing to accept her, but it was Myrna Lou, herself, who was being difficult. I mean, she'd try to play it up...you know, present herself as someone she wasn't with the other girls. She tried to act like she was a bit better than them. I'm not stupid, you know? It was evident that she felt inferior to them. She actually envied them; maybe even resented them. I tried to talk to her about it. A few times—I don't know, maybe four or five times—after youth group activities, she'd stay behind and we would talk. She told me about her father's death from some illness when she was five or six. It really affected her. The girl told me about her stepfather and what a jerk he was toward her—things like that."

He stopped talking and I patiently waited for him to go on with his story. When he didn't, I slapped the top of his desk with my opened palm and he jumped.

"Come on, Coady! What's the rest of it?" I snapped.

"The last time she stayed behind was after we'd handed out flyers in the community. The day was nice and sunny, so we took a ride over to Belle Isle. My wife was in Arizona. It wasn't like I had to be home for anything. We sat on one of the benches in the park and I tried to boost her confidence. Mr. Flanagan, Myrna Lou needed someone to love her. She felt abandoned by her father, even though it wasn't the man's fault. For God's sake, he became ill and died! She felt rejected by her mother's choice in a second husband. She just felt alone and displaced. I stupidly told her that if I weren't married, she would be just the type of gal I'd want in a wife."

He hung his head in shame and became quiet. What wasn't I getting here? There had to be more to the story. I still was banking on the fact that Matthew Coady had killed the girl. But I couldn't see how it went from encouraging the girl to rage and wanting to get rid of her. There *had* to be *more*. Everything he was telling me about the young woman's character seemed to fit with what I'd learned from others so far. We all agreed that she was needing affection in her life, but one didn't feel enough anger at that to want to crack her skull open with a rock! What if she voiced to Matthew Coady that she was falling in love with him? What if she threatened to tell his wife? But that didn't make sense. The young man had done nothing, as far as I could see, to feel that his marriage would be in danger from such information had his wife found out. At least, he hadn't admitted to any wrong doing *yet*. Certainly he could explain it all to his wife if this had come to light. Certainly that sort of thing might be common among youth pastors, especially when they were as young as Matthew Coady. Surely there was always the case or two where a young girl would become smitten with someone who was instructing her. It happened all the time.

"What else?" I said, breaking our silence. "There's got to be more. You can't tell me that you withheld all of this because it was so damning. Tell me the rest."

He turned his head, looking off to the side. I got the impression he didn't want to look me straight in the eye. He was having a difficult time getting out what he had to say.

"She kissed me," he said, barely above a whisper.

"What?"

"She kissed me. When I told her that stuff about wanting her for my wife, she kissed me."

His lip was quivering again and his eyes began to water. I drew my eyebrows together in a frown. I hated to admit it, but I still wasn't seeing the whole picture. I mean—so what? Okay, so she kissed him. What was the big deal here? This guy actually got angry enough about that to want to murder her over it? It didn't make any sense.

"Okay, so she kissed you. It wasn't the end of the world," I said.

He slammed his fist down on the top of the desk and shouted, "I didn't *stop* her! Don't you see? I *let* her do it; I *didn't* pull away!

I'd been alone for weeks. My wife was across the country and we hadn't been married all that long. Do you know what that's like? To have needs, and your wife is more than two thousand miles away? I didn't stop her. It felt good, Mr. Flanagan! I just let it happen—how would that look to my wife and Bertram Mayhew and the whole congregation if it ever got out? None of them would ever trust me again! And how does it look to Jesus? And how about the other kids? Oh God!"

He covered his face with his hands and moaned. I stood and leaned toward him, placing the palms of my hands on his desk.

"So you led her to believe you were falling for her, and then you killed her to keep your screw up a secret! You make me sick, Coady! You're playing adult when you're just an immature jerk! Who do you think you are, playing with people's lives like that?"

I knew what it was like to have the woman you love a world apart from where you were. I knew what it was like to have needs and desires; but I also knew you didn't toy with the emotions of others—especially not someone as young and vulnerable and needy as Myna Lou had been.

He looked up. "No, no! It wasn't like that! When she came in here that night she told me she wasn't going to camp if I wasn't going. She told me she thought we had a future together; that we could deal with anything. She thought I could get a divorce and we could go away together and start all over. Truly, I was shocked. I explained to her how I loved my wife. I explained the best I could that she and I could never be, and I was sorry about the kiss. I knew she was upset and angry, but she never made any threats. Even if she *had*, I wouldn't have *killed* her over it. You've got to believe me! I didn't kill her!"

Suddenly, his eyes darted to the left over my right shoulder. He hurriedly wiped the tears from his eyes and turned to me with a panicked look on his face.

"Shh! Please, Mr. Flanagan, don't say another word. I beg of you. Please," he pleaded in a whisper.

His eyes returned to the wall behind me and I followed his gaze. The light was now on in Pastor Mayhew's office. When I'd arrived, the door was open a few inches, but it had been dark and vacant. Now light streamed from within and I heard movement. Within seconds, the senior pastor filled the doorway with his presence. He looked pale, and his face wore a frightened look. Even from where I stood, I could see he was broken out in a sweat. Matthew slowly rose from where he was sitting and just stared at the man, as I was doing. Finally, the older gentleman spoke.

"Matthew," he said, his voice shaky. "I just received a call at the house." He then turned to me. "Thank God you're here, Mr. Flanagan. Lonnie Orwick called me in quite an agitated state. He's out on Belle Isle and wants me to come to him to hear his confession. He says it was he who killed Myrna Lou Stevic!"

Judith White

# Chapter Thirty-Three

At the mention of Lonnie's name, a jolt of electricity went through me. *Lonnie Orwick? He killed Myrna Lou?* I turned to look at Matthew Coady and could see he was just as confused as I was. I was feeling so much at this announcement, and I needed a bit of time to sort it all out, but knew there was no time. I was stunned, to say the least. Bertram Mayhew turned to me.

"Will you make the drive with me?" he asked.

I silently nodded as Matthew spoke up. "I'm coming, too, Bertram."

"No, Matthew. Stay here. We don't want to scare the boy off."

"Don't be silly. I've had him in class here for more than a year. I've talked to him and had a certain kind of relationship with him. Why would my presence scare him off?"

"I don't know...I just thought...well, isn't it better if you stay behind in case he changes his mind and calls again?" asked the senior pastor.

"No. Bertram, I'm coming along."

"I really think it's best if you stay here in case he calls," the pastor said again, but Matthew ignored him.

The youth pastor moved to get his coat from the back of his chair. Pastor Mayhew lifted my overcoat off the back of the chair at Duane Whelan's desk, and was about to hand it to me when he stopped and turned toward his office.

"Let me just turn out the light in here," he said.

****

We were crossing the parking lot to the black car I'd seen at Woodmere Cemetery. It belonged to Bertram Mayhew. The only other auto visible in the lot was my own. Matthew climbed into the passenger seat up front while I eased into the back. Once inside, I asked Matthew where his car was.

"Sheila dropped me off tonight. She's going to pick me up later. Gee, I probably should've called her before we left," he said, and then added, "I can't *believe* Lonnie did this!"

The blue car I'd seen earlier in the lot must've belonged to Mrs. Rousch, the elderly woman who'd been playing the organ earlier tonight. I was uneasy. Something wasn't right and I couldn't put my finger on it. *Lonnie Orwick?* I couldn't believe he'd done this, either. I knew the boy had the strength to commit this crime, but I didn't believe he had the mentality for it—not that I'd seen, anyway. Something was definitely off. I leaned a bit forward and tapped Matthew on the shoulder.

"What's the color of your car?" I asked him.

"Huh?"

"The color of your car—what is it?"

He turned slightly, aiming his words over his shoulder. "Brown, why?"

I sat back without answering him. His car was brown. Suddenly, I felt trapped. I was in a car with Bertram Mayhew and Matthew Coady, who was a murderer. Was Pastor Mayhew in cahoots with him? As we headed toward Belle Isle, I thought of the very strong possibility that Lonnie Orwick wouldn't be there to meet us.

My grandmother's words suddenly surfaced in my mind. She spoke of going to her youth pastor with any problems because the senior pastor was much too scary. Lonnie Orwick, himself, had spoken of not really knowing Pastor Mayhew all that well. I now realized that Lonnie hadn't called Bertram Mayhew at all. He wouldn't call the man with a confession. If he felt the urge to confess something, he would've called the man he knew and trusted...Matthew Coady. How long had the pastor been in his office, standing in the dark listening to our conversation, overhearing Matthew Coady's words? He'd been there, taking in the situation, I was sure of it. He was coming to Matthew's rescue in luring me to a darkened Belle Isle. Would he allow the youth pastor to kill me, too? How could he go on, preaching from the pulpit, knowing he was protecting a murderer? I now knew I'd made a grave mistake in accompanying them to the small island.

I had one hope, though. My mind traveled back to the day of the funeral at Woodmere Cemetery. My uncle had pulled my Luger out of the glove compartment and I'd taken it from him and put it in my pocket. I patted the outside of my overcoat pockets now. I felt nothing. Had I taken it out and placed it somewhere in the house? I couldn't remember.

Sweat formed along my brow as we traveled over the bridge to the island and I realized I was defenseless. The car headed toward the north end. We drove to the farthest point and then Mayhew turned the engine off. He sat for a few moments as Matthew opened his door and began to get out.

"No, Matthew. Stay here."

But it was too late. The younger man was out of the car and scanning the area. "Bertram, are you sure this is where he said he'd be? I don't see anyone."

Pastor Mayhew didn't answer. He got out of the car himself and started walking toward the water's edge. I sat where I was for a moment more, but finally got out of the car, too. Coady was following Mayhew and I hesitantly followed Coady. I looked around for signs of anyone else on this section of the island, but saw no one. It was pitch black on this part of Belle Isle. The only lights I saw came from a freighter moving slowly a mile out on the Detroit River. The wind was cold and brisk. How I was going to get out of this, I wasn't sure.

Finally, Pastor Mayhew could go no further. He stopped but didn't turn around.

"Where is he?" Matthew asked.

The older man didn't answer. Confusion engulfed me. If Coady was playing a part, he was playing it very well. Maybe he didn't know that his senior pastor was onto him and helping to cover his crime.

"Bertram, where is Lonnie?" he asked again.

"He isn't coming, Matthew," I said. "Lonnie never called him."

As I stared at the pastor's back, I saw his shoulders begin to shake and his head bend forward. He was weeping softly.

Matthew looked confused and his frowning face traveled from me to the pastor's back and to me again. Then it was as if a veil were lifted from my eyes. Matthew Coady hadn't killed Myrna Lou—Bertram Mayhew had killed her. But *why*, for God's sake? Was I missing something? Why on earth would the pastor of Christ the Divine Lutheran Church want to end the life of one of its congregants?

"Bertram, what is going on?" Matthew asked. "I don't understand. Is it true the boy never called you? And if not, what are we doing here?"

It was I who answered while the older man continued to shake with tears. "He didn't call him because there was nothing for him to confess. Lonnie didn't kill Myrna Lou." My gaze returned to Mayhew. "Why don't you tell him who did, Pastor?"

"I didn't mean to kill her, but she wouldn't listen. She laughed in my face. The little fool wouldn't listen to me!" His words were barely audible.

"Bertram! Do you know what you're *saying*?" Matthew gasped.

The older man turned slowly toward us now, his hands in his overcoat pockets.

"You're a fool, too, Matthew," the man spit out of his mouth. "*Such a fool*! I overheard her that night in your office. She made me sick telling you that she loved you and that kiss meant everything to her! I heard her tell you the two of you could go away together and start all over again. I couldn't stand it! I left the office when I heard that. I needed to get out of there. *You* make me sick, Matthew! How could you do it? How could you do it to my little girl?"

*His little girl?* What on earth was he talking about? I recalled sitting in Pastor Mayhew's office—the photo on the desk of his daughter—he'd called her Sheila. *Sheila!* My God, Matthew Coady was married to Bertram Mayhew's daughter, and no one had ever mentioned it! That was the connection! I suddenly knew why Myrna Lou had been killed. It all made sense now. "There is nothing I wouldn't do for the girl, nothing," I had heard the man say. He hadn't stayed in his office long enough to hear Matthew tell Myrna Lou of the love he had for his wife. He'd left too soon. He was protecting his daughter from pain.

"So what happened on that Monday, Pastor?" I asked him.

Surprisingly, he didn't hesitate in telling me. Pastor Bertram Mayhew had had an appointment with Karen Wieboldt that afternoon to discuss details of the baptismal service that would take place sometime after the baby's arrival. The baby had been due at anytime. Somehow, he'd misplaced his keys. The man had gone into his son-in-law's office wanting to borrow the young man's car, but Matthew had been in the church's gymnasium, leading the group of boys in prayer prior to their basketball game. Not wanting to disturb them, he made his way back to Matthew's office and took the keys, taking the youth pastor's car without approval. He hadn't planned on being gone long, and he was sure it would be alright. In taking his leave from the Wieboldt home, he'd noticed Myrna Lou sitting on the front steps with the young Bonnie, and stopped in front of the house to call to her. He told her he wanted to talk to her about her relationship with Matthew, but she got snide with him and started to walk back to the steps. So, he told her that Matthew had sent him to get her; that the young man wanted to see her badly.

"I remember feeling disgust toward her as she got into the car with me. I mean, she just left her little cousin to sit alone on the steps of the house. She was an evil girl, Mr. Flanagan. I didn't mean to kill her, but when we got here and I tried to talk sense into her, she laughed at me and told me it was high time Sheila knew about her and Matthew's love for each other. She told me if Matthew didn't have the courage to tell her, she would. She told me our conversation was over. She started to walk back toward the car…and well, I *had* to stop her, didn't I? I *couldn't* let her ruin my baby's life! Sheila means the world to me!"

"My God, Bertram," Matthew said, looking shocked. "There was nothing between us—nothing! I love Sheila! Had Myrna Lou gone to her, I would've explained. Sheila would've understood. *Oh my God*!"

The young man buried his face in his hands and began to weep. He then fell to his knees, rocking back and forth on them. I turned from him and looked at Mayhew.

"Well, now what?" I asked him.

"I'm sorry," he whispered as he removed his right hand from his pocket and brought with it a gun. He pointed it straight at me.

*Aw, damn it*! It looked like *my* gun—*my* Luger! How the hell—and then I remembered him carrying my overcoat into his office to turn out the lights. He'd lifted it from me then. I held up the palms of my hands, as if in surrender.

"Hey, you really don't want to do this. Don't make things worse than they already are. You said yourself you didn't mean to kill her. They'll take that into account."

"I'm sorry," he whispered again.

Matthew took his hands away from his face and his eyes grew wide with fear at the sight of his father-in-law holding a gun.

"He's right, Bertram; don't do this!"

"Shut up you fool! I should kill you, too!" Mayhew screamed.

"Listen," I said. "You can't do this. I have a date Sunday afternoon."

As soon as I said it, I knew how ridiculous it sounded. But, as God is my witness, that is what was truly on my mind. I was thinking of Patti Ann and how rotten it would be if I was to be robbed of this possible relationship. Bringing myself down to more practical thoughts, I'd noticed a large stone, which was lying close to my right foot. If I could make a dive and grab it, maybe I could hurl it, throwing Mayhew off guard; or maybe I'd be lucky enough to knock the Luger out of his hand. There was no time like the present.

I went down; heard Mayhew whisper, "Dear Father, please forgive me," and almost immediately heard a shot. At the sound of it, I flattened out on my stomach, facing away from Mayhew. I simultaneously heard a gasp and a grunt from Matthew. I felt no pain, though. *My God*, I thought. *He's shot his own son-in-law!* And I was to be next! I kept my head turned for what seemed to be an eternity, waiting for the next bullet to pierce me. I was afraid to look—I didn't want it in the face—but I heard no other sound. He hadn't fired off another round at me. I *had* to look, and turned my head slowly.

My gaze first went to Matthew for some reason. He was still on his knees, rocking back and forth. His mouth was wide open and the look on his face was one of horror. I saw no blood seeping from any wound. I looked up to where Bertram Mayhew had been standing, but didn't see him. Lowering my gaze, I saw his lifeless body lying on the ground. The Luger he'd been holding was a few feet away from him now and was smoking. I caught movement out of the corner of my right eye and turned just in time to see the top of the senior pastors head sink below the surface of the water.

Judith White

# Chapter Thirty-Four

It was 11: 50 p.m. by the time I drove by the White Castle in Dearborn. There was no vehicle in the parking lot and the restaurant was dark and vacant. I headed for home, finding Joe and Derwood playing poker for change when I arrived. Both had glasses of whiskey over ice sitting in front of them, with my now half empty bottle sitting on the table, too. I told them of the night's events while hearing soft snores coming from Gran's bedroom. When I was done with my story, Derwood was quiet and the restaurant owner shook his head in disbelief. Then my uncle told me to sleep in my own bed—he and Joe were going to continue their game for a while yet. I took him up on his offer. The last thing I remember before drifting off to sleep was thanking the Lord for Matthew's presence that night on Belle Isle. There was no doubt in my mind that Bertram Mayhew's plan was to take me there and kill me, blaming it on Lonnie or making up another lie for my demise. Matthew's insistence on coming along foiled those plans, and the pastor could see no way out other than to end his own life.

\*\*\*\*

On Saturday, Gran woke me at 10:00 a.m. Aunt Pearl and Uncle Derwood were ready to leave for home, and she wanted me to say goodbye. I watched as they climbed into their car and pulled away from the curb. Aunt Pearl needed to get home—she was happiest in her own environment—but Uncle Derwood...well, I would miss him.

After they were gone, Gran ran to the phone in the kitchen and dialed Helen's number. She wanted to bring her up to date on Myrna Lou's murder. I, on the other hand, returned to my bed and slept the day away.

****

It was the second day of May, and it was going to be a glorious Sunday. The paper reported the weather was expected to be a sunny seventy three degrees with a mild breeze blowing out of the west. I showered early, dressing in my best black suit and splashing my face and neck with a manly smelling aftershave.

Leaving the house a few minutes after 1:00 p.m., I wanted to swing by Johnny's place first. I'd found a ten dollar bill in my suit pocket and a short note from him telling me he'd give me more of my fee later. He must've slipped it to me at the funeral. Gran had a few blank cards on hand and I took one, using it as a sympathy card. I put his ten dollars inside, along with a five of my own. Johnny was going to have a hard time paying off the funeral expenses, let alone paying the ten dollars a day for my services. The investigation I'd done for him was going to be pro bono. He was my dearest friend.

I pulled up to the house on Garrison and parked at the curb. Johnny's vehicle wasn't in sight. Knocking on the door, I waited. No one answered, so I knocked a little harder.

"Hey there, young fella, they ain't ta home!" I heard someone shout from down the street, and knew right away it was Onus Higby.

The old man was sitting on his porch, and when I meandered on over to him, he attempted to rise from the metal chair he was sitting in. I put up my hand, silently telling him to stay seated, and he did. I sat on the chair next to him and decided he deserved to hear the conclusion to the mystery of Myrna Lou's disappearance.

"You means ta tells me that it was that there pastor of that church?" he asked, astounded. He shook his head sadly when I confirmed that that's what I meant.

"Well," he said, struggling to rise. "I was just gonna go in ta fix scrambled egg sanniches. You mights well ta eat one, too."

"Eh, I can't really stay, sir," I said. "But if you don't mind, I would like to use your phone. It's a local call."

"Well, follow me inta the kitchen," he said.

Once inside, I dialed the boutique. I just wanted Patti Ann to know I'd be on my way. Butterflies filled my stomach...I felt like a schoolboy. Lucy picked up after the second ring.

"Oh, Mr. Flanagan, I am so glad you called. This way, I'll save you the trip out here."

"What do you mean?" I asked.

"Well, Patti Ann got word of that building she's been eying in New York and she flew out late last night. She told me to tell you that she should be back in a week or two."

I frowned. I had no idea what she was talking about.

"Didn't she tell you that she's been wanting to open a second boutique in New York City?"

After finding out that Patti Ann was in the Big Apple, my heart sank. I looked over at the old man, stirring eggs in a frying pan, and suddenly felt that I knew how he felt on a daily basis—lonely.

"Hey," I said, "is it too late for me to get one of those sandwiches?"

"Now yer talkin' young fella," he said with his back to me, and I could feel his smile from across the room.

I'd stay there with the old man and have lunch with him. Maybe after that, he'd have a deck of cards or a checkerboard handy. After a couple hours of visiting, I'd make my departure, leaving the card with him to give to Johnny. Then I'd go home, pack an overnight bag, and call a man about a dog named Daisy. Taking a drive to Cleveland would be kind of nice.

Judith White

# Epilogue

Christ the Divine Lutheran Church lost quite a few members in the aftermath of the case, including Grace Delbeck and her children. Gran called her and invited her to the church she attended, but Grace hasn't taken her up on the invitation yet. The church also lost their youth pastor, not surprisingly. Matthew and Sheila Coady left the house they were renting, and no one knows where they went. It's been rumored that those who have stayed in attendance are hoping Duane Whalen will take on the duties of senior pastor after he finishes his schooling. In my opinion, they'd be lucky to have him.

In the days following Pastor Mayhew's death, I spent some time with the Lord. I told Him where I thought He went wrong—how I thought He screwed up in allowing Myrna Lou to leave this earth and her mother at such a young age. She'd never had the chance to experience the feeling of love and the sense of belonging that she so desperately needed. He, in turn, assured me that where she was now, she was being bathed in the ultimate unconditional love. My anger toward Him then dissipated.

Patti Ann came back ten days after she'd left. She's got quite a bit to do in opening her new boutique, so she won't be in the Detroit area all that much in the coming months. We did, however, get to see one another when she returned. I took her out to dinner and then to the Grande Ballroom for a night of dancing. She's a wonderful dancer and an even better kisser. I can't wait to see her again.

On a side note, my forearm is healing well. Forty-five miles out of Cleveland, heading west again, a driver cut me off and I retaliated with the blowing of my horn. This spooked Daisy, the Rottweiler, who was sitting beside me in the front seat. She lunged and bit into my arm. After a shot and seventeen stitches, we were on our way again, but not until I made a detour to a local butcher and bought a nice steak bone for the dog to chew on. I threw it in the back seat, where Daisy stayed the rest of the trip home. Her owner made good on his promise and paid me fifteen dollars a day, and even threw in an extra five for all my trouble. Yep, life is good!

## Other books in
## The Case Files of Sam Flanagan:

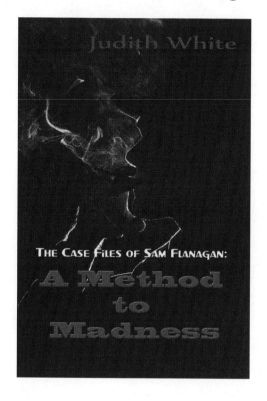

Judith White

## About the Author

Judith G. White holds a degree in secondary education with a major in history from Western Michigan University. She currently works part time at The Henry Ford, America's Greatest History Attraction, where her life has been enriched by meeting dignitaries, entertainment personalities and leaders in business and industry. She's traveled throughout the lower forty eight states and toured Great Britain. History, reading, playing word and trivia games and, of course, writing, is what she likes to do best. She makes her home in a southern suburb of Detroit along with her husband, Jim; two children, Brandon and Erin; and two dogs, Sadie and Orie.

Made in the USA
Charleston, SC
11 March 2013